NIGHT LIGHT:

MEMOIR OF AN ARSON

By Margaret Conway

Book Layout for publication, 2024 by Jerri-Jo Idarius
https://Creation-Designs.com

ISBN 9798877650817

Praised be my Lord for Brother Fire
    who lights up the night,
    and he is bright and playful and robust and strong.

Saint Francis of Assisi,
Canticle of the Sun

INTRODUCTION

Fire is as old as creation, yet its power, ruthlessness and sheer beauty keep us enthralled. Fire can pose as enemy or friend, can provide warmth or be the cause of death. The nicest, most compassionate folks will rubberneck at a fire—the sight of six-foot flames devouring a roof is simply too mesmerizing.

There is scarcely an area of life untouched by fire, scarcely a person who has not survived a fire or had a friend or relative devastated by fire. In *Night Light: Memoir of an Arson*, Ms. Conway writes of her experience surviving an arson fire motivated by revenge.

The dark side of fire—arson—routinely involves police departments, arson investigators, courts, lawyers, and prisons. West Coast wildfires alone would justify a five-city media tour to this region, and San Francisco, is a fire-fighters' nightmare due to its narrow hilly streets and wood frame buildings.

While researching this book, Ms. Conway talked to fire-fighters and investigators, all expressing great interest in the project and readily offered advice and information. The San Francisco police investigator featured in this book was a liaison with the Police and Fire Departments—all being thoroughly familiar with the individual who set the arson fire that Ms. Conway and her husband survived.

TABLE OF CONTENTS

CHAPTER ONE

SURVIVAL TEA

A man threatens to kill me. And I know, the way you sometimes know these things, that he will do it by fire.

The night he chooses is moonless. Bristling with wind. Heavy fog has made the days gray and the nights white. Night in our neighborhood sinks into silence only after two, when the Abbey Tavern and other pubs have ushered out their last customers. Then comes the great crash of empties into the Abbey's dumpster. Gradually, like a give-up sigh, traffic along Geary Boulevard thins to nothing. Small sounds become distinct: a cat's cry, an arpeggio of wind chimes.

Lying awake, I'm tuned to an eerily familiar frequency, the kind that creeps up the spine, begging to be identified. A sort of hissing. Or a crackling. I visualize strips of bark, or paper, curling upward.

Could be rain.

But rain—in May?

Anything is possible in this city of microclimates and shifting tectonic plates. Surrounded on three sides by water, we live astride the San Andreas Fault. Great danger underpins the surface glamour of San Francisco, and some of us actually savor this edgy sense of threat. Yet within loose parameters our weather is predictable. By late May, a mountain of cool air known as the Eastern Pacific High sits offshore, blocking any storms that might otherwise slam into our coast. In summer we don't get rain; we get fog.

Behind a tall gate and well back from the street, we seem to be deep in the country, drifting asleep to the rain's music on our roof.

Our flat roof: a tar-and-gravel expanse that cats and raccoons use as a thruway to other backyards. Whatever I'm hearing—that curling, crackling—is coming not just from the roof but from behind our heads as well, the wall connecting us to an abandoned cottage where for six months a homeless man has been squatting.

High up in our loft bed, my husband Shorey faces away from me.

Suddenly I'm alert. "Better get up!" I say.

"Wha—?"

"Something's happening. Something bad, I think."

Never has it taken so long to scramble down six rungs of a ladder. I trip over Bridie, our cat, who darts ahead of me out the front door. If I had the least hope that this was my imagination, that hope dies when I see Madeleine, our neighbor, striding toward me, a cell phone clapped to her ear.

"I've called 911 twice!" she cries.

My upper arms go weak. A cold vapor invades my throat. Staring up, I see that our roof is in flames. Big, shooting, six-foot flames. For one stunning moment I fail to comprehend. Then the facts rain down: My husband, asleep inside. Our things, all we've accumulated over nineteen years of marriage, nineteen years in that cottage. "Pleez." My voice squeaks into the coloratura range. "Could you call them again?"

"I'm on it," says Madeleine. "Go! Get Shorey out!"

Her boy watches from their back doorway that opens onto a patio we all share. A tiny figure in one-piece pajamas, he points to the tall flames that rush northward ahead of the wind. Madeleine turns him round and leads him back inside, into the well-lit kitchen.

"Ma'am," comes a voice. "I need to ask some questions."

Improbably, a man stands in the shadows by Madeleine's flat, near the narrow walkway that leads to an atrium where tenants keep plants and potting materials. I am struck by the brilliance of his badge, the crisp dark outline of his uniform. So well turned out, for the middle of the night. The sudden sensation of an icicle against my thigh, and I realize I'm wearing my worst nightgown, the one with a long rip down the side. Hardly the time for vanity, but the fact is, I'm in bare feet on concrete, my hair a tumbleweed.

"Ma'am? Questions?"

I have read, possibly in one of the Sunday supplements, that a wood frame house such as ours can become "fully involved" within ten minutes: burnt beyond repair, a pile of char. The unusually hot spring we've just enjoyed has baked those hundred-year-old boards to pure tinder. I step over to this guy and flap my arms to emphasize each word: "Why–are–you–talking? Put some water on that roof!"

"I'm a police officer," he says. "Not a firefighter."

Another man appears: Wayne, a neighbor from across the street. Seeing the flames, he claps a hand to his forehead.

Our roof is alive, seething, and Shorey's in a loft bed three feet from the ceiling of the one-story structure. Coils of sooty smoke rise upward, as if to obscure the flames.

I bound up the front steps and into the bedroom. "We're on fire! Hurry!"

Hair thrusting up like a cockscomb, he descends the ladder quick as a firefighter sliding down the brass pole, even managing to slip his feet into Birkenstocks.

Disaster calls forth a calmness and clarity that Shorey is not always able to summon in lesser situations. The larger the disaster, the greater the calm. Lifting his pants from the dresser where he laid them out for work, he drapes them over his forearm, creases lined up perfectly, and plods off to the bathroom.

Seeing me staring, he declares, "I am not going out there in PJs."

Before I can respond, he has closed the bathroom door, for privacy, as if this were any other morning. He's running water. Is he planning to shave?

Smoke has pooled in the back room. As I enter, calculating that there's time enough to grab a few things, I hear Shorey bounding from the house. Switching on the lamp, I see that the air in here has thickened to a yellowish gray. Our place has been breached, its uninsulated walls leaking fire and fumes. From somewhere comes a soft crash, like the sound of spent logs tumbling off their andirons into the embers.

I yank open the roll-away storage bin where I've cached a steel box containing a third draft of my novel, the product of three years' work, as well as my passport, birth certificate, and family photos. I had squirreled the box at the bottom of the bin, under drawers clogged with items. Now, in an act of radical anti-housekeeping, I reach in and begin tossing out envelopes, pens, legal pads, Post-its, paper clips, scissors, folders. I'm ankle-deep in stationery, kicking stuff to the side, coughing.

Rolls of narrow satin ribbon in shades of ecru, olive, burgundy; Florentine paper; address labels done up in Carolingian calligraphy—all this must be abandoned.

"Maggie, get out NOW!" My husband's voice. "This is no time to be farting around."

A loud crack, like a branch ripping loose from the mother tree.

"Come the hell out of there!

Surely he realizes I can't leave without my manuscript. I start to speak, but smoke thick as solid matter absorbs the words. Smoke, containing carbon dioxide that causes asphyxiation. I'm going as fast as I can.

Bending to lift the fireproof box, I nearly pitch forward into the bin. Though I'm lightheaded, my eyeballs feel like lead in their sockets. The living room, roiling with smoke, has lost its outlines. The mirror over the mantel appears dull as tin. To my left, I catch flickers of red in our bedroom.

Having rescued the book, I suddenly feel defeated. Our cottage, burning up behind me, is worth ten of this novel. A nest, a haven, it has seen us through nineteen years, some of them rugged. The very floorboards are imbued with our union: two headstrong, solitude-loving individuals.

Once outside, I ask Shorey about the cop.

"Which cop was that?"

"He was standing right over there."

Shorey turns toward Madeleine's place, where all is as usual, lights blazing at two in the morning. Luckily for us, she does work nights.

He throws up his hands in bewilderment. "No cop," he says. "And look at you: no shoes!"

Cinders underfoot. I hadn't been aware. Our roof is self-destructing, throwing down gravel and big black flakes.

The front gate spans fifteen feet and stands wide open. Someone thought to do that for us, probably Wayne. The firemen will need access. I see that people have congregated on the pavement out in front.

Under a ceiling of fog the firefighters deploy hose lines across our street. The lines are flat, as yet uninflated by water. They snake along wet macadam made iridescent by streetlights. Lights, everywhere: strobes, flashers, revolving colors atop an official car. Engines and ladder trucks take up the entire block, some parked diagonally so no traffic can make it through. Men, dark moving forms defined by reflective strips on their clothing, go about their business with utter focus. One carries an ax, another an unlit flashlight. The car radio erupts with static, and a man who's unmistakably the chief steps out. He walks around, checking on equipment. The cottage back there: it's his now. For tonight, at least, he's God, and I have to believe in him. Shouts, radio, water being discharged under pressure: I hear it all, and then I don't. I'm very far inside, no longer cold.

On the front steps facing the street I am surrounded by women: Jean, Cindy, Madeleine. Jean, our landlady, assures me that everything will be okay. They all offer snippets of hope that strike me as wildly implausible. Cindy tells me I mustn't hesitate to ask for help. Madeleine offers a room—a bed—for the night. I feel myself on the far side of a divide where I'll be forced to depend on the generosity of others. But the trouble is, at some bedrock level I don't trust others.

People mill about, probably folks from the Abbey. A fireman, politely, almost apologetically, asks that they please clear the gate. Remembering times when I myself have rubbernecked at fires, I do not despise these people for copping some free entertainment on a foggy night.

What I do note is the absolute irony of all this. Ten years in school, and this was meant to have been the summer of relaxation, renewal.

I mumble that I was due to graduate in four days.

"You'll graduate," says Jean.

A woman comes charging from behind the engine. Sidestepping a fireman who's stretching a hoseline, she drops a nylon haversack at my feet. She plucks out a polar fleece pullover and asks me to raise my arms, please. Over my head and down onto my body goes the warm garment. Out from the bag comes a pair of fleecy pants that she manages to ease up under my nightgown without exposing any bare flesh. Coaxing thick gray socks onto my frozen feet, she wedges each into a leather clog.

Hunkered down in front of me, she pats the black bag. "I threw in a couple of sports bras and other items you might need. And I've plenty more at home. You've only to ask."

It's the sort of face made even lovelier by a sheen of mist.

"Where in Ireland are you from?"

"Dublin," she says.

"My grandparents—"

"Look, you're cold. You're in shock. Why don't I fix you some tea."

"Irish tea?" I say, inanely.

"More like . . . survival tea. You survived. Just don't think too far ahead."

Springing to her feet, she brings her palms together. "What's it to be, then—caf or decaf?"

On a night like this, such delicate distinctions hardly seem to matter, but I ask for caffeinated.

"Milk and sugar?"

"Yes, please."

"Hold tight. Be back in a bit."

As she disappears behind Engine 31, I call out, "Who are you?"

Mary Dawson," she calls over her shoulder.

Briefly out of sight, she reappears behind the elongated ladder truck with its raised pillion at the back. She's climbing the steep steps to a house across the street. How is it that we have never met? I can't recall even passing her on the sidewalk.

Within minutes she's back, threading her way between the big red vehicles. She could have offered Styrofoam or a chipped mug, but instead hands me a porcelain cup and saucer patterned with intertwining ivy. She has tucked a linen napkin alongside the cup. It would not be good for me to go all weepy over a serving of tea, so I merely say thanks. I can taste each component: the milk, the sweetness, the tannic bite of the tea itself. I drink it quickly so I can return the cup.

"Keep it," she says.

But I have no idea where the weeks ahead will take us. What if I were to lose or break this delicate china? I continue to hold out the cup.

"Keep it," she repeats. "For luck." And then she's off.

Cindy, too, heads for home. And Madeleine, before returning to her son, hands me a key and says, "Second door down the hall."

Wayne offers me his card. This man, who has always been simply Wayne-from-across-the-street, now emerges as a person with a last name and a phone number.

"Where's Shorey?" I ask.

"Out back, taking photos."

"Taking *photos* of our burning house?"

Wayne bites his lower lip. His eyes shift to the side.

"Before you go, Wayne, would you ask him to come out here?"

"You bet."

Shorey appears in excellent spirits, a camera slung round his neck. "I've been getting to know the firemen," he says. "*Really* nice guys."

"Back there politicking, at a time like this?"

"No. *Talking.* And—I got some amazing shots."

"Like, why would we want pictures?"

"To document the experience." He throws up a hand, as if to say, What other logical reason could there be?

He indicates that I should nudge closer to Jean so he can snap a photo.

"Don't. I look like hell."

"But that's the point: phoenix, rising from the ashes."

I lower my voice. "How bad is it?"

"Bad."

"Think we'll ever—"

"I guess it's up to Jean."

Jean peers up at him, her face the very picture of exhaustion. Mired in my own misery, I'd forgotten that it was her property burning up back there. And on such a gusty night, who's to say whether the fire will turn rogue and jump to the front building?

Shorey asks softly if Jean will rebuild.

Despite Mary Dawson's warm clothing, I begin to shiver. Our entire future in San Francisco depends on the answer to this question. Were we to lose our rent-controlled place, we'd be forced to leave this overpriced city.

"If I can," says Jean. "If the damage isn't too extensive."

"Let me just say that the fire's out," offers Shorey. "Right now they're looking for hot spots. They had to vent the roof, break some windows. The top half of the cottage is pretty much trashed." He expels a hard breath. "That's the extent."

Jean says nothing. I lower my head to my hands.

I would give a lot to have the top half of our house back. In that house, on a shelf, sits Hiroshige's *Tokaido*, my first book, purchased with babysitting money when I was thirteen. The *Tokaido*—recounting in words and woodblock prints an artist's journey through the Japan of the Tokugawa Period—has traveled with me to more than twenty residences, East Coast and West. In a minute, though, I'd relinquish old Hiroshige. I'd give up my rare volumes of British domestic architecture and my collection of antique fabrics: watered silk, black bombazine, beaded satin. I run my mental inventory until one article starts to glow in the blackness of the burnt-out cottage: the graduation gown I rented yesterday. A paper warned of late penalties, but what if a person actually lost the garment?

"Shorey, my graduation gown's still inside!"

"They really doused that back room, but lemme go see."

He soon returns, holding the dripping plastic bag like Exhibit A. "A miracle," he says. "Gown didn't even get wet."

Now he insists on a photo of me in my cap, windblown hair feathering out from beneath the mortarboard.

A car noses in close to the curb, next to the rescue squad's van. The man wears full fire regalia and carries a clipboard. Introducing himself as the arson investigator, he slides in next to me on the tiled step. He's encased in massive clothing including the traditional leather fireman's helmet. I feel like a peanut beside him. "I'll make this short," he says.

At this moment, the policeman who tried to question me earlier now horns in with the fact that he, too, has questions.

"Get him away from me."

The arson man glances from me to the officer.

I don't care if this cop, whom I now recognize, can hear me. "A week ago he came around, after I was threatened. He and his buddy did nothing."

"Should've called Fire Prevention," says the investigator. "They take these things very seriously."

"I had no idea there was such a thing as Fire Prevention."

"Most folks don't. Not till there's a fire."

He tells me what he means to accomplish by means of this interview, but the cop lurks in the background, hands folded over his abdomen.

I answer the questions mechanically, but when he introduces the phrase, "point of ignition," there's a prickling at the back of my neck, the same sensation I would feel whenever Ajax, the one who threatened my life, was in our vicinity. The feeling came to remind me of a *Peter and the Wolf* leitmotif: the tune that heralds the wolf.

And there he is, down by the Abbey Tavern, by the hydrant to which one of the hoses is attached. Ajax, the man who set the fire.

CHAPTER TWO

AJAX 101

Even before Ajax appeared on the scene, the year had turned ominous. There came a creeping realization of something not quite right in my left lower abdomen. Then, on a rainy afternoon in November, I got a call from Kaiser. I was in the middle of writing. Setting down my teacup on a coaster, I tried to grasp what the man was telling me.

"But why an MRI?" I wanted to know.

I had worked in medical offices, and in a hospital. I knew about insurance constraints, how they'd try anything before offering an MRI, the king of scans that costs real money. MRIs are the big guns that don't get hauled out until the final sortie.

"You're being screened for ovarian cancer," he said.

For months, I'd felt unwell. However, I considered myself too busy to be sick. One day, during a class I was teaching at San Francisco State, a student took me aside and pointed out that I seemed to be gripping my abdomen.

"Really? Do I do that a lot?"

"All the time."

An inconvenient truth came to light: I was in pain. On a roll and barreling toward my MFA degree, I had no time to deal with the donkey of the body. Let it keep carrying its load, was my motto. Don't bother me with details. Except that now I remembered what a Chinese acupressurist had told me two years previously. With his hand hovering like a Geiger counter over my left lower abdomen, he'd said,

"I don't know what's in there, but it's bad."

"How can you tell?"

"Energy not flowing."

"Could it be the ovary?"

"Don't know. Go see a doctor."

I did, and had some tests. One clinician speculated about fibroids, another about the colon. No one mentioned my ovaries. And that's what I told the man who now called about the MRI.

"Sorry, but I don't understand," I protested.

"All I know is what's written on this order."

"Excuse me, but who am I speaking to?"

"A medical assistant. You'll have to talk to your physician."

"Can't you tell me anything? I won't be able to get through to a doctor until Monday."

"Sorry," he said, and hung up.

I recall the keyboard under my fingers, the dark brown walls and deep chill in the unheated garage where I sat working. Rain rat-a-tatted the low roof, slopping into a puddle outside the door. I tried to summon statistics: the percentage of women who survived ovarian cancer. I hadn't the slightest. As with most cancers, didn't your chances go up with early detection, before the onset of pain? God, ovarian cancer. What if it turned out to be true? And—what was the point of slogging away on a master's thesis when I might, in fact, die?

Tears welled up. I mean, hell, over the past ten years I'd done every single thing that every teacher asked me to do. I learned to write English compositions. I endured a year of math tutoring. For a biology paper I forced myself to sit in the sun for hours until I grasped the principle behind DNA and the double helix, the genetic code. The hot sun had a melting effect that allowed the arcane knowledge to seep into my brain, and I became ecstatic, as if it were I and not Watson and Crick who had cracked the code. I became fluent in Spanish, drew topographical maps, ventured outside with a team of students who carried tall surveyor's rods and measured the campus. I studied geology, anthropology, American history, political science. And that was just for the bachelor's. Now, nearing the end of graduate school, I'd become so burnt-out, so sleep-deprived, I could make it through only by telling myself that I was the first woman in all four branches of my family to have gone to college.

Some days, dead on my feet after four hours' sleep, a veil of sweat before my eyes, I'd walk the campus, seeing not the fresh-faced students who lay about on the broad green lawn, napping or studying or socializing, but rather the women of the family: Byzantine Greeks from central Turkey with their handwoven clothes and weatherbeaten faces, and on my father's side, child-bearing champs from Western Ireland. What these women had in common were the huge numbers of children they had produced, and the fact that no one alive on earth knows their names.

I see my mother, with her seven kids, and my sister, a disabled waitress. They send me cards. My mother will slip in a fiver, "For coffee and a donut when you're out at school." They view a college degree as an exotic prize, one that will significantly alter my life, even though I did not enter a university until the age of forty-six.

Carrying all these histories on my back, I vowed that no way would I let allow myself to be sidetracked. I might die, I told myself that day in the garage, but I will die possessed of a master's degree.

∽

After the fellow from Kaiser dropped his bomb, I sat and stared at my fingers, poised on the keys. Fictional characters more real than family or friends lived in those fingers, waiting to be actualized. A second draft of this book was to be my master's thesis. Because I'd been juggling school and a job, I had taken too long and run bump up against the seven-year deadline for the master's. The task seemed un-doable. I had less than six months in which to finish.

I took a sip of Earl Grey. The tea had turned cold.

I started to type. I typed for the next three and a half hours. Under the circumstances, I felt quite proud. The writing seemed incandescent.

Later on that rainy, sloppy afternoon, during which I wrote some kick-ass dialogue, I heard the gate creak open to the property next-door. A cement walk led past the far side of the garage to an abandoned cottage. Thus, the man would have been no more than five feet from me as he shuffled along to the back. I heard him cough, softly. He'd taken up residence the previous week. A homeless drunk, he had nothing to do with me. Live and let live.

The next day I looked over the pages I'd written. The narrative meandered wildly. The dialogue might have been written by someone on LSD.

The MRI proved inconclusive. Before excusing herself from the exam room, the gynecologist handed me a pamphlet to study: ovarian tumors and cysts in dreamy pastel shades. Glancing at these big globules about to burst and spill their load of girlie pink or lavender poison, I felt like throwing up. One evil-looking tumor contained two discrete teeth and a strand of hair: an incipient baby gone horribly wrong. Tossing the pamphlet onto a chair, I stalked the small space, muttering, "Shit, shit, shit."

Why must exam rooms be kept at freezing temperatures? And the cheerful posters felt like an assault: four generations of women engaged in a group hug, a run on the beach. The moral, I guess, being: Life's a lark, even if you are eaten up by cancer.

I thought of my mother's mother, dead at forty-eight from a tumor in her belly the size of a nine-month fetus. No group hug for her. And my own mother had undergone a total hysterectomy at thirty-five.

The OB/GYN returned. "Sorry to be so long. Did you read through the pamphlet?"

"Oh, yes. Very interesting."

"I'm afraid I won't know till I go in at surgery whether there's any cancer. So we'll need to talk beforehand about our choices."

"One thing," I told her. "I will not submit to chemo or radiation."

Not that I doubted the efficacy of these modalities, but I did not want to be throwing-my guts up or losing my hair. Instead, I would try Chinese herbs. The macrobiotic diet. Homeopathy. Crystals. Whatever.

"Fine," said the doc. "But in that case if I find even one cancer cell in your pelvic cavity, everything's coming out: uterus, ovaries, pelvic lymph nodes. Agreed?"

Deep breath. "Agreed."

The surgery was to be done laparoscopically via three small incisions. In the case of cancer, she'd make a longer incision to remove the uterus.

"So if I wake up after surgery and see only three little incisions, I'll know there was no cancer?" It seemed important to nail this fact.

"Right you are," she said, nodding and smiling at my correct assessment.

"Oh, and doctor? I'm pushing to finish a master's thesis. So I hope all this won't take too long."

She flashed me a shrewd look, pressing her lips together and shifting in her seat. "You do realize there has to be a recovery period."

"But I'm up against a deadline. I'll recover fast."

"Your surgery is scheduled for December 17th."

"That's three weeks from now! I can't possibly—"

"Actually, my surgery schedule's completely booked for the next two months." She scribbled a note on the inside of my chart. "Which is why I left the room: to see about scheduling your operation on one of my days off. So—the 17th, it is."

Rain fell. The garage turned frigid. The intruder in my lower abdomen caused such pain and pressure, I had to bind myself with a strip of cotton cloth in order to keep working. Whatever had lodged inside of me seemed about to explode, and the cloth, to my way of thinking, kept things neatly in place. By nine each morning the neighborhood emptied, kids off to school, adults to their jobs. Real work, while I was left to craft sentences. The dark, dripping days matched my mood.

Oddly, I found myself looking forward to surgery. Since seeing the doctor, I felt cloistered in a medical limbo that was not entirely unpleasant. Life, death, cancer, no cancer: all a crap shoot. Out of my control. As December 17th drew near, I counted the days I'd be unable to work in this freezing room. One day for pre-op, another for the surgery itself, then three, maybe four days to recuperate.

I laundered sheets, pillowcases, and a comforter, preparing the sofa bed for occupancy. I screwed a pink lightbulb into the lamp and placed John Donne's *Devotions upon Emergent Occasions* on the bedside table.

Serenity lasted two weeks. During the count-down week, I found myself caring a great deal whether I lived or died. After all, I reckoned, death was not supposed to happen until later in life. I began reading medical articles. I called people who had known people who'd had ovarian cancer. Chopping vegetables for dinner, I'd start to weep, then feel like a fool. I phoned the Neptune Society for a price quote on their cheapest cremation package. The only place of peace was the garage. In there, the writer took over from the quivering, self-pitying woman.

Sometimes I'd work straight through, sometimes I'd break for lunch at around one, when the homeless man came creaking through the gate to his hovel.

"Who is he?" I asked Shorey.

"That's Ajax."

"The one who used to sing on the street?"

"The very one."

"But he's so altered."

I remembered the old Ajax roistering along Clement, our shopping street, the sun on his ruddy face, a striped shirt that gapped over his belly. In those days he appeared sleek and well fed. Flinging his arms overhead like Frankie Pentangeli in *Godfather II*, he'd belt out a song for the street. He had the gravelly voice of Frankie Five Angels, the same rascally charm.

Even on such a crowded street, even when blasted by booze, he could pick out the individual. He knew his people. And I was one of them—the Mary of his imagination.

"Maaary," he'd roar. "Lemme sing you one."

"Should I tell him my name's not Mary?"

Shorey grabbed my arm. "Don't ever speak to him, you hear? Don't even make eye contact. The guy is dangerous."

"Oh, come on. Poor, funny old drunk."

We then rounded the corner as Ajax continued along Clement, serenading the mostly Asian shoppers with one of his many songs honoring the Marys of this world.

"Granted he's cute," said Shorey, "when he's in the first blush of a bender. But he can turn nasty."

The name Ajax figures in mythology. A Greek chieftain, he fought against Troy. Big, brave but simple-minded, he was nearly the equal of Achilles. He dueled with the great Hector and managed to retrieve the body of Achilles, whose armor he coveted. When the chestplate was award-ed instead to Odysseus, Ajax ran himself through with his own sword, and where his blood soaked the soil a red flower sprang up, a flower that bore the first two letters of his name, in Greek: AI, onomatopoeic for "lament."

When I first encountered Ajax, I thought I detected glints of nobility, but fifteen additional years of drink had left him mean, vengeful. While I awaited surgery, though, he was no more on my mind than the acacia sprouting by the side of his ruined cottage.

Friends warned that when I came out from under anesthesia I wouldn't know a thing. Not my name, they told me, or where I was. Not true. As soon as I broke through into consciousness, I eased up the green hospital gown and checked my belly.

Three small incisions.

My doctor came by while I was in the recovery room. What I'd had, she said, was a very large but benign ovarian tumor. The tumor, ovary and fallopian tube had been extracted through the navel. I could expect the region to remain sore for quite a while.

After two days of thrashing about on the sofa bed, trying to keep body and mind unpolluted by narcotic analgesics, I gave in and swallowed a pain pill. I began to enjoy my convalescence. Friends came by dropping off fruit, flowers and soup. Everybody called. I could hear Shorey in the other room, speaking sotto voce into the phone: "She's resting now. Sure, rice porridge would be nice. She'd like that."

The pain became manageable, but I attributed the overwhelming weakness to the fact that I'd been in bad shape when I went into the hospital. For several reasons, surgery under general anesthesia becomes dangerous when a person has a cold or flu because a cold or flu can impair breathing, and general anesthesia depresses the autonomic nervous system that controls respiration. With an already compromised immune system, there's also a danger of infection.

The pre-surgery pamphlet urged me to advise my doctor of any such illness, in which case surgery would have to be postponed. No time in my schedule for postponements. I reported to Ambulatory Surgery at 6:30 a.m. on December 17th with a sore throat, cold, and low-grade fever, trying to look as perky as possible.

Had any friend said they were about to do what I did that morning, I'd have told them flat out that they were a lunatic. And looking back, I can say only a lunatic would have gone into a freezing garage just days after surgery, while still weak, with surgical dressings on her belly, and sat typing for seven straight hours.

I am not quite in my body when I'm writing, and therefore oblivious to pain. I normally put in six hours, but to make up for lost time that first day back, I kept going. When finally I closed up the garage it was black night, with a biting wind. Staggering across the garden and up the steps into the cottage, I collapsed onto the living-room floor.

Fact is, I didn't believe I'd ever get the master's. Though I'd graduated summa cum laude for my bachelor's degree, and as a grad student had done well, having been given the opportunity to teach writing classes at the university—still, underlying all this effort there remained an *idee fixe* that I'd somehow gotten above my station. Who did I think I was, aiming to be different than my mother or sister, or our female forebears who'd had no time for books, let alone university degrees?

An incident in my father's life kept cropping up like a cautionary tale. When I was twelve, the local librarian, who enjoyed talking with my father, invited him to lead the Great Books Discussion Group in our town. My father was a self-taught man with a good grasp of literature and the classics. I'd been begging him to accept because I felt the very future of our family hinged on his decision. He had in his hands the power to gain us some respect.

We lived in Jeffersonville, Pennsylvania, a village thick with neo-Colonial mansions and dignified stone homes. We, the newcomers, were fresh from the mill town with our five-hundred-dollar deposit for a Levittown-style box in a spanking new housing tract that dared to intrude on the leafy serenity of Whitehall Road, down which British troops had marched In 1778 on their way to encounter General George Washington and his men at nearby Valley Forge.

Long-time residents had no time for "the Whitehall Park people," with our hordes of kids who ran around half-naked in the summer heat and whose day revolved around the arrival of the Good Humor man. There was an enclave called Halford Tract, a section so exclusive we didn't dare walk through the hush of its unpeopled streets. Jeffersonville businessmen took off each morning in Lincolns or Chryslers, or boarded the train for Philadelphia, wearing suits and ties. These were the 1950s. Men wore fedoras and carried leather briefcases, while my father wore faded broadcloth and toted a lunch pail.

How I craved the respect of those regal people in the Colonial homes. They struck me as authentic, in a way that we were not. In the mill town I had never known such people existed, but now I could not survive without their approval, their imprimatur.

In the days while my father pondered his decision about the Great Books group, the house sizzled with expectancy. He, however, seemed to have forgotten the whole thing. Then, as if stating what should have been obvious to all of us, he simply said, "There may be executives, even teachers in such a group. Why would they hearken to the words of a factory worker? No, I will not make myself an object of scorn."

I despised him for this betrayal. My father, in front of a Great Books group—I could have made much of that in my desperate attempt to climb Jeffersonville's social ladder. Only later did I come to understand how he must have felt. He claimed our family was jinxed, and on this subject he spoke with stunning authority. But even when talking about the weather, say, or salad greens, my father employed an elevated diction not common to our working-class milieu. We sometimes laughed behind his back, but we listened. Coming from his mouth, the notion of a jinx seemed entirely believable.

And, in the days before my surgery, continued to be believable. I mean, did I have in my belly a cancer that would cause me to die before I got my degree, thus proving him right?

I needed someone who would dispel this phantasm, this jinx.

I called Maxine, my thesis mentor, and made an appointment.

Riding the bus out to State, surrounded by others carrying backpacks and book bags, I thought of my father, who had worked his hated job at the B. F. Goodrich factory to put food on our table. I started to weep. Through the smeared bus window, I saw trees and rich green foliage that concealed the stately homes of St. Francis Wood (the Halford Tract of San Francisco). "Dad," I whispered to my long-dead father, not caring that the young student next to me obviously saw me as a nutcase.

The third floor of the Humanities Building, with its long cloistral corridor where professors have their offices, also houses the Creative Writing Department, a place I avoided like poison. Just stepping into the anteroom where the secretary sat, occasioned in me the most paralyzing feelings of inadequacy. I imagined that every teacher who passed through on the way to the mailroom, every funky writing student, even the secretary herself, looked at me and thought, *You fraud. Do you seriously think you're a writer?*

Maxine's office, computer humming and everything in its place, always made for a rational encounter.

"Come on in," she said, and enveloped me in a motherly hug. She'd never done that before. "Any news?"

"My surgery's on the 17th."

"Good. Get it over with."

"It's just that I was looking at the time I've got left. Less than five months to finish up."

"Yes?"

"What I meant—"

The phone rang. Maxine dealt crisply with the student, the way my mother dispatched my six younger siblings whenever she and I needed to have one of our little chats.

"What you meant was?" said Maxine, picking up my thread.

"Considering the time crunch, I wonder if you'd maybe accept a *partial* second draft for my thesis?"

Maxine, who had big hair, a shimmering black aureole round her pale face, formed her hands into a steeple. No mistaking her disappointment. In fact, I hated my quavering voice and the no doubt piteous expression on my face.

She let the moment pass. "You promised me a second draft," she said, drubbing the desk with a fingernail. "And that's what I want."

Actually, I felt relieved. She believed I could do it. Therefore, I began to believe I could do it. Playing coy, though, I had to add, "You know, there'll be a recovery period, so that's bound to set me back a bit."

"Keep writing," she snapped.

Her face then softened, and she betrayed a look of concern.

"I'm a little nervous, Maxine."

"Anyone would be. Even the thought of cancer."

"Also, I'm a sissy about gynecologic procedures."

"We all are."

"Look, thanks for seeing me. Believing in me."

"I do believe in you. All you need is confidence."

The phone again. Before picking up, she gave me a parting hug and whispered, "You will get through this."

I was not one to argue with Maxine.

I kept to a schedule: seven days a week, six to seven hours a day. I had twenty-six of thirty chapters to re-write. I consoled myself that each day I'd feel stronger, but the weakness hung on, in the manner of chronic illnesses.

By March, though, I was really cooking. As I saw the pages pile up, I knew I'd get my thesis in under the wire. Short of a cataclysm, I'd be able to polish off this baby by the end of April.

Something eerily free of family haplessness, the way my thesis readers tore through the manuscript in record time; the way the perfectly amiable advisor in the Grad Division signed me off without a quibble, even congratulating me and wishing me a great summer; the way the bored young man in Rapid Copy merely checked to make sure I'd used twenty-pound bond, then scrawled a receipt for the binding fee.

As of that moment, I had graduated.

It was over. If I never again set foot on the campus, not even for commencement, still, they could not cheat me of my achievement. And if I chose not to attend the May 29th graduation, they'd simply mail me the diploma.

In one moment I had progressed from student to alumna. I longed to celebrate, at the very least to get giddy over coffee in the Student Union, but had no one with whom to do so. The Rapid Copy Center lodges in a far corner of the library's first floor. For ten years the J. Paul Leonard Library had been for me a study space, shelter from the rain, and hideout in which to nurse the wounds of student life.

Not the time, though, to hole up in a library.

Awaiting me outside was a full-blown May afternoon. Northwesterly winds had skimmed across the Pacific, scouring the city, leaving the sky a searing blue. In the eighty-five degree weather, students lay sprawled all over the lawn while Brewer's blackbirds dove and swooped, warning people away from trees and shrubs where their chicks nested. The campus smelled of fresh-cut grass and of fried onions from an outdoor food concession.

Walking around, nowhere in particular to go, no twenty-pound bookbag slung over my shoulder, I felt free, filled with prana. All these years, charging from class to class, building to building, I had forgotten to breathe. Now, standing in the middle of the quad, hot sun on my head, I sucked in the good ocean air and the scent of wet soil.

Though this is a state school, often short on funds, the campus has been beautifully landscaped, a pleasing mix of green sward and hidden grotto with some fairly decent herbaceous borders. Whenever I had a minute I'd stop and bug the gardeners, asking the name of this or that tree or flower. From one woman I learned all about dianthus, including the Greek etymology of the word. Over time, I racked up a free botanical education. Now I went to check on the dianthus, and saw that it was doing fine, a phalanx of chaste white blooms by the entrance to Student Health.

I went by Thornton Hall, recalling three long-ago weeks when I'd crammed for the geology exam, and then by Hensill where I'd studied holistic health with the magnificent Dr. Araki. I had passed a lifetime on this campus.

My geology professor once told us the greatest gift you could give a person was the gift of time. Some of the students had blinked at him uncomprehendingly, so that he added, "When you get to be as old as I am, you'll understand." On that day in early May, my thesis having cleared the barrier ahead of deadline, I'd been handed three wide-open weeks.

My friend Bernadette O'Neill had called to say she'd be arriving from Arizona before the graduation, and I needed to get her room ready. Declaring May a write-free month, I tackled the house, cleaning, airing, dusting, scrubbing. No more biology exhibits in the high corners. No more dirty grout.

I spent languorous afternoons with old friends. The days drew out, hot and dry, the apricot light flooding through till sunset.

Days, I worked on the house. Nights, I read: whatever happened to grab my interest, after all the years of assigned reading. I gobbled up a thriller by William Trevor, then a book on bees by Sue Hubbell, then moseyed through a volume on Belgian lace-making that I'd taken out of the library simply because I liked the smell of the yellowed pages.

Starting in June, I would write all summer, see how it felt to work without a deadline staring me down. In the fall, I'd scout out a job. For now, though, who needed anything beyond the slow pull of the days and the blessed restful nights?

One day, taking a break from cleaning, I bopped down the front steps with a frosty glass of tea and headed for the green plastic chair. My landlady had gotten up to stretch her back after yanking wild grasses, clumps of which lay here and there, bleaching in the sun. Another hot, blue afternoon. Jean and I greeted each other, then admired the trumpet vine, its fleshy red flowers that tumbled over forty feet of redwood fence—all that biomass from one single plant. Through slits in the fence we spied some movement, jerky and staccato. We both froze.

"He's getting worse," Jean whispered.

Shouting, hurling curses at hallucinatory spirits that peopled the inner and outer darkness in which he lived, Ajax seemed to have lost all human connection. At night, through our flimsy walls, I could hear every feral sound.

"And," said Jean, "he smokes." She advised me that from her upstairs window she had seen him enter the place, dragging on a cigarette.

"Not okay," I said. "That place is a tinderbox. If he should fall asleep with a lighted cigarette . . ."

I described the nightly antics. Told her I had rationalized, said to myself, Poor old booze-hound: he, too, deserves a roof, some shelter. And since I no longer kept up such a brutalizing schedule, so what if I lost a little sleep on nights when Ajax had tied one on? But smoking, while drunk, in that wooden cottage? That could not continue.

Perhaps he sensed the changed tenor of our conversation, the fact that at first Jean and I had talked in a normal tone and then begun whispering like conspirators. Must have, because right then he surged toward the fence and rattled the one by sixes.

"You bitches!" he roared. "I'll come over there and beat the shit out of you!"

A watercolor sky, air so soft you seemed to be walking through folds of silk, yet Ajax was declaring war.

"Bitches," he muttered, and slunk inside his doorless den.

The Ajax who had once serenaded his "Mary," was now prepared to knock her block off. Whenever I saw him approaching, I beat it across the street. Frankie Five Angels of fifteen years ago had morphed into a man whose flesh had melted from his bones, whose iron-gray hair and beard had gone white and shaggy. A Kris Kringle effect except for the big dark Mediterranean eyes that beamed forth lasers of pure hatred.

I did my utmost to avoid the man, but he had on his side the advantage of surprise. One day, passing the 540 Club on Clement Street, I spotted him at a café table in the recessed entryway under the dark green awning. No drink in front of him. According to the neighborhood grapevine, he'd once again been barred from this club. Still, he laid claim to an outside table and apparently no one dared to dislodge him. And like a jungle cat who'd caught my scent, he sat crouched and waiting. Flashing me a sinister smile, he raised a hand and sang "Hello" in three lilting syllables.

I picked up my pace. Wrong thing to do because from behind me I heard the bark of laughter, then the words, "Don't want to talk to Santa Claus?"

"Not your kind," I muttered.

My nights he turned into the sound-track of a horror movie. Shorey slept through it all, even the night when another drunk forced his way into the place. Clutching the blanket to my neck, I *cringed* at the bestial roaring and sounds of men grabbing each other. Each time the pair of them slammed into our wall, the bedroom rocked with seismic tremors.

I told myself I could handle the occasional street encounter. As for the wild nights, no white-haired man could keep up that level of violence for long. I did worry about his smoking, but reasoned that all over town homeless were squatting in abandoned houses, smoking in abandoned houses, and not all of those houses had gone up in flames. The statistical probability that our place would catch fire seemed low to nil. Then there were my politics. Since 1970 when I'd first arrived in the city, I had done my little bit for the homeless, donating money and clothing, forking over a dollar for the *Street Sheet*, never losing an opportunity to raise my liberal voice defending the rights of homeless persons. But those homeless persons had been faceless, anonymous—until Ajax. Maybe the grandfatherly white hair, or maybe the simple fact of his homelessness caused me to feel squeamish about bringing down the authorities on the dude. I let things ride.

May 21st, eight days before graduation, and I'm walking along the Ajax stretch of Clement Street. The day had started out bright and sunny, but a trifle cool. I looked around me. No Ajax under the awning of the 540. No drunken Ajax hunkered outside the bookstore. Then, just as my shoulders relaxed, it happened. Like a tiger he leapt from a step in a narrow doorway and yelled, "I'm going to kill you!"

An older woman ambling by stared at him and put her hand to her throat, but her he ignored. Instead, he repeated, this time as if mouthing an intimacy, "I am going to kill you."

Oddly, I felt like laughing. Who the hell did he think he was? The Irish side of me reared up and I was about to fire back with something like, "Shut up, Ajax, you jerk," when a cold current went through me. I stood like a stone, cars passing, people passing, Ajax frozen in his predatory stance. That's when I knew. Drink talks, and often talks big, but in this case the guy was not bluffing. He'd said he was going to kill me, and he meant just that.

I sensed him following me down the street, turning in at our block and continuing to follow. Climbing my front steps, I heard his gate clang shut.

When Shorey opened the front door, having seen me come up the walk, I said, "I'm calling the cops."

Though the station house is barely two blocks away, it took them forty minutes. Meanwhile, Shorey stood on our porch from which he could see over the fence with its rich thickness of red blooms into the yard beyond where Ajax prowled back and forth among the weeds. Having been arrested many times—for brawling, for assaulting women including a female police officer whom he'd cold-cocked into unconsciousness while in custody at our local police station—Ajax no doubt had a well-developed sixth sense that warned him when cops were on the way.

To remain outside and watch while they hauled him away seemed to me a breach of etiquette, so I peeked from behind the living-room curtain.

"You can't scare me with those eyes!" I heard him yell at Shorey.

There's not a person, a cat, or any living creature who can outstare Shorey. He has a most level, penetrating gaze and can go three minutes without blinking. He hated hearing that I'd been threatened, and without saying a word was making his displeasure felt.

I heard, "What're you looking at, mister?"—then the usual epithets as Ajax retreated into his cottage.

Considering Ajax's known record of aggression against women, how to explain the fact that two towering male cops stood lounging against our open front gate as they watched, from a distance of seventy-five or eight feet, while a young blond officer beat her way through the weeds that surrounded the rotting cottage? The older of the two men, his head a mass of tight gray curls, leaned in to make an apparently amusing remark to his fellow officer.

The woman called out, "Anyone in there? *Anyone?*" Folding herself into a smaller package, she ducked inside the low opening. The men made no move to back her up. How she got Ajax cuffed and into the car, I could not imagine. He would have tried to throw a punch, even though she had a gun.

Now here comes Gray Curls up the walk, wanting to question me since it was I who'd placed the call. What had I heard, what had I seen, why particularly did I feel threatened, he wanted to know. He then told me they could hold Ajax for only one night. "But if he ever comes back," he said, "just call 911."

"If he ever comes back? I've been trying to tell you: the man lives in there. He's there day and night."

"Like I said, give us a call."

"But then I'd be calling every day, wouldn't I?"

"Best I can do," he said.

"Officer, he's living there illegally. Trespassing." I hated using these terms. "Can't you just get him out—for good?"

"No can do," said the younger cop. "That would be violating his civil rights."

So ironic did this statement seem, in the circumstances, I figured it had to be tongue-in-cheek, an officer bemoaning the system that's stacked against the ordinary law-abiding citizen. But on the off-chance that he hadn't intended any irony, I said, "What about our civil rights when he burns us down one of these nights? You know, he smokes in there."

We were now out on the street, the men's navy-blue backs to me as they strode toward the patrol car where Ajax sat caged behind the grille. Gray Curls turns to younger cop with a look that says, *Another hysterical woman.*

The next evening I had dinner with two friends, Karin and Virginia. All a part of my coming out of hibernation. Sitting in Karin's postmodernist dining room at a triangular metal table, the matching seats as high-backed as bishops' chairs, we were relaxing over coffee and baklava. Karin switched off the overheads, and we kept on chatting in the chapel-like ambiance of lit tapers and a tasty arrangement of yellow freesias and ornamental grasses. Candlelight caught the rim of my water goblet and trembled there. This was the life. Our talk hovered around Karin's recent trip to Italy and a must-see exhibit, "The Treasury of Saint Francis of Assisi," due in July at the Legion of Honor. We three agreed to see the exhibit together, then have lunch on the museum patio under the olive trees.

"So," said Virginia. "A week till graduation."

"Yep. If I'm still alive."

"Of course you'll be alive." Karin laughed, leaning over to pat my arm.

I lifted my water glass, setting it back down so awkwardly that it tipped over, spilling water and ice chips across the damask tablecloth. I saw that my hand was shaking.

Virginia gave me an *Everything all right?* look.

"Things have gotten . . . a little weird," I said, reckoning I'd better come right out and say that Ajax had made a threat on my life. When they both gasped, I regretted having injected such ruinous words into the lighthearted atmosphere.

Both of my friends assured me the guy was shooting his mouth off, drunks did it all the time, nothing to worry about, think on the bright side: the upcoming graduation. Later, though, when Virginia was driving me home, she suddenly braked the car a little distance from my place. Both hands on the wheel, she peered over at me and confessed that she was worried. "I think maybe he did mean what he said," she told me. "I think you'd better call the police."

"I already have, Virginia. They're not interested."

Chastened by his night in jail, Ajax became the ideal neighbor. That was enough for me. I was back to, Live and let live. He crept in and out of his place, made no noise, entertained no visitors.

The days clicked by. Monday morning, the 24th, I went out to school to rent the cap and gown, royal purple in honor of the school's centennial. I paid an extra ten dollars for the gold-edged mantle worn by master's candidates.

Back home, in the voluptuous afternoon light, I sat on the divan where Bernadette would sleep during her visit and looked around at my room: new white rug, comforter freshly washed and smelling of Bounce, new curtain with a pattern of floating lotus flowers that scattered elongated shadows over the comforter and rug. I had steam-pressed an antique pillowcase and placed three green-wrapped Andes chocolates in the center of the pillow.

Sitting there, I breathed in the smell of cleanliness: the evaporating scrub-water, the negatively charged aroma reminiscent of the seaside. I tried to summon up my fore-mothers, invite their spirits into this spotless chamber. For years I had hitchhiked on their hard lives, turned these nameless women into metaphors, but what could I ever know about women living under old-world strictures, forced to obey, to bear fifteen children? Time to let them rest.

During this grind of a year, when friends asked what I meant to do after graduation, I'd tell them, "Right now, I'm climbing K2. When I get to the summit, I'll know what's on the other side." This room *is* the other side. In this white room I'll spend the coming summer months, writing my heart out.

The very existence of the room was never in question.

How could I know that in fewer than twelve hours it would be destroyed?

CHAPTER THREE

HOMELESS

By late afternoon on the day of the fire, we seem to have entered a parallel reality that feels like a dream from which we will–must–awaken. We are in the car.

Shorey attributes human traits to his cars, even naming them. Tillie Tercel, having intuited that we're somehow without volition, takes us on an impromptu tour of the quiet, tree-lined streets of Pacific Heights. Our '82 Toyota has groaned up a Matterhorn of a hill and now sits becalmed in a wide intersection surrounded by neoclassical and Tudor castles topped with clusters of English-style chimney pots. Brick and masonry establishments built to last. Not a leaf or blade of grass is out of place in this fastidiously tended part of town. I can hear in the distance the sound of a power-mower: an unseen gardener at work. Tillie must have known we needed the order and safety that such a neighborhood conveys. The Marina lies spread out below, its yacht harbor a dazzling sweep of blue and white on this glamorous afternoon.

We are not moving. We are the only car in the intersection, the only car in sight. I start to say something when I notice Shorey gripping the wheel so fiercely, it seems he will yank it free of the steering column.

"Hey, there."

He shudders.

"Why don't we go home," I say.

But wait—we have no home. In the past twelve hours we've seen our house incinerated, have slept three or four hours in a strange bed, entered the emergency room due to smoke inhalation, and afterwards ate breakfast at a diner where the waitress backed away from us because we stank of smoke.

"Where's 'home'?" says Shorey tonelessly.

The nice ride, the shade trees and breezes redolent of fresh lawn-clippings have momentarily lulled me into assuming that our reference point, the place we started out from and returned to each day, is still intact: the stage on which we enacted the daily drama of marriage, where disagreements were adjudicated and love was maintained. Who am I—or what—without a home?

And where are we supposed to go, right now for instance? Do we curl up and take a much-needed nap in the Toyota? It seems crucial that we put together some sort of plan, so I say, "We'll stay at Madeleine's again. She said we could."

"Bed's too narrow. Do what you want," says Shorey, "but I'm crashing on the floor of the garage."

"It's dirty in there. You can't."

"Watch me."

Before marriage, Shorey lived a semi-nomadic life and, it's entirely possible that, given enough time without a fixed residence, he might revert, might find it pleasant to sleep in a down bag and hopscotch from place to place —with or without a wife in tow. Over the years we have developed rituals and routines that bind us together. The very act of visiting the bathroom in the middle of the night involves sidestepping the jungle of potted plants on our living-room floor. In the absence of a familiar bathroom, Shorey might just as happily pee in the park.

"Then I'll sleep in the garage, too," I tell him.

"There's not enough room."

The ease with which he seems to be shutting me out feels ominous. As if twenty years have been the dream of a moment.

And what about Bridie? We haven't mentioned her since this morning after we called out her name until our vocal cords went numb, then crawled around for half an hour in her favorite hiding-place, the atrium, where Jean reported having last seen her. But who knows if that was Bridie or the neighborhood tomcat with similar markings?

Two days from now a friend will tell us the obvious: Go to the Red Cross. This afternoon, though, we don't have a clue.

All I can think is: Establish a routine, no matter how flimsy.

Eat, drink, sleep.

Gas, food, lodgings.

We can't go around like bums.

Paralyzed at our intersection in Pacific Heights, we're going nowhere.

Then the car slips into gear and I feel a surge of horse-power beneath us, as Tillie turns us to the right, past the mansion where Danielle Steel resides and the manor houses too discreet to display any evidence of human life except for service vans that disgorge carpet steamers, leaf-blowers and men in coveralls who clamber over these magnificent structures, up walkways, onto lawns and scaffolding like so many bees maintaining a great hive.

The afternoon burns with a rare loveliness, even for San Francisco. It's a Lawrence Durrell kind of day that cries out for an al fresco celebration.

"Where are we going?" I ask.

"To the hot tubs."

I think fleetingly of the price, the fact that a private hot tub, including tip, will run nearly as much as a week's worth of groceries. I'm also thinking we don't want to turn this into a habit, a Roman indulgence during the weeks or months we might be out of a home. We don't want to land ourselves in debt. Yet all around us, as we speed downhill towards Van Ness, are the signs of good living. Couldn't we partake, just a little?

"And don't say one word about the money," warns Shorey. "I need to clean up for work tomorrow."

In the dim, chlorine-smelling lobby, where we pay for our two towels and bottles of spring water, Shorey has started telling the Hispanic attendant about the fire, just as he did earlier today to our waitress at the diner. It's plain to me the woman knows barely enough English to negotiate the communication necessary to take our forty dollars and point us in the direction of our room, but Shorey plods on with the tale of Ajax and his depredations.

"*Fe*," he emphasizes, to make sure she understands this is about fire.

"*Fe* means 'faith,'" I say.

"So what's 'fire'?"

"I think that's *vega*."

Apparently, it's not *vega*, and I say, "Shorey, she doesn't care."

"Of course she cares. Who wouldn't?"

In fact, I told pretty much the same story to the medical personnel at the E.R. this morning, gloating over the same horrific details. We seem to have lost our envelope of self-containment and become nothing more than this wretched story. Besides which, we stink.

A buff young couple bounces past us into the back, wafting a fresh lemony fragrance, while another couple approaches the desk. I'm concerned that Shorey will start telling *them*, too.

"Could we go clean up," I plead.

The room is womb-like: black walls with gold detailing and a sunken tub bubbling quietly in the corner. The piped-in classical music abruptly becomes Haydn, so Shorey reaches for the knob.

"Do we need music?"

"No," I say. "Just the water."

I want water so badly that, dirty as I am, I step into the tub and sink to my shoulders. Shorey feels he must shower first, wash away the smoke and trauma. I watch as he soaps his hair, wriggles wet forefingers inside his ear canals, bows his head to let the steaming water stream down the smoothness of his back, the rills illuminated by what little light there is in here. Then he lathers himself as if this will be the last shower of his lifetime.

And I, too, have to wonder where we'll take our next bath.

The tub, lit from below, is the light-source, bringing out the subtly different greens of the ceramic tiles. The room around us recedes like night. When Shorey gets in, finally, he puts a finger to his lips. We're all talked out. Too tired to turn on the hard jets, too wasted to have them blasting against our bodies. One small jet pulsates beneath our legs and, that's all the stimulus we need.

Other than listening for the buzzer that will warn us we've got ten minutes left, we have nothing to do.

Eat, drink, sleep.

Clean ourselves, from time to time.

Try not to make each other miserable.

And have faith–*fe*–that we'll make it through.

CHAPTER FOUR

DOLLHOUSE

Back in February Shorey bought me a garden: six tiny terracotta pots under a plastic greenhouse in the shape of a church without the steeple. The directions said to sprinkle seed onto the soil pellet in each pot, mist with a spray bottle, then keep on misting until some green broke through. During the non-green phase, I needed to have faith that what had happened for every other purchaser of this $6.99 herb garden would happen for me, as well.

I was to be alert for the first set of "true leaves," the sign that my parsley, marjoram and basil were ready for transplanting. And I must not confuse a mere sprout with a true leaf. Somehow I cleared this intellectual hurdle, and on the porch my plants bushed out, crowding the wide-rimmed pot. Each morning I went out with my watering can. So simple, the needs of these plants. You gave them water and they grew. The payback seemed disproportionate to my puny effort. By the time I turned in my thesis, I was pinching off basil leaves for a marinara sauce.

And it's basil that Shorey now nudges with his shoe, mashed basil in a carbonaceous sludge. The pot has burst apart, a block of soil and parsley still clinging to its interior.

"Firemen must have thrown it down," says Shorey, as we tiptoe around shards of terracotta.

"My plants," I moan.

"They had to clear the porch. It's nothing personal."

"Sure. What're a few plants—I fling up my arm—in light of *that*?"

The sorry remains of our cottage. We'd decided to avoid the place until after the graduation. For those few days, pretend it hadn't happened. Miles away in a motel room I steam-pressed my purple gown on the polyester bedspread with an iron I'd borrowed from Mr. Vyas, the manager. When I explained to Mr. Vyas that the next day I'd be receiving my master's degree, his eyes registered shock, then a flicker of sadness, knowing as he did that we'd had a fire, but he composed himself and said, "Just remember to return the iron. It's my wife's, and I don't usually lend it out."

On the patio the firemen have heaped charred timbers into a great pyre. From underneath, grayish water leaks onto the concrete. They would have hosed down the pile, and a rainstorm two days later added more water. We could have used that rain the night of the fire, but what we got was wind. This morning's sun picks out every ugly detail, and the heat draws a creosote odor from the hundred-year-old boards.

Heartsick, we're reduced to phrases that state the obvious.

"Jean's flowers," says Shorey. In cutting across the garden to get to the fence, the firemen trampled a rosebush and the *H. buxifolia*.

"The fence," I say. Boards have been yanked to clear a passage to Ajax's place. Easier than trying to negotiate his narrow walkway.

Bits of blackened roof and gravel litter the front steps. One of the banisters has broken loose. Everywhere, there's debris. I count eight smashed windowpanes. Considering the total of thirty-six panes in our Victorian-style windows, I'd say the firemen used great restraint when they vented the cottage.

Our door lolls open, its lock having been axed off.

"How will we lock the door?" I want to know. Shorey lets out a mirthless laugh, and says, "That's supposed to be a joke?"

As if a bellows were at work, puffs of dust escape the black cavity that used to be the façade of our cottage.

Near the door we're driven back by a burnt-rubber stench reminiscent of my father's work-clothes after he'd put in a shift at the tire factory. In a house-fire it's not only boards that burn: synthetics add their own noxious fumes. I had stayed inside to get my metal box, and I paid for that. Brain swelling inside my cranium, the world tilted and I started to vomit. At the E. R., they administered two liters of oxygen, and while I lay on the cool white sheet, curtains drawn around me, the doctor and medical tech ate up the story of Ajax and our fire, even motioning a male nurse to hurry over to "hear about this arson."

Not so fast, I said, repeating what the arson investigator had told me: "The crime of arson is notoriously hard to prove unless you can locate an incendiary device."

"A what?"

"Doesn't matter," I said dully, closing my eyes. I hadn't slept in a hundred years.

Hands clamped over nose and mouth, I follow Shorey inside. Except for a coating of soot over every surface and each leaf of the ten-foot Schleffera, our living-room's not too bad. Up near the ceiling, though, a dark ooze has moved down the walls—like the horror-movie scenario where the sunny little bungalow begins to exhibit underpinnings of evil. And why the brilliant light blasting from our right front room? Is the house having a spiritual experience? The curtains in there have been torn from the windows, and hang like Halloween ghosts from the dangling brass rods. Crunch and squish with every step, plaster and lath in a thick, filthy soup. I see that my collection of video-tapes has been doused, likewise the TV and VCR. Probing the VCR's tape receptacle, my fingers dip into a small lake. Clearly, the firefighters directed a fierce stream at the wall that's no longer there, the one that divided us from Ajax. I can't allow myself to see into the gloomy squalor of his hideout. From our loft bed in this room, I spent too many nights imagining the place.

"Unreal," says Shorey, shielding his eyes against the noon sky.

The ceiling's gone, the roof above it obliterated. In its place, a vast sheet of clear plastic sags with rainwater. Our lid has lifted. There is something like grandeur in that unexpected opening, and I can only gaze up in awe.

"Could be the first time anyone's seen sky from this room since they built the place," I say. "Before the roof went on some workman probably stood on this spot looking up, maybe a hundred years ago."

More than a hundred years ago. In the late nineteenth century cottages like this one, modular housing shipped by rail from Sears in Chicago, were going up all over San Francisco's Richmond District. You could buy one for three hundred dollars.

"And isn't it cool," says Shorey, "to see the old structural beams."

There are exactly two remaining structural beams.

"Let's get this over with. Really."

"Okay, okay," he says. "But I like what just happened."

"What just happened?"

"You forgot your misery for a minute."

Since the fire I've been trapped inside a waking nightmare where I seem to slip off the continental shelf and go plunging down till I collide with the sea-floor. The dead, silt-covered abyssal plain. Above me, miles of water impose a deafening pressure. No use fighting my way toward the surface. Better to lie flat out like a flounder.

For me, home equals sanity. How will I make it without my clawfoot tub, my lavender soak and four a.m. cup of tea? Pre-dawn in the back room with a chenille throw over my legs and a favorite text on my lap, something from Donne or Jacob Boehm, or my old standby, the Duino Elegies. The lonely, silent hour puts each day into context.

I am feeling a fair amount of self-pity, but I'm not the only one in this sorry fix.

As we move from room to room assessing the damage, I try to remember this is also Shorey's loss. The shambles we moved into nineteen years ago, in the days before Jean took over as landlady, had no kitchen ceiling, a rotted-out bathroom floor, road-cone orange on three of its walls, and some eager beaver had Varathaned the living-room floor, slathered matte black over beautiful blond hardwood. The plumbing was unspeakable, but no complaints from us. We were renting potential. With our own money and mostly Shorey's labor, we spent a year transforming the place. Shunted around as a child, nomadic for most of his adult years, Shorey had lived in forty-two domiciles before this one. By the time we married, he felt a nesting bird's need to settle, and was willing to do whatever it took to create a home.

With all the caution in the world, a house, especially a wood frame house, remains vulnerable to the wrong combination of oxygen, heat and fuel: the fire triangle. In the room I fixed up for Bernadette, firefighters' boots have ground fire's products—char, soot, ash—into the absorbent fibers of the white cotton rug. The lotus curtain hangs like a sad gray flag, and every bin on the wall stands open, having been blasted with pressurized water because one live ember in one of those bins could have flowered into flames amid the combustibles, the dozens of file folders bulging with research materials that are now sodden, useless. The manuscript of a friend's novel that I'd promised to read and critique: gluey pulp, the inkjet print running down its title page like wet mascara. And my burnt-out closet's now an open portal to Ajax's place.

Shorey tells me the entire roof will need to be replaced. We figure six weeks to rebuild.

"How will I make it through six long weeks?"

"Try," he says.

"But you're talking to a husk."

"Things'll be better when Bernadette arrives."

Bernadette descends from a warrior clan that includes ancient kings of Ireland. It took millennia to craft a Bernadette O'Neill, and she has carved a life for herself in the Arizona desert—not Phoenix or Tucson or even Sedona, but remote, dirt-track Arizona where one's close associates are wind and sky and lone predatory birds. A master potter who draws inspiration from desert tones, lichen colors, she's not into flash. Her bowls and wind bells incised with faux fossils and other prehistoric designs seem lifted from rock-face or the walls of Lascaux. Her first three years in the desert, she lived, winter and summer, in a canvas tent that eventually collapsed under heavy snow. She has been bitten by scorpions.

Bernadette was not fazed on hearing that because of fire she had lost her place to stay in San Francisco. When I reached her cell phone shortly after she'd crossed from Arizona into California, somewhere near Blythe, she said not to sweat the situation. She'd find another place—she had friends in the area—or sleep in the car. No biggie. I was to hang tight. She'd be along in a jif, and would spend her eight days here in town helping me to pack up the house.

"No way," I told her. "Not *every* day. That's no vacation."

"You don't get to say what constitutes a vacation . . . for me."

"All right, Bernadette. I know how stubborn you can be."

Now she's striding up the walk. No backpack: she must have left it in the car. The day is cruelly, mockingly beautiful with clear fresh air and sapphire sky. I'm on the bottom step, our blackened ruin as backdrop. If I were to snap a photo, it would show a woman barely five feet tall with a tumble of nut-brown hair and a blue-eyed, open expression. Clothing that says she's ready for work. Arizona sun has ruddied her fair, Celtic skin, but otherwise she's a walking advertisement for health.

Rather than comment as I take her on the excruciating tour, she merely nods to herself the way doctors do when patients reel off a litany of symptoms. "O-kay," she finally says, pivoting away from my ruined closet. "Got any boxes?"

"Only about a hundred. Used ones. Can you believe even used boxes cost two-something apiece?"

"So. You got a deal. Good. Let's start putting them together. We can do that while we talk."

"No boxes. Not today. I swept the steps and washed them down, and we're going to sit in the sun and eat Tofutti."

"Fine with me, but why waste an entire day?"

"Because tomorrow they're turning off our gas and electric. Because I've got two pints of Tofutti in the freezer that need to be eaten. Because I'm really freaked that they're shutting off power to the garage. That's where I work on the computer. Just for one day I want to hang onto the illusion of a grand and glorious summer."

"But when you called you said the rebuild would take six weeks. That leaves plenty of summer."

Pant-legs rolled, our bare feet dip into the afternoon as if into warm surf. Under us the enamel-red steps have cooled down, now that the sun has eased behind the house on its way west. Precise black shadows drag from the base of each bush and plant, though the garden's still bathed in high-noon brightness. Bright and still, not even breeze enough to stir the wind chimes. Bernadette and I concentrate on spooning the silky frozen dessert from our individual cartons.

Jean starts down her back stairs, hand never leaving the banister. A considerate landlady, she moves among her tenants in a way that's friendly but never intrusive. I see her hesitate before approaching us. Sunlight dazzles her froth of white hair.

She's looking serious. Serious is what I can do without right now. "It's been five days," she reminds me. "Shouldn't you begin emptying out this cottage?"

"Emptying out?" I hear the sun-drenched stupidity in my voice. Bernadette keeps on spooning Tofutti.

"Why, yes. Otherwise the contractor can't get started."

"But, Jean, the kitchen's pretty much untouched. Couldn't I leave it as-is? We've got millions of items in there. Why fill up more boxes than we need to?"

"Because they won't budge until everything's out. And the sooner they start, the sooner you'll be back in."

"I'm here to help," pipes up Bernadette, without glancing up from her vanilla treat.

The phone rings. Strange, walking through the foul-smelling house toward our kitchen phone, as if this were a normal day and I were about to embark on a normal conversation.

"Hello, dear," says Ruby, my mother-in-law, from three thousand miles away in Connecticut. "There's something you really need to know."

Beside the fact that I should have beaten down every door at City Hall till I got Ajax evicted? Beside the fact that we should have had renters' insurance? But I merely say, "Oh?"

"You'll have to wash every bit of fabric in strong detergent, and right away."

I have the nicest of mothers-in-law, a real peach. Like Jean, helpful but not intrusive. But this information, at this juncture, is almost too much to take in.

"Ruby, there's no *time*. I've got to get everything in boxes."

"Sorry, dear, but I'm afraid you'll have to make time. If you don't do it now, if you put your things into storage without washing them, they'll forever smell of smoke."

I'd always considered books to be our main freight, but now that I'm forced to gather up "every bit of fabric," it's clear that cloth dominates our lives. The laundromat is four blocks away, and to that laundromat I'll be hauling all our clothing, every towel and washcloth, the kitchen linens, bed linens including blankets and heavy comforters, the undamaged curtains and cotton throw rugs. With books, which are permanently on display, you know what you've got, but cloth hides in cupboards, closets, hampers, drawers. When I pluck these items from their neat, flat, discreetly stored piles, they expand to form a multicolored mountain on the living-room floor. Much that is fabric has been destroyed, but not enough. Dear God, not nearly enough.

I sort according to type of fabric: linen, cotton, silk, wool, as well as the various synthetics. Some fabrics are so finicky they die in anything but cold water. Others you can boil. Blankets and comforters get tumbled in the big, front-loading machines that take eighteen quarters. I live in terror of these machines, that after inserting my $4.50 they will refuse to start. This has happened. And in terms of cost alone, I can't concern myself with whether this or that item requires dry cleaning. I'm doing triage. Anything I deem worthy of saving goes to Bubble Factory. What doesn't survive gets tossed.

We possess one laundry cart, and I'm looking at a mound of wash that will translate to at least sixty to seventy-five loads.

"Logistics," says Bernadette. "You wash while I pack up the house."

She's willing to stay behind in the stink and filth while I frolic among the suds. Sounds good, but it won't work. Each day I'll need to commandeer nine or ten washers and nearly as many dryers, and that I can't handle alone. I tell Bernadette we'll fill up the cart and schlepp loads on our backs.

We agree. I go to the bank for a hundred dollars' worth of quarters. I know that before long I'll be buying another hundred.

Our first day out, we thump the cart over the threshold of an empty, sun-filled Bubble Factory. A line of thirteen washers waits with raised lids, and a wide-open table invites us to sort and fold. Next day, the place is thronged with people who shoot us evil looks for hogging so many machines, buying up so many little boxes of Tide that we threaten the general supply. Responding to these hostile vibes, Bernadette jogs over to Smart & Final for an SUV-sized container of generic detergent.

Once our things get stuffed into dryers, the worst is over. Then I sink into a chair and slip into no-think mode, my head automatically rotating in synch with the clock-wise, comic tumble of wash in seven or eight contiguous machines.

With an operation this big, we can't simply go bopping off for coffee. A washer might flash "Unbalanced," so that you need to reach in and readjust the tangled wet mess. Or a front-loader will balk like a donkey and refuse to move. A dryer will suddenly turn cold.

Mornings, we're Irish washerwomen. Afternoons, we pack. Somewhere in between, I treat Bernadette to brunch. Our golden hour, a ritual I will miss after she leaves.

Friends offer to help, but except for Bernadette all draw the line at working inside the cottage. One person cites the "toxic atmosphere," the danger of free-floating carcinogenic particles. Another cites the smell. Well, yes. Time has not diminished the stench. Or the soot. Try as we might to keep clean, Bernadette and I emerge at the end of each day looking like Dickensian chimney-sweeps.

We can't afford to be fastidious. We just heave to, and do our best to ignore the surroundings.

While my summer's been cut off at its green roots, life blooms for others in rich, luxuriant dailiness. They've got things to do, full schedules. I do understand, but how dare my friend call to tell me she can spare "forty minutes, on Friday," between lunch and her chiropractic appointment?

"Keep it up," says Shorey, "and you'll lose everyone."

"Not *you*, I hope."

"No, not me. Only, I wish you'd . . . grow up. Shit happens."

"Yeah. To *me*."

"To me, too, only you don't hear me bellyaching."

"So what's your message?"

"Take what you get and says thanks."

A minister's son, and the grandson of a minister, he's a twelfth-generation American descended from a line of preachers and pulpit-thumpers stretching back to the Puritans and Church of England dissenters. If I live to be a hundred, he'll never stop interposing a Christian perspective. Though no longer a churchgoer, he tries hard in this regard, holding himself to high standards, although the day after the fire I did hear him declare that, given the chance, he'd like to spread Ajax all over the pavement.

"You're not really mad at *people*," he now says. "You're pissed at God."

"And that's bad?"

"No. That's what he's there for. I mean, he lets some funky things go on. Just give your friends a break, okay?"

Packing's the main job, an enormous task that for reasons of convenience has to be done indoors. But we don't want to turn away willing workers, so have set up a box-assembly operation on the patio. Sam supervises the part-time assemblers, who come and go. Today they've all gone, and there's only Sam. Unless I insist that he take a break, he'll keep at it for five or six hours in the hot sun, stacking newly constructed boxes until they rise up around him like fortifications. He wears a brimmed hat, but the heat has dyed his face a shrimp pink.

I make a joke about mad dogs and Englishmen.

"This ain't the tropics," he says, "and it's way past noon."

I assure him that he's done more than enough. Time to go home.

"Do I smell age discrimination?"

Sam is eighty-six years old.

"Lots of smells around here, but that's not one of them."

He chuckles. "Like I said, I'll leave when I'm ready."

Besides Sam, I've got Bernadette to worry about. This morning she underwent dental surgery. When she phoned from downtown, I told her to stay away for a day or so, get some rest at her friend's place. Take baby sips of melted sorbet.

She countered with, "I'll be by when I'm done at the dentist's."

"Like hell you will."

"Expect me around one."

"Forget it, Bernadette. Laundry's all done. I can handle the rest."

"So. You're shutting me out."

"You can't be in all this filth after surgery! Ever hear of infection?"

I suspect Bernadette thinks infection is a self-induced state of mind. In her faded denim shirt and drawstringers, she sits in a half-lotus on our encrusted rug, wrapping kitchen gadgets in newspaper and placing them side by side in crosswise layers like kindling twigs in one of Sam's newly constructed boxes. She, who has pared down her own life, treats my myriad possessions, my redundant bits and pieces, with exaggerated respect. The fire has forced me to see how much I've hoarded, how little breathing room I've left in this poor cottage. When I tell Bernadette I'd like to throw all this shit out on the street for the scavengers who come by in the night who sift through our recycling bin, she flashes me a wry smile.

Pausing for a moment, she presses her palm to her cheek. The pain-killer must be wearing off.

Sam sticks his head in the doorway to say there's now a surfeit of boxes. If it's okay with me, he'll shut down the operation. Anything else I need?

"No, Sam. You've been a brick."

Two days later, and Bernadette's hugging the northern coast route on her way to Washington State. A circuit-rider who spends her vacation ministering to those in trouble, she will rescue yet another friend, a single mother who lives tucked away in the Yakima Valley.

"But I'll see you," she says, pointing, "when I swing back down this way in two weeks."

"Where will you sleep?"

"In the van. At a rest stop."

"Is that . . . safe?"

"As safe as the city," and she glances round at our burnt-out hovel.

I try to make her take money for a motel, but all she'll accept is bread, fruit and bottled water for the trip. Pretty thin fare, so I dash over to Smart & Final for a family-size jar of peanut butter and a block of cheese.

I'm on my own. No Bernadette, no Sam, no box-makers. No Shorey. He's at work across the bay, in Mill Valley. He says interacting with customers helps him to forget for a while.

I'm picking up where Bernadette left off, packing up the kitchen. But I don't wrap each item. Except for glassware and crockery, I dump stuff in boxes and shut my ears to the teeth-tingling jangle of metal on metal. Why does any couple need *three* can-openers? And here's the knife that cut the wedding cake nineteen years ago: never used since that day. So what if it's got a mother-of-pearl handle? The blade's gone rusty.

I hear a clawing sound on the other side of the cardboard arroyo leading from the front door to the living-room corner where my cat's food and water bowls used to be. Packing creates its own architecture, structures that rise up without design or intent: walls made of storage boxes, book-pile buttresses. They'll be dismantled in a day, but a cat doesn't know that, sees them as a threat to the permanent order. Bridie has been more or less missing for a week. Once she did appear, but as soon as I blurted out, "Oh, my poor baby!" she bolted. I've seen her black tail flicking round the corner to the atrium, a restricted space where gray light filters down and one tenant has been brave enough to try and force tomato plants, a "fog-tolerant" variety. So as not to spook my cat, I tiptoed back there, along a passage so narrow I had to draw in my shoulders and shimmy past a vertical pipe entwined with desiccated weeds, only to find—nothing. I lay on my belly on cold concrete, peering through the place where two missing bricks provide entryway under the main house. Cats do squeeze through, vaulting down into the dark maw, but they have a tough time making their way out again.

I know she's around. I know she hears me. I also know I'm being punished for having let Ajax destroy her habitat.

Innumerable times I've called her name, only to have it absorbed into the white fog of early June. I've transferred her bowls to the garage and created a cat-bed on the couch in there. I leave the door open for hours. Other cats have crept in and eaten her food.

Sick with worry, I've stood in the garage doorway brandishing her bowl, reminding her of skeletal cats I saw in Delhi who'd likely worship me as a deity for providing such a warm, dry place, with an unending supply of fresh kibble. Will she take my words as an ultimatum? I think not. She knows where her power lies: in silence, stonewalling.

Now she's scratching at the other side of the cardboard tunnel where I sit. I set down the wedding knife, and wait. I don't call her name or go "Tsk-tsk-tsk." Anything I say will be taken as patronizing baby-talk.

Soon enough she comes padding towards me, the furry white bib and boots gone dingy from sleeping rough. She sniffs at the boxes, pretends the gravelly bits lodged in the carpet-pile are oh-so-interesting. I do not move, do not breathe. We are ever so close to a rapprochement. With her nose she nudges something that looks like a cocklebur. I see the tiny nares twitch and contract. Another step forward, and she's sniffing at a pancake of mud from the bottom of somebody's shoe. The moment she raises her head, acknowledging that I'm there, an air-horn blares up Geary

Boulevard. Might be a fire-truck or an ordinary truck, but that's all it takes. Bridie lets out a howl, a primal cry that speaks of all the terrors she's experienced in the past week, the misery brought on by her dufus owners. She turns and run, but instead of heading for the front door, force of habit takes her into the back where, whenever she wanted, I would open the window so she could leap onto the railing and then down into the Sixth Avenue backyard that forms a part of her territory.

I don't want her in that room. Where the wall's been burnt away and the floorboards end is charred spurs, there's a sheer drop-off into Ajax's place.

Scrambling to my feet, I follow along, though not too closely.

Her cries are no longer a cat's but an infant's. They start as a mewling, but as she stares into the void that surely points to the end of life as she's known it, she breaks into an all-out squall worthy of a human two-year-old. I can't let her jump.

Inching closer, I try to keep my voice level. "Bridie, honey? Stay away from there, okay?"

From the back, she's mostly black. Only her boots hint at the cute white configuration seen on frontal view. She's a small, sturdy, butch sort of cat, born under the Sign of Taurus. The palm of my hand fits neatly over the rounded cap of her head, and this is normally the only endearment she'll permit. She's on the brink of the ragged boards, moaning, inconsolable.

"Sweetie?" I venture. "Would you please move away from there?"

I know my cat. One wrong move on my part, and just to demonstrate her independence she will dive into that jagged, filth-laden lair.

This takes all the skill—a skill I'm not sure I possess—of a firefighter trying to coax the suicide away from the ledge. You let them know you're there and that you care, and then it's a question of which instinct will prevail. Bridie's a smart little girl. She knows danger when she sees it. On the other hand, she's angry with me for obvious reasons, and no doubt for cat-gripes she has nurtured since kittenhood. Hurling herself over the edge would represent the perfect way to pay me back.

She stops crying. We are locked in the moment.

What does she see? Does she know, on a preconscious level, that she was born in that cottage? Long before Ajax came, before the negligent absentee owner bought the place from the previous negligent absentee owner who began gutting the cottage for renovation but stopped midway when the City refused to issue the permit—before all that, a nice Christian Scientist lady owned the property. She lived in front, and was not interested in making a bundle but in having a decent tenant who'd do a little yardwork and keep an eye out for her, now that she was ninety. She got the perfect twosome: a young physicist and his artist girlfriend. Over the next six months they revamped the place, and when they were done they invited us to dinner: homemade deep-dish Chicago pizza served on mismatched thrift-store plates in primary colors. We dined by candlelight. I recall a magical evening, warm weather and crickets. Somewhere in there they told us their cat was pregnant. Would we be interested in a kitten?

She came to us at six weeks, with a red ribbon round her neck and a birth certificate. They had named her Bridie. Six weeks old. I figured I was her mother.

"Please," I say. "Mommy wants you to come away from there."

Before jog-trotting from the room, she fixes me with a look that can only mean, *You are such a moron.*

After she leaves I let myself look. The sight is awful, mesmerizing. In the same way that I don't really want to see the guys with food-flecked beards and the brown on the back of their pants, or their rat's-nest sleeping arrangements under the marquee of the defunct movie theater up the street—in that same way, I've packed and sorted these past ten days with my back to the place where he lived, this man I initially pitied, then feared.

Before the fire there would have been the same barn-like duskiness, cut off from outside and percolating its own stinks, but now his place borrows light from ours. Daylight shafts down from the tall windows and the opening where our roof used to be. We did not exactly share a wall with Ajax; a sliver of San Francisco air separated the two wood frame dwellings. With his left wall gone, though, and our right one obliterated, we seem to have merged: light with dark, civilization with all that's feral. And feral is what our home has become: smoke-black, smelly, a den fit for hoboes.

His flies now swarm into our place. After feasting on whatever's in the galvanized bucket down below, they make lazy sorties across the open border, but only after buzzing round the stovepipe that still protrudes from the wall. That pipe was once connected to the stove in which our friends baked pizza for us in their newly enlarged kitchen.

They had knocked out an interior wall, laid down carpet, installed shelves, painted, decorated, cleared out a dumpster's worth of garbage from the basement and begun creating an office down there when their landlady died.

The new owner gave them the boot, then had her relatives gut the place, leaving only the outer shell, so that the eventual incumbent, Ajax, had a cathedral ceiling, sixteen feet of festering gloom from ground-level clear through to the roof.

Space, flies, shit in a bucket: that's where the story ends. Well, maybe.

My friend, Annette, who seasons her talk with Yiddish, likes to quote a saying that translates into English as, *If you look, you find.* The very sound of Yiddish conveys a meaning that's bound up with the cynical humor of those who've suffered greatly and have good reason to be wary. The saying is not an exhortation to look more deeply. In fact, Annette will use it as an excuse to stay away from doctors, who, she claims, have a way of unearthing ailments you'd rather not know about.

I'm afraid that if I look, I'll find. Much easier to hate the little Mary-singing bastard who set us on fire. I don't care to know about his sad childhood or his drink-related craziness. I don't want to feel sorry for the guy.

But I don't seem to be moving.

From where I sit, I can see the stovepipe, the glinting slop-bucket, the fairly decent mattress that might be a Sealy Posturepedic®. I see Venetian red on the far wall, a smoky-café shade that ends abruptly, six feet above Ajax's encampment. I remember when that paint was new.

I've seen photos of houses bombed out during the London Blitz. Typically, there will be a rubbled crater beside a ragged cutaway of room stacked on top of room, three walls remaining, the fourth having crashed into the abyss. A private world, now brutally exposed. Passersby stood gaping at the flowered wallpaper, the glass-fronted cupboard with its teacups and standing plates, the toilet with its pull-chain where the master of the house might have sat reading the *Times* while he strained for a bowel movement that final morning before a doodlebug destroyed his home. The photos took me back to a time when I would stare, for hours, into my girlhood dollhouse. A house with no inhabitants, only furnishings. It was I who created the people and made them speak to each other in the miniature tin rooms. My people never raised their voices above a civilized contralto. Nor did they have dozens of kids and endless money problems. They had plenty to eat, and sang songs round the piano. They did not come home drunk.

I graduated from dollhouse to books. My five brothers rampaged through the rooms, but I was far away with Nancy Drew or the March sisters, then even farther afield with Martin and Osa Johnson, in Borneo, or with Henry Stanley, struggling up the Congo.

Not much of a dwelling, Ajax's place, with the puckered blue mattress and the shit-bucket, but he fought like hell to keep out the man who'd tried to bust in that night. I'd have to say, he was fighting to save his home. Just as we tried to have Ajax arrested in order to save our own.

We have not only merged with Ajax, we've traded places. In jail, he's got three hots and a cot, while we are essentially homeless.

The packing done, our stuff goes into storage. Shorey's boss offers a corner of the company warehouse, partly open to the elements. All day, trucks and vans come and go through the wide portal. Anyone could pick off our TV. Possessions that the fire has spared now stand unprotected. *Que sera, sera.*

After some jousting with the contractor, I'm permitted to keep one item in the cottage: the eight-foot umbrella plant. While Shorey talks with the man, I take off up the street for two coffees.

When I back get, Shorey's slumped in the garden chair, head in his hands. I set the coffees down on the concrete. "What's the matter?"

"We're fucked." His face has taken the white imprint of his fingers.

"Now what?"

"Contractor says it'll take not six weeks but three months."

"That can't be. Shorey, you've gotta talk to the guy."

"He won't budge."

"We can't rattle around in limbo for three whole months."

"Actually, what he said was, *At least* three months."

CHAPTER FIVE

ANAPEST

Our first night at the Ocean Breeze, a stiff Pacific wind pursued us up the street and into the parking lot behind the motel where it wailed like a banshee across the vacant space. We were the only car. We were soon to learn, though, that here at the Breeze people tended to tumble in late, vehicles piling into the lot around eleven, their comings and goings linked to the action at Mister Bo's, the bar that animated a front corner of the ground floor.

Hauling our bags from the trunk, tired and grimy, we let ourselves be blown across the macadam by the salt wind that really did seem that night to be a *bean sidhe*, the keening ghost-woman of Irish folklore. The motel office, cramped but warm, smelled of basmati rice and the biting mix of spices that told us someone would soon be dining on a good, strong, reviving curry.

Shorey asked if I had the voucher. I said yes, but checked my purse to make certain.

No one at the front desk. From inside came a staccato exchange, in Hindi, the woman's voice overriding the man's as she settled in for what sounded like a frayedat-the-edges complaint, words to keep herself energized while she cooked the dinner. A sudden sizzle of hot oil, and the place began to fill with a fried-onion fragrance.

Rearranging the bags at my feet, I let my gaze travel across the tourist brochures: fun things to do in San Francisco. Outside, the wind had picked up.

"They have to take us in, don't they, Shorey? They can't turn us away?"

"Calm down. That paper you've got is the same as money."

"You're sure of that."

"Red Cross called and confirmed. You were there. You heard the guy."

"God, I just want a bath. Or a shower—I don't care."

"Me first in the shower. I can smell myself."

And he popped the bell a second time.

The living quarters went silent except for the steady sizzle of the fry-pan. A tall, gaunt man brushed aside the paisley curtain and took us in—suitcases, plastic bags, bedraggled appearance—with one practiced glance. He wore a dark gray stocking cap pulled low over his brow that accentuated the sunken cheeks and dusky half-moons under his eyes. He had the world-weary look of someone living on intimate terms with disillusionment. Peering at Shorey, he merely said, "Yes?"

Shorey, who'd spent a lifetime working with the public, had also seen a bit of the world. Tired as he was, he turned on the charm, remarking about the fresh ocean breeze and therefore the aptness of the motel's name.

Waving dismissively, the man said, "I did not name this place."

"Well, we're awfully glad to be here," and Shorey slid the Red Cross form across the counter until it came just short of the man's fingertips.

"Ah. Red Cross people."

We admitted that we were.

"We are presently filled to capacity. I do have something, but you won't like it. Very noisy. Right over the bar."

Shorey assured him we'd be grateful for any accommodation he could offer.

"Hah. Well, in that case . . ."

We introduced ourselves, filled out a motel form, and the owner, Mr. Vyas, studied it line by line.

"I see you are not from Sixth Street," he said.

"No, no," I confirmed. "Not from Sixth Street."

"Inner Richmond," added Shorey. "Nineteen years at the same address."

The man's jaw muscles relaxed visibly. "You see, they come here, these Sixth-Street people—" and he stopped short.

We knew the rest. We had read the exposes. In the downtown's underbelly, near the old bus station, filthy, roach-ridden hotels lined Sixth Street. You had to have dropped right through the bottom of your life to seek a room in one of these places. And they were not cheap. The articles spoke of rats and discarded needles, feces on bathroom walls, the usual urban horrors, not to mention the fire danger in such tumbledown warrens. Inevitably, there'd be a five-alarmer, with fifty or sixty residents needing beds for a night, a week, a month. In a way, I empathized with Mr. Vyas. They came to his place, and they made a mess. On the other hand, our man at the Red Cross had warned us that when our benefits ran out, we, too, might have to seek out a south-of-Market hotel. And he had named two that were affordable and "not too bad."

"But will we be safe there at night?" I asked.

Avoiding our eyes, he said, "Safer than on the street."

The only person who now stood between us and a flea-bag hotel was Mr. Vyas. And so, kicking aside our compassionate ideals, we distanced ourselves from the "Sixth-Street people." Not because we looked down on them, but because we didn't want to end up as one of them. When Shorey divulged that the next day I'd be receiving a master's degree, I chirped right up and asked if I could borrow an iron to press my graduation gown, thus establishing myself as a decent, fastidious sort of woman, no different, essentially, than Mrs. Vyas herself—who could be heard banging plates onto a table—and certainly bearing no resemblance to anyone on Sixth Street.

We were in.

Mr. Vyas looked us up and down. "You know," he said, "I can do better for you. Not tonight, I'm afraid. You will have to put up with it. But tomorrow a good room will come vacant on the top floor. Much less noise. More privacy."

Like two who were spiking a fever, red-faced, heat breathing from every pore after our showers, we slid into bed from opposite sides and sat stiffly against the padded headboard. Our hands, composed on the white sheet-flap as if for a Flemish portrait, seemed to be asking, Now what? The TV's blank screen stared back at us, but we didn't feel like watching. While Shorey showered I had pressed my graduation gown on the quilted comforter and returned the iron to Mr. Vyas. Winding the cord more carefully than I had done, he reminded me that local calls would be billed at fifty cents each. "I am only telling you," he said, "because if you are here long-term the charges do tend to mount." I asked whether Mill Valley, where Shorey worked, was considered local, and he answered, "Most definitely not."

Shorey kneaded his pillow into the shape of a sourdough batard before wedging it behind his lower back. He was wearing his Breathe Right® strip that tugged at and widened his nostrils. I asked if he had remembered to apply his Lanacane®, and those were the first words either of us uttered since entering the place. Off to the right, in the steam-whitened bathroom, our wet towels hung from a nub of metal, the vestige of a towel bar from some long-ago time. I had rammed the thermostat to eighty-five, and the heater fired up, churning away dramatically in its corner. Our suitcases sat with open flaps on the recessed table. Underneath we'd placed the bulging plastic bags, two for each of us, and lined up our shoes, Shorey's 15s jutting out beyond my size 7s.

In arranging the bags and setting out our toiletries, we had completed our housekeeping. Made a home. Not even a cloistered monk could have boasted such a simple routine. I mentioned this insight to Shorey.

"True enough, but no monk has to listen to that hell-wagon going by every fifteen minutes."

Every fifteen minutes, a minor earthquake. The city had been experimenting with Italian streetcars—if it's from Europe it must be better—and people along the routes had to endure the metallic screech and seismic tremors each time one of these monsters rumbled by. Complaints had poured into the newspapers.

"Should we turn off the lights?" It was 10:45.

"Not yet," said Shorey.

"Want to watch the news?"

"Not right now."

For a long moment he compressed his lips, then dove for the drawer of his night-table. Out came the white-covered Gideon Bible.

I could have predicted this.

At times of great strain, Shorey forgets his opposition to the Christian fundamentalism in which he grew up, and to bible-thumping in general, and will reach, reflexively, for the Good Book. I've got nothing against the Bible. Truth is, I've never read it except to pick away at well-known sections: the Psalms, the Song of Solomon, first chapters of Genesis. I am not proud of this gap in my education. My only defense is that I grew up in an era when Catholics did not read the Bible and, moreover, were not encouraged to read the Bible. I never saw any of my friends or any Catholic adult toting a Bible. We carried missals, big fat St. Joseph's missals, thick with holy cards. As for the Holy Bible, there seemed to be an unspoken rule: better to let the priest interpret the Gospel from the pulpit on Sunday. That way you won't get into trouble, interpret something incorrectly and thus sail off the edge of the earth into the boiling seas of doctrinal error. During the 1950s, the Church did not exactly forbid, but neither did it look with favor upon laypersons studying what most of us viewed as a Protestant book.

I love hearing Shorey read from the Bible in his deep baritone voice, though in the early, tempestuous days of our marriage he tended to use it as a weapon: waving the book about and stridently quoting passages that bolstered his point of view whenever we'd have an argument. At such times he favored Jeremiah 31 (*But every one shall die for his own iniquity: every man that eateth the sour grape, his teeth shall be set on edge*). When the argument naturally escalated he'd lick a finger and frantically flip the tissue-thin pages until he came to the Lamentations of Jeremiah (*All our enemies have opened their mouths against us*), his voice soaring inside the tiny cottage so that I'd feel I was at a tent revival. In those moments he seemed to have become his father, the evangelical minister, employing homiletic inflections to dramatize the sermon and drive home his point.

In time, we settled into a greater felicity and I enjoyed hearing him read, though the book always did feel a little foreign. Twice I tried to plow through to the end, but got bogged down in Genesis 10 and 11 with the generations of the sons of Noah and all the begats. What did I care who begat whom? I didn't know these people, who had weird names like Serug and Nahor. Maybe it was too late for me to imbibe the Scriptures, which came across as alien, the way a painted plaster saint or smoking censer would have seemed to Shorey, who'd grown up worshipping in austere chambers that were bare of graven images.

Tonight, though, my nerves were tweaking, and I didn't want TV. I wanted to be read to. His voice pitched low, Shorey chose only the most lyrical passages from Ecclesiastes and First Corinthians (*Beareth all things, believeth all things, hopeth all things, endureth all things*).

Gliding high above our troubles, we set forth into the blue-white world of Judea and heard the words of Jesus. *But after that I am risen. I will go before you into Galilee.* I then felt on my neck and shoulders the hot desert breath, a fiercely therapeutic heat that melted my trapezius muscles. I was truly into it, eyes shut, breathing serenely, when the music began thundering up from Mister Bo's. Eleven o'clock, party time at the bar. Our room rocked with the *boom-boom-BANG* of the anapestic beat, the disco meter that had insinuated itself into the culture via the Bee Gees and *Saturday Night Fever*, the "deadly anapestic," a martial rhythm that set scientists to writing articles in the late seventies and early eighties, warning us that even to hear this wretched beat from a distance—say, the radio of some low-rider's car—would compromise one's health. Studies were performed. Laboratory mice were said to have become homosexual from extended exposure to *Stayin' Alive*.

Shorey kept on reading. Jesus had attained the Mount and begun delivering the Beatitudes. One of our wet towels fell from the vestigial towel-rack. The music penetrated the floor like so many pneumatic drills. No wonder some of the Sixth-Street folks had gone postal and started tearing up the place. I could no longer hear Shorey's words, so he placed the silk ribbon at Matthew 5 and closed the book. We turned off the lights.

"He did say that tomorrow we'd get a better room."

"If we don't," said Shorey, "I'll go down there and remind him."

"But I wouldn't be . . . too assertive."

"I'll do whatever it takes to get some sleep. I've got to work." And he fluffed up the pillow, easing it under his head.

Too tired to remonstrate, too tired to worry that tomorrow he'd raise his voice to Mr. Vyas and get us thrown out, I closed my eyes. Under the covers, we held hands. We stayed that way until the banshee came alive in the form of a siren that tore us from sleep.

Sitting straight up, I began shaking, hyperventilating. "What in the world? That was right outside!"

A drawn-out, electric silence. Like a wire stretched far beyond its tensile capacity. 2:10, said the white digits on the TV. Since the fire I'd been having this dream: Ajax, coming at me from out of the dark, the twin beams of his eyes like miners' headlamps. Now this: a siren.

"I'm not dreaming? You heard it, too?"

Without answering, Shorey made for the door.

Ours was the last unit on the second floor; all other doors remained shut, the rooms dark, curtains drawn. No wind now, just the shadowy murmur of the surf, four blocks away. I looked down on a full lot, car-roofs gleaming dully. One person had wedged their vehicle into a space that didn't exist, blocking our car. Others, too, had parked erratically.

Mr. Vyas, still wearing his knitted cap, came sprinting along the passage. "Most dreadfully sorry," he said, winded from climbing the stairs. "They come up from the bar and they do this mischief. Always it is happening." And he fiddled with the fire-alarm on the wall outside our room.

"So you're saying it was a false alarm?" Shorey tucked his sweatshirt into his plaid pajama bottoms.

"False alarm, yes. These drunkards—they will do anything."

"Well, one of them seems to have blocked my car."

Mr. Vyas turned on us a look of utter weariness. "Can it wait till morning? Or should I rouse the person?"

"It can wait."

He kept at his task. The alarm made a brief, premonitory squeak before going silent. "It will be okay," he said, folding his arms over his sweater vest. "No further trouble tonight."

Not the case.

Back in bed, we turned away from the window side, each settling into a fetal curl. The darkness sifted down, softly weighting the covers, our faces, our eyelids. Far away was the fire scene, and our missing cat. They had Ajax in custody, in the County slammer. A brief thought drifted past as to whether he, too, might be lying awake, not between ironed sheets, of course, but in some sort of bed, and maybe thinking about his blue mattress and his old hideout. The heater, now set to seventy, came on intermittently. It had just done its stint, and shuddered into silence.

Mister Bo's had closed for the night. No streetcar at this hour, only an owl-bus that ran but rarely. All man-made noise seemed to have been sucked out to sea, and the surf itself sounded like distant freeway traffic: dull, soothing, sleep-inducing. I was nearly under when a woman started to shriek and a man yelled an obscenity, then came the splintery sound of something wooden being heaved against the adjoining wall.

I nudged Shorey. "Think we should do something?"

"Do?" Groaning, he flipped himself over.

"Call the cops, maybe?"

In the next room, a man might be throttling a woman.

Before getting into bed I'd cracked open the window and inch or so, and the breeze parted the heavy brown curtains. With the aid of his BreatheRight® strip, Shorey took in long, even draughts of ocean air. Tomorrow he'd have to make it through my commencement, speech after boring speech. Let the poor guy sleep.

After the graduation, seven thousand students sitting on a football field in the fog, Shorey took me to dinner at a Thai restaurant two blocks from the motel. Over pad thai and salad, a red votive candle flickering between us on the inlaid table, he told me how proud he felt. "When I saw you walk across that stage," he said, "it almost felt like I was graduating. I never finished, but you did it—twice."

Doing it twice had taken years—ten years of wanting each day to be the next because the next day would bring me that much closer to the finale. But the finale had slipped by without my noticing. Was it the moment when the Dean of Humanities handed me my diploma? Was it when we graduates marched off the field, already breaking rank, zigzagging between other graduates on the sodden grass to reach the bleachers where friends and family waited? Or had the finale, the real finale, taken place four days before when Ajax set fire to our house? I looked across the table at the man for whom I'd had so little time or attention these past ten years, and realized—though I couldn't have said why—that it was just possible I'd been a fool.

We stepped out into a radiant morning, the ocean alive with white breakers. As if the night of the anapest had never happened, the parking lot was empty of all cars except ours. Far off by the horizon, the sea scintillated with what appeared to be liquid lava, so brilliant I had to close my eyes. It was barely eight, but the sky had attained a deep peacock blue. "Let's climb," said Shorey, and so we hiked to the third floor for a more panoramic view. Our own neighborhood was flat as a pool table, but in this part of town we saw houses in orderly rows dipping down to the beach. Under the sun, a certain flat blue roof resembled a reservoir.

I put my hand out and touched the topmost leaves and sticky red flowers of a bottlebrush tree. From inside the foliage came an incredible bird chorus. Every moment more birds, wrens and plump little finches, alighted all over the treetop. The whole canopy quivered with their delicate weight. I had looked on trees from above, when flying low before a landing, but never like this, at such close range.

"If only I could stay here all day," I said to Shorey.

"Then do it."

"I can't."

"Come on, you just graduated. Enjoy yourself."

But what about Bridie, her food bowls? Also, the contractor might show. I should talk to our landlady, and before PG&E turned off the juice to our place I needed to call my mom and sister in Pennsylvania—on our own phone line, not the one here at the motel where Mr. Vyas would likely dun us a hundred bucks for such a call.

Though I'd rather have holed up at the Ocean Breeze, reading fiction and drinking take-out tea, I had to return each day to the scene. Even after Bernadette and I finished packing, sorting and washing everything washable, even after she'd taken off, finally, for Washington State— I needed to remain on-site, at least for the sake of my cat who would not have been welcome at the motel. Each day I faced the spectacle of our sad, blackened house in order to be there for Bridie, to feed her and provide a reassuring human presence. And since, by some quirky circumstance, PG&E had turned off the gas but not our electric, I was back to sitting all day in the brown-walled garage, tapping away on my book.

Some mornings I couldn't stomach the prospect of another ten-hour stretch in The Dungeon, as I had come to call the place, and I'd ask Shorey to please feed Bridie on his way to work so I could stay behind at the Breeze.

"Get some writing done," he'd say, patting my head.

And I really did mean to. I asked myself: Where is it ordained that in order to produce, a writer must remain in brown seclusion, manacled to a computer? Sitting on the comfy bed, I faulted my Catholic training for implanting in me the belief that only through suffering could I bring forth anything of beauty. Stashing a couple of pillows behind my back, I scribbled some Notes to Myself, then crafted a few sentences—real writing, as opposed to motivational notes. Peering round the room, desperate for the next idea to detach itself from the wall or spring from one of the open suitcases, I noticed that even this place had taken on the gloomy aspect of the garage. Those brown curtains!

I really meant to keep writing, but the maid, having seen the open drapes, came by to announce she was about to start cleaning our room. And how long would that take? *Una hora, mas o menos.*

The previous day I had spied a nautical-looking café at the bottom of our street, across from where the dunes hummocked above the beach. The Sea Dog featured sun-bleached boards, swags of torn netting, and a ship's figurehead mounted over the door. Coffeehouses, in my experience, were not conducive to writing. Too much sensory barrage. But here, at least, I'd be left alone. I didn't know a soul in this part of town. I stepped into a cozy jumble of stained pillows, gimpy chairs, even an old red banquette. The smell of burnt coffee and clam chowder. They sold cheese danishes and glazed donuts. Right away, I liked the place. Ordering tea—they didn't ask what kind, just handed me a Lipton's®—I listened in on a couple of world travelers, b.s. artists trying to outshine one another. A bookcase, dangerously aslant, contained old Penguin paperbacks. When finally I picked up my pen, I saw that two hours had melted away.

Though I learned to work around the vagaries of the cleaning schedule, I never got any writing done at the motel. Nevertheless, I gave myself one day a week there and began burrowing into the neighborhood. Don't, said the little voice. This is not your home. I hauled our clothing to a nearby launderette with pre-electronic washers that actually had a Wool cycle. I began to think of a certain corner table at The Sea Dog as my own. I catalogued the different types of birds that visited the bottlebrush tree.

The motel's main attraction lay in its sheer distance from the fire scene. Nobody knew us. We didn't have to smile or socialize. Evenings, we were free to be as miserable as we liked. Our furnishings and possessions had been reduced to a minimum, and I believe we both found a sere beauty in that enforced simplicity.

We rarely went out at night, not even to take a walk. Had we been able to barricade ourselves inside Room 39, we would have. Behind the brown curtains we watched the News; we read, sometimes to each other; wrote in our journals; and slept. There were only two places to be: in the bathroom or on the bed. Whenever the phone rang, we'd glance at each other, big-eyed, as if it might be the Gestapo calling.

Sunday night, and I've cranked open the bathroom window to let out the steam. Wisps of sound from Mister Bo's. It's only nine: still early. I can see all the way along 45th Avenue to the dark forest of Golden Gate Park. The night outside has the grainy look of a Noir film. Aureoles of mist surround the streetlights. The street itself, beetle-black and wet, shines under the misty lights.

Warm from my shower, I'm about to start reading a library book: an Indian author I've just discovered. Suddenly my chest tightens. There's a clenched fist under the breastbone. This has happened before, so I know it's not a heart attack. I hunch forward, my forehead against the clammy wall. If there were a towel rack, I'd grab hold.

I don't have to look too far to figure out why I'm having an anxiety attack. Tomorrow morning, while Shorey's at work, I will have to go downtown to ask for another week's lodgings. In order to place people who've been made homeless by fire or other disasters, the Red Cross works in tandem with a City agency called Central Relocation. You may get a total of a month out of these agencies, but you will have to visit one or the other at the beginning of each week to obtain your authorization form.

You will have to—and here's the hard part—play the supplicant. My first time in the supplicant's chair, while the Red Cross worker jotted down our data, I thought for a moment of those forced to beg routinely such as Welfare people who have to face the blatant scrutiny and possible innuendoes from a bored or burnt-out caseworker, as well as the seediness of the facility itself. Our homelessness was viewed as temporary, and in no way our "fault." Yet by the second week I was being asked, gently enough, if we'd managed to find ourselves a place. No one we knew who had a spare room?

By Week Three, I'd become acutely conscious of my knees. I felt I should be down on them, thumping my chest in a mea culpa. I noted that the cup of coffee offered on my first visit was not given again. And why should it be? Big blaze yesterday on Sixth Street, and those folks needed rooms—one of which we happened to be hogging. Knees together, hands folded in my lap, I waited while the man filled out our form. Four coffee mugs sat clustered by the In-Box on his desk. From the wall, Cezanne's Woman in Blue looked down on me with a quizzical tilt of the head.

Monday morning, and the signs are favorable. I leave early, allowing two hours to make it to my 10:15 appointment at Central Relocation. Bustling over to Judah, I find an N sitting quietly at the corner, empty and waiting. This means a straight shot downtown, with time to spare. I might stop at that kiosk for a latte and sip the froth as I amble up Gough Street to the agency.

A group has gathered by the front door of the streetcar, one of those Italian jobs that breathes fire even when it idles. I hear no sound. See no driver inside. A woman angrily denounces the MUNI, our transit system, while other people stand around dispiritedly, not much interested in her fulminations. She sees me coming, and calls out, "Don't even bother. Nothing's running."

"Nothing's *running*?"

"No *streetcars* are running. Electrical's down. Better get a bus."

"But where?" I do a 360 right there in the street. "I've got an important appointment!"

"Then go grab a 71," she says, waving me away from the N-Judah as if it were about to explode. "Over on Noriega. It's only four blocks."

Four extremely long blocks. Finally, I break into a run, but it still takes twenty minutes to reach Noriega. On the gray, windblown corner, two old Asian ladies with shopping bags stand with their backs to the ocean. Each has the resolute look that says she's prepared to wait forever. Good thing, too, because the 71 doesn't show for half an hour. Downtown, it drops me off in a thicket of unfamiliar streets where I see dozens of homeless—scarcely a doorway without its sleeper. A man gathers up his belongings, at the insistence of a store-owner, but most remain burrowed inside their bags or under ratty blankets, in the middle of the morning, while members of the parallel society, myself included, simply sidestep these impediments to get where we're going.

Not a good feeling, to be stepping over recumbent bodies.

I dash into a coffee shop for directions, which turn out to be wrong. I then approach a suited man on Van Ness, who gives me directions contrary to those I received in the coffee shop. I arrive at Central Relocation by 10:20. Alone in the elevator, a narrow but well-lit chamber, I push "2." Nothing happens. I push "3," just to get things going. Nothing. I jab the red emergency button. Shouldn't that set off an alarm, or something? I push "Open Door," figuring I'll run up the stairs. I push "Close Door," since that's the only remaining button.

Trying not to start bawling because that would mess up my face, I implore God to deliver me from this upended coffin. I pound on the door. Shout for help. Beg forgiveness for all the times I made light of my mother's elevator phobia.

A door opens. A young man enters. He presses "2." With a serene glissade, the elevator conveys us to the second floor.

I explain why I'm late to Ms. Jamison, omitting the elevator debacle. She listens impassively, then reminds me that this will be our final week at the Ocean Breeze.

"But if I asked at the Red Cross?"

"You can ask, but he'll almost certainly say 'No.'"

I file away that "almost" for next Monday. For now, I've got a signed form and feel like winged Mercury as I tear down the stairway and out into the breezy morning. So many ways to celebrate, without spending much at all. A latte. A visit to one of the rooftop gardens in the business district, with my latte. That same visit, with latte and a copy of *Martha Stewart LIVING*. But Central Relocation is a long way from the business district, and if I'm going to board a bus, why not just go home? Walk down to The Sea Dog. Order a Lipton's and spend two hours with my Indian author.

Back at the motel, I can't wait to call Shorey and report the good news. The open drapes cast a swath of creamy light over the comforter. I settle myself on the freshly made bed and pick up the phone. There is no dial tone. I tap the button, repeatedly tap the freaking button. Still no dial tone.

Grabbing my purse, I practically cascade down the two floors to the office. No one at the counter. I pop the bell. Mr. Vyas shows little surprise on seeing me.

"You see"—and he clears his throat—"you have not paid your telephone bill."

"I thought we were supposed to pay at the end, before we left."

"If I allowed that sort of thing, some people would skip out without paying so much as a penny."

"But we're not like that."

"Still. Your bill. It's very high."

He hands me the itemized invoice. Twenty-two dollars. I see that one local call has been billed at five dollars instead of the agreed-upon fifty cents. A typo, no doubt, that extra zero, but I don't argue, just fish in my purse for the cash.

"Hah. Good," he says. "You are reinstated."

Mr. Vyas steps out of the office and around to the back, where he stops in his tracks. San Francisco is simmering in 95-degree heat, the seamless blue sky about to liquefy and melt into the sea. It's late afternoon, nearly six. The saffron light that bathes his face seems to emanate from inside, making the man appear almost healthy. This is the light of his native India, and I realize it's maybe the lack of light in this foggy town that makes him so mournful. His white shirt is open at the throat. For once, he's not wearing the cap. Frowning, he stares at us, then breaks into a bashful smile.

"I see you are . . . enjoying yourselves."

"Yes, thank you. We are."

Bernadette and I, barefooted and bare-armed, are sitting astride the low concrete wall that borders the parking lot. I'm aware of how we must look to someone from a more decorous culture: two mature women with skirts hiked above the knees, eating Tofutti straight from the container. Once we've had our fill of the sun, we'll have a Thai dinner. Bernadette will drive all night along thinly traveled roads to Arizona. She likes driving at night, windows open, the rush of air, the pre-dawn cool-ness in the desert. I sense that she finds leaving places as exhilarating as arriving.

She blew in this morning, having dozed at a rest stop for a couple of hours. I took her down to The Sea Dog for breakfast. The rest of the day we walked the beach, trekking for miles along the hot gray sand, and the cool wet darker sand by the shoreline, finally dipping into the surf, letting the sea-foam lap our ankles. I couldn't say what we talked about. Bernadette's not caught up in the past or future. She will listen politely to recitations of what has happened, what might happen, what should happen if there were any justice in the world—then draws your attention to the perfectly red plastic pail with matching scoop; the gaggle of sandpipers, the way they all talk at once; the two children dashing into the water, in spite of the posted warning about riptides, and how we'd better get over there, just in case. Deftly, she kept pulling me into the present. A day spent in this mode has its effect.

I longed to draw out the experience. "Let's keep going," I said. "Keep on walking till we drop."

"No," said Bernadette. "Time to eat. I've got a long drive ahead."

We struggled up the crumbling concrete steps and slipped into our sandals, picking our way through razor-sharp grasses along the top. The sun, lower in the sky, warmed our backs. At the foot of the dune just across the street from The Sea Dog, a homeless man held court. I had seen him before. Huge, wild-haired and white-bearded, wearing a tattersall garment that resembled a wizard's robe, he sat surrounded by a spillage of colorful possessions that overflowed his shopping cart, the wheels of which were half-buried in the sand. He seemed to have emerged from the sand, or from the sea, a scruffy Poseidon who startled passersby with his gruff spontaneity. All he needed to complete the effect was a silver trident.

Raising his white mane, he peered up at Bernadette as she tried to step past the clutter of his belongings. "And what did you learn today?"

"The day's not over yet," she said.

He nodded sagely. "Very good. You may pass."

We've taken so long with dinner that now it's dark. I decide not to let Bernadette drive me home. It's an easy walk, and I'd rather say goodbye in front of this fairy-lit restaurant with its slim gold bodhisattva in the window. After a brief hug, she speeds away in her Nissan Pathfinder. I'm not ready for the motel, the shapeless drapes, the day's heat trapped inside our top-floor room. This day deserves some sort of culmination. On a rare impulse, I cut to the beach: across the Great Highway, up over the dunes, then down a steep stairless embankment. I kick off my sandals. The sand has retained its earlier heat. I can barely believe I'm out here, barefooted and alone. People claim it's unsafe to walk the beach at night, but in such soft weather, the air emptied of all turbulence and a fair number of folks still clumped in the sandy hollows—I see nothing to fear.

I'm scuffling along, kicking sand, exulting in the fact that on this tropical night I don't even need a sweater. I see fire after fire all the way to where the earth curves into total darkness somewhere beyond Fort Funston. Illegal campfires—a beach tradition. I tell myself that nothing about fire has changed in the past four weeks. It's I who have changed. I can no longer imagine lighting a candle indoors, or even a stick of incense. I try to be still and appreciate the tall bright jet that shoots upward just in front of me, discharging sparks, any one of which could catch at my clothing or lodge in my hair. Outside the orbit of the flames, the night throbs behind its cover of darkness. I don't know what I'm doing here. In the hollows of the dunes, young people are making out. I'm as much outside their world as those downtown homeless were outside of mine. They die, and no one cares. Will death be like a walk on a dark beach? My heart starts thumping. I stifle the urge to run, to keep running till I pass Fort Funston and then Pacifica, down the land mass to Santa

Cruz and Capitola, running and running till there's no more fire. But I don't run. Instead, I step past the bodies and around the many campfires. I exit the beach in a dignified manner, befitting my age, then hurry back to Room 39 where I burrow under the covers.

On the News next morning, a woman in a bathrobe fills the screen. The frame widens to include a fire-blackened home, smoke draining from the upstairs windows. The woman's voice breaks as she recounts how she woke up surrounded by smoke and flames, with just enough time to stuff her cat into the carrier. The newscaster announces the location: three blocks from our own ruined home.

I scoot to the bottom of the bed, to get closer to the screen. Shorey's sitting rigid against his pillow, carefully peeling the Breathe Right® strip from his nose.

I say, "Are you thinking what I'm thinking?"

"Let's not go there."

"Think they let him out? Or maybe he escaped."

"Or maybe used his supernatural powers and flew off in his Santa Claus sleigh loaded with incendiary devices. I don't know."

The woman on the TV is obviously in shock, totally focused on her cat, Sparky—of all names.

"Poor kid," says Shorey. "She's only at the beginning. Whereas we're four weeks into it."

"Four weeks into *what*? Where's the progress? That contractor's stalling, and come Sunday night, we're likely to be tossed out of here."

"Talk them into giving us a couple more weeks."

"Shorey—*both* agencies have made it clear that's not happening."

"Wave your wand. Make it happen." He rubs the place where the adhesive reddened his nose. "For the sake of our sanity, we need this place."

CHAPTER SIX

BROTHER FIRE

Drumming on our file folder, then dog-earing a corner, the man at the Red Cross makes the mistake of asking me how I'm doing.

"Not too well," I tell him. "I can't sleep. I have nightmares. All day I smell charred wood, and the taste of it —this oily, acrid taste—stays in my mouth. I blame all the unsafe hibachis. No covers, flames shooting high in the air, sparks flying everywhere. One spark in the weeds out back, one spark on the roof—and there goes what's left of our cottage. Our *rent-controlled* cottage. We'd have to kiss this city goodbye and relocate to who-knows-where, maybe to some godawful—"

"Whoa!" says the Red Cross man. Speed-rolling his swivel chair in one fluid backward movement, he reaches behind himself and whisks a form from one of the bins. "Go see this lady," he says. "She's a therapist who specializes in fire victims. She gives four free visits to people we refer. And here's your motel voucher. This is absolutely your last, understand?"

"Do you think Central Relocation will give us a final week as well?"

"*That* you'll have to take up with Cora Jamison."

I tuck the referral slip and voucher into my purse.

"Now go out and do something fun with the rest of your day."

My *day*? Does he not understand? I no longer have "days." What I have are minutes, or rather moments when, if I'm lucky, my mind stops doing the Indy 500.

A week from now we'll no doubt be on some friend's doorstep with our two suitcases and four plastic bags. I cringe to think of sharing quarters with a more normal person who might find our presence a burden. And right now we *are* a burden—even to each other. What if we weirded out, as we sometimes do these days, in front of people unaccustomed to such behavior?

Out of nowhere an argument will flare, as if a bad wind, a mistral or Santa Ana, had dropped a load of pure discord between us and we were helpless to do anything but succumb to the noxious influence. Yesterday, as we speeded along Portola near Twin Peaks, I spied a fire on someone's balcony. A *wooden* balcony. Actually, a stair-landing at the back of a three-story wood frame apartment house, the kind where the landing above becomes the roof of the unit immediately below.

"Look!" I cried. "Over there!"

"Some asshole," said Shorey. "Barbecuing."

"You think it's really a barbecue, or should we call the Fire Department?"

"We're not calling anyone, and you're not Smoky the Bear. I'm hungry. I want my dinner."

He had just come from work. We'd been to the Mission for takeout burritos which we intended to eat in the park, to keep from having to buy another pricey restaurant meal. I could see that he was beat, so kept quiet.

Slowly, we drove around Stow Lake until we nosed the car into a shaded parking space by one of our favorite spots. Here, an overhanging willow draped its feathery branches along the surface of the water, and in the dim green shelter of the trailing branches a few mallards paddled back and forth, well fed ducks that showed no interest in the bits of warm tortilla we flung in their direction.

"Yuppie ducks," muttered Shorey.

We sat on a bench, munching our burritos, while behind us an ancient couple toddled by, speaking a liquid, intimate Russian utterly consonant with the peaceful evening. Her arm hooked in his, they appeared to drag each other down under the weight of their infirmities, but they looked happy enough.

"In some ways," I mused, "this is an odd city."

"Uh-huh." Shorey was staring beyond the ducks, through the fringe of willow branches to the open water.

"Ducks that don't want perfectly good food. Fires on wooden balconies."

"Uh-huh."

"San Francisco may be a romp for the tourists, but think of the nightmare for firefighters: the wind, the hills, all those narrow streets where a fire truck can barely get through. Wooden buildings jammed together—a conflagration waiting to happen."

Stoically, Shorey finished off his burrito, picking at every last bean and bit of salsa that had escaped the roll, then squeezing the foil wrap into a tight silver ball which he pitched toward a nearby trash can. The ball made a lazy arc before falling into the wide green mouth of the can. "Michael Jordan," he said, smiling wistfully.

We sat in silence, as the sky began to gray over and the air turned cool from the incoming fog, and then I said,

"I think we were wrong. We should have called the Fire Department about that balcony. What if it wasn't a barbecue? What if it was a real fire? We should have called, Shorey."

"Shut up."

"What was that?"

"You heard me. Shut your mouth. You ruin everything."

"*I* ruin everything? Because I have a sense of civic duty? Wouldn't it be our fault if the folks in that house were made homeless because we failed to make a phone call?"

Shorey shot up from his seat and surged toward the car. I followed behind, angry, contrite, lost in a welter of emotions.

Half a block from the Red Cross, I pause by the Rand-Mc Nally store, the seductive display windows that wrap around the corner of Second and Market, windows filled with maps and globes and travel guides, vicarious nibbles of Paris, Rome, Barcelona. Turning onto Market Street, I'm assaulted by the interweaving crowds and massive office towers with their blinding reflective surfaces. And there it is, like a slap in the face: the silver monolith in which I slaved for three miserable years in a bond firm where I shared a cubicle with another clerk. Even now, I'm not certain as to what a municipal bond might be. A bicycle messenger goes by in a blur, cursing the car that nearly cut him off. The brassy, late-morning sun hurts my eyes. I stink of the fear brought on by my begging expedition to the Red Cross. I'm sweaty, my back feels covered in sandy particles I can't reach, and I'm choking in my clothes. In fact, it's 88 degrees downtown, and I'm wearing fleece, the gray pullover and pants that Mary Dawson gave me the night of the fire. I have two outfits, three if I mix and match. I'm in polar fleece, on a day when others are displaying acres of flesh.

The purse strap digs into my left shoulder. The purse itself, not a large one, must weigh fifteen pounds. Crammed to the max, it resembles a black bomb. I hand-carry a green spiral notebook: my portable office.

I am passing an obnoxious preening bank headquarters, when I spot two young nuns: Daughters of Charity, followers of Mother Teresa, who look cool and serene in habits designed for the tropics: white cotton saris edged with a delicate blue stripe. Chins lifted, cheeks flushed from the heat, they speak in broad Midwestern accents. Laughing in a spontaneous, unguarded way, they shield their eyes to gaze up at the bank façade in outright admiration, as if to say, *Just see what man has wrought!* Now they're going inside. Making way for others, they proceed one at a time through the double doors. What will they do in there—deposit s small sack of change, the contents of their convent's piggybank?

I happen to know that members of their order possess not much more than the clothes on their backs. These women convey such a lightness and grace that once they're inside the street seems meaner, noisier. I'm tempted to follow them, stand in line behind them in the gloom and hush of this temple of money. I'm sure *they* do not trail a list of worries in a green notebook. Nor do they hit the pillow each night obsessing about the birdshit accumulating on their possessions in a warehouse partially open to the sky. If their convent were to burn down tomorrow, if they lost their prayer books, their sandals—no big deal.

In winter duds and dusty Birkenstocks, I feel so layered, swaddled in heavy clothes and dragged down by a mind that will not let me rest. On this, one of the busiest streetcorners in the city, I'm a boulder in a stream. As people sail past or jostle me out of their way, I'm lashed by a silk scarf, enveloped in a toxic cloud of perfume.

I wait a bit. It's lunchtime. The sidewalk thickens with officer workers.

The nuns are not coming out.

The trees along Market are in full green leaf, waiting for one bright little breeze to spangle their foliage. The brick sidewalk looks freshly swept. I watch as a merchant hoses down the section in front of his store. As soon as water hits the hot brick surface, steam rises up.

I have no desire to go back to the motel. The Red Cross man ordered me to have fun, so I decide to follow my feet, see where they lead. They lead up over the humpbacked hill to Chinatown, whose alleys I explored minutely during the years I worked there. Entering the afternoon effulgence along Grant Avenue, I encounter a different quality of light and a thinness to the air, as if autumn had intruded into summer.

I don't linger over the sidewalk bins except to buy a journal covered in peach silk brocade. Its pages smell of the white paste I remember from grade school, the kind of paste you felt tempted to taste, and sometimes did. I've often had six or seven journals going at once, each devoted to a different theme. A journal must have limp, easily turnable pages. The paper must be absorbent enough to drink up the ink so that it doesn't smear when I write my left-handed bird-script. I collect journals the way certain tribespeople collect cowrie shells, as a form of wealth. I rarely know my deeper thoughts until I take up my pen and see words spilling across the pale blue lines.

I turn down at Clay to avoid the next several blocks of Grant, a repetitive stretch of souvenir shops and pungent fish markets. Clay Street maintains some of its Asian flavor even as it snakes into the business district. An open doorway reveals a smoky room where a group of elderly men sits practicing a complicated piece on Chinese zither, flute, drums, gong, and a two-stringed violin that produces the most searingly mournful sounds. The scene, musicians in black silk robes, could be from a hundred years back, in San Francisco or in China's Guangdong Province. This is the music that issues from noodle houses, sewing factories, Mahjongg parlors. This is the music of Cantonese movies. The atonal melody draws me in, after all the nights of anapestic songs thumping up from Mister Bo's.

One of the men makes me aware that I've been staring, so I cross the street and dodge into a park that runs canyon-like between Clay and Washington. The fountain, ferns and many trees make it cooler here. I love the weird scale of the place: sixty-foot redwoods that look like houseplants at the base of the Transamerica Pyramid.

I arrive just as a group has finished setting up for a noontime concert: the bossa nova sounds of the late Antonio Carlos Jobim. Chairs have been placed. Downtown workers have claimed the front rows, so I take a seat in the shade, off in a corner where I'm surrounded by ferns with enormous swaying fronds. Tuning up, the brass section blows a sunny spray of Brazilian jazz into the clear air. Girl from Ipanema music—a bit sad, considering the passage of time, the fact that the girl from Ipanema would now be a grandmother.

I lean back, close my eyes. A breeze stirs the ferns. The plash and gurgle of the low-lying fountain only adds to the day's voluptuous softness. Following Jobim's easy rhythms, I realize I was a naked wire during the decade as a middle-aged student at San Francisco State.

And where was the music all those years?

Even now, it doesn't last. The music of Brazil, cheerful as a yellow kitchen, thins out and fades into the trees.

I like remaining at a place—a concert hall, movie theater, church—after others have left. I don't stay long enough to become a nuisance to janitors, but I enjoy luxuriating in the charged atmosphere that others seem eager to leave behind. Today, though, I'm ready to head out with the crowd. It's growing chilly under the redwoods.

Just as I stand up, I hear sirens and the bull roar of an air-horn exploding down Clay Street from Chinatown. A ladder truck, fire engine and rescue van scream past in a flash of red. The fierce, competing sounds blot out the gentle memory of Brazilian music, the lightsome riffs and glassy tinkle of the high notes that made me feel I was perched on a sunny cliff above Rio.

Shorey can say what he likes, but I know fire has me in its sights.

I'm going back to the motel, the only place where I feel safe. I will draw the curtains, sit on the bed and read Amit Chaudhuri, my Indian author. Only he, with his plotless novels, can restore my spirit. An hour with Amit, and I'm myself again. Forget dramatic tension—protagonist, antagonist, ruling passion, conflict resolution. I crave minutiae, nuance, petty details. The geologic pace of the hourglass, where time is dispensed in grains of sand. I want to stroll with the main character along a back street in Calcutta, noticing every stone in the road, every shifting cloud pattern.

On my way to the BART station, I pass a Catholic bookstore. I'm a sucker for any bookstore, even the Russian one in my neighborhood that contains only volumes in Cyrillic script. Just put some text between two covers, and I'll turn the pages.

Catholic bookstores are never simply bookstores. This one contains racks of holy cards, bookmarks, statuettes, miniature grottos and other gift items. There's a revolving display of saints' medals. And the rosaries: everything from the cheapest plastic numbers to ones made of semi-precious stones or fashioned from petrified rose petals.

Not that I attribute any inherent holiness to such sacramentals, I simply find them beautiful. In childhood, these mass-produced artifacts were all I knew of Art. Even the phosphorescent crucifix given me by my great-uncle, the one that glowed green above my bed in the dark—this eerie reminder of the supernatural added a mysterious dimension to the unadorned room in which I slept.

Shorey, with his roots in Puritan tradition, scoffs at my delight in "pagan trinkets," but the blue of a holy-card sky still stands, for me, as the blue of Eden. Not even Giotto can compare, or the Impressionists. High art, low art—it's hard for me to make the distinction. I've experienced the same degree of esthetic pleasure on seeing the spice market in Delhi—conical mounds of saturated, unambiguous color—as I have at the Guggenheim or the Met. I love the cheap thrill of carnival colors. I love baubles that support my superstitions. Whenever I fly I still carry a St. Christopher medal, though he's no longer a patron saint of travelers, or even a saint at all. One pope had him canonized; another had him struck from the roster. And when I lose anything, I still chant, ten times: *Dear Saint Anthony, come around / Something's been lost and can't be found.*

I hadn't expected to see actual nuns running a bookstore. Nuns are thin on the ground these days, going about their business incognito, in street clothes, or sequestered in some administrative post in a university or hospital. You just don't come upon two sets of nuns in one day, not in downtown San Francisco. I don't know which order these belong to, with their cotton/poly dresses and abbreviated veils. I'm browsing the Mary section, the long aisle of books on "Marian Studies," when a tall young nun comes up behind me. Flipping through a picture book of madonnas, my page open to the Black Madonna of Czestochowa, I'm sure the sister can tell by my vibes that I haven't been to mass in decades. I imagine she's about to ask what I'm doing here, what it is that I want, but she only says, "Pardon me," and replaces a book on the shelf.

"This is a nice store," I murmur.

"Yes, it is. People seem to like coming here."

Where is this going? How can I say that this morning I started to bliss out after seeing a couple of Mother Teresa nuns, and that now it's happening again? Should I admit that I'm a lapsed Catholic, that I said goodbye to Rome nearly forty years ago, but that I do believe in *her*, and in the nun behind the counter—the purity and one-pointedness of their commitment? I believe, too, in the elderly nun who's lurking by the spider plant, pretending to rearrange a display of books by Thomas Merton while scrutinizing my movements.

"I have to catch a bus," I tell the tall one.

She simply nods. To leave immediately after pawing an expensive book seems rude, so I rummage through some bookmarks on the front counter.

I find a green card with a crude woodcut of St. Francis of Assisi among the birds and his poem, *Canticle of the Sun*. Ten cents apiece. I buy ten because I've taken up space in the store, listened for half an hour to the mood-altering music that's heavy on harps, synthesizer and angelic sopranos, and I figure I'd better part with at least a buck.

As I'm handed my change, the old nun, white hair bristling from under her veil in front, abandons her display table and comes rushing over. "*Ecco!*" she cries, continuing ecstatically in Italian. She grabs me up, pins me to her bosom before taking hold of my shoulders and saying insistently, "You are back!" The woman is clearly senile. In fact, the nun behind the counter appears faintly worried, but doesn't intervene, just goes on shuffling receipts while out on the street people stream past the plate-glass windows. Through her tears, the nun croons in a singsong voice, "*Cara mia*, you've come back!"

What had begun as a sweet encounter is turning surreal. She shakes my shoulders, as if to reassure herself that I'm real. Or is she trying to loosen me from the obduracy that she senses?

"Okay." I hear the quaver in my voice. "But I have to leave."

"She's come back!" she calls out to the other nuns. Raising a hand, she gestures to the ceiling as if bearing witness before God.

Gently, I disengage myself. "Nice meeting you. Really."

Patting my cheek, she keeps her hand in place while whispering in my ear, "*Finita la commedia!*"

Speeding along underground on the N-Judah, I take out the green card with the poem by St. Francis and place it on my lap. I am living in the city of St. Francis, which in turn is a sister-city to Assisi. In my hometown I belonged to St. Francis of Assisi parish. During mass I'd let my gaze shift to the stained-glass window depicting Francis with the bird on his outstretched hand. Not until adulthood did I read a serious account of his life. Reading about him, I was right there for the ecstasies and the stigmata, but he and the early Franciscans took the life of poverty to such an extent they did not even own books. How could people live without books? Francis praised the death of the body but not the body itself, so it followed that he would not have a lot to say in favor of bodily comforts.

In his poem, Francis personifies wind and water, fruits, flowers and grasses. He sees these as his sisters and brothers. About Fire, he says:

> *Praised be my Lord for Brother Fire*
> *who lights up the night,*
> *and he is bright and playful and robust and strong.*

In fact, Francis so revered Brother Fire that he refused to roll in the grass or beat out the flames when his tunic caught fire. To do so would have been to extinguish—or kill—his brother. Had his monks not rescued him, he might have burnt to death.

I'm not yet ready to make friends with Brother Fire, but neither can I let the fear of him dominate my life. I phone the woman on the Red Cross referral slip.

Her name is Meredith, she's an MFCC, and the only sound in her waiting room is the whir of an air purifier. From magazines fanned out across a tabletop, I choose *Architectural Digest,* an issue featuring an article on carriage-house conversions.

The inner door opens, and Meredith introduces herself. She's about fifty. I can't help staring into the crystalline eyes that possess a glitter rarely seen in captivity. Ash-blond hair, gold accessories, and as for her clothes, there's not an artificial fiber in sight. She invites me to sit in a pretty chintz armchair.

I breeze through recent events in about three minutes, then settle in for a cozy session regarding my family: my father and the family curse, the tire factory, my mother's phobias including her mortal fear of birds. I'm not so naïve as to believe these revelations will make me a better, saner person, but Conway history—so painful to have lived through—always yields a few laughs in the telling.

Meredith lets me run on for a bit, then leans forward, smoothing the linen skirt over her knees. "All very interesting," she says, "but there are things we need to talk about."

I had expected, for starters, to cry on her psychotherapeutic shoulder and garner a bit of sympathy. I figured that by the second visit I'd be submitting to formal headshrinkery, which I envisioned as a nonlinear Joycean verbal flight: myself circling hawk-like over the refuse-pile of feelings and problems before swooping down on a core issue that I could pick apart for the remaining two sessions.

"We need to get you a working strategy," says Meredith, transfixing me with those eyes.

Strategy? All I'd hoped for was to endure this rotten summer. No great victories—just get me to September, and back into my house.

"Meredith, I'm so *tired*." (Didn't she get what I told her about the grueling school year, the abdominal surgery, the six-month Ajax saga?) "I feel like I've got nothing left to give."

"I know. It's as if you just finished running the 26-mile marathon, and here I am, telling you to keep on running."

"But—where am I running to?"

"What I'm trying to say—" And she takes a deep yogic breath. I am certain this lady does yoga. Every. Single. Day. I can see her executing a cobra pose on her redwood deck.

"Please. Tell me."

"You said earlier that this was no ordinary fire: faulty electrical wiring or a pot burning on the stove or old newspapers combusting. You said the fire had been *set*. So there's something more we need to deal with. I'm referring to the criminal element."

My skin recoils. I may be exuding an odor. I don't want to make the criminal element any more real by talking about it.

"You told me this man had a record. You said he threatened to kill you, then set fire to your house. Isn't that what you said?"

Dumbly, I nod. "I'd rather not focus on Ajax. Anyway, he's locked up someplace."

"For now. But he may get out. He could come back."

"Don't say that!"

Meredith leans forward, props her elbows on her thighs. "Sorry to have made you nervous, but you really can't *afford* to remain passive. You've got to be proactive."

A hateful word, an abortion of a word, right up there with *prioritize*.

"I'm here to help you get through this, make sure you stay safe. That's the purpose of these four visits."

She's classy enough not to have said four *free* visits. But nothing's free. So now I'll have to be "proactive."

"Have you brought something to write on?"

I hold up the spiral notebook.

We then discuss restraining orders. A week or so ago the D.A. informed me that a Stay-Away Order was in place, in the police computer, and that I needn't worry because a Stay-Away was an effective safeguard. However, Meredith has nothing but contempt for SAOs, as she calls them, because with an SAO you've got to wait until the cops pick up the miscreant, and the cops may or may not put him in jail. No, indeed. The only way to go is a formal restraining order, and if we can get an RO under the SL, or Stalking Law—call Women, Inc. for info—and Ajax violates the RO, then he goes to jail for a long time. But an RO costs money, so I should contact the Collective Restraining Order Clinic about a possible discount. And I should also know that an RO normally takes 45 days and that we don't *have* 45 days because what if he's let out on his own recognizance while the ineffectual little SAO is still in place? One possible solution: There's an attorney who works out of her home in Berkeley. I should call her and explain the urgency of the situation: the fact that Ajax must be served with the RO while he's still in jail, because if he cops a plea and gets back on the street we won't be able to find him, since homeless people are notoriously hard to locate.

"How much will the Berkeley lawyer charge?"

"I don't know," says Meredith. "But not as much as others would. Maybe fifteen hundred."

So much for *that* idea.

My forehead's dripping. I have broken into Gregg shorthand in order to get every word down in the green notebook. Sitting primly in my secretarial pose, I tell myself that Meredith can rattle on all she likes, but I'm not doing any of this stuff because I know what it's like out there in arson-land. Restraining orders, SAOs, stalking laws— there's not a law on earth that will keep Ajax away if he chooses to stagger up our street, blind-drunk, on his way to the 540 Club. And there's not a cop in the precinct who will help.

Now we move on to the State Attorney's office, and the fact that I must type up a chronology because under no circumstances must Ajax be allowed out on his own recog. I'll need the case number and the name of the felony supervisor. Eventually, I'd do well to get involved with the San Francisco Tenants Union. Later, after the smoke clears—and she immediately apologizes for alluding to smoke—we must take out renters' insurance.

"Am I correct," says Meredith, "in sensing some resistance on your part?"

"I don't know."

"What had you expected in coming here?"

"I don't know."

"Are you willing to do these things that I've suggested?

"I don't know."

One thing I do know: Amit Chaudhuri is beckoning, like a figure in the mist in a Grade B movie. He's calling out to me from page 265, where I've placed the sandalwood bookmark. By way of his hypnotic prose I will return to Calcutta and doze on a woven charpoy on the rooftop while waiting for an afternoon breeze to blow in off the Hooghly River.

Meredith crosses her shapely legs. She seems far away, in a country where grandfather clocks tick away the moments and no one truly misbehaves. My only ally is Shorey, mostly because he's as beaten down as I am.

Out of nowhere, Meredith says, "I should tell you that once I was stalked. I hid out in my house for two days, in total terror. I got no help from the police. In fact, one sergeant insinuated that I'd brought it on myself. I have never felt more alone. And that's when I decided to get up off the floor and fight back."

"But I don't have money for an RO."

"Then do what you can," she says. "Make as many calls as you can because, next week I'll be expecting a progress report."

The clock bongs once. Meredith gazes up at the clock face with its delicate black numerals. On the wall the palomino in the painting has cleared the hurdle and remains suspended, with its rider, in mid-air.

Meredith tells me she likes to end each session on a positive note. "Think back on your day," she says. "Anything *nice* happen?"

The memory is not exactly "nice," but I tell her about the old Italian nun, the way she came running over and whispered those words in my ear: *Finita la commedia.*

"The game's up," says Meredith.

"Pardon?"

"That's what it means, in Italian. More literally, "The farce is over."

"She was senile."

"Perhaps."

"Of course, my summer is turning out pretty farcical."

"And the worst part is—"

"Not knowing where we'll be living from week to week."

"I meant to talk about that. And this is important. You should try to get established someplace, then stay put. Moving here and there will only delay the healing process."

I have no control over where we live. And now that her antique clock has struck, there's no time to talk about the Red Cross, or Cora Jamison at Central Relocation, or how it makes me feel to beg. "I'm sorry, Meredith, but I don't know what to do with your suggestion."

"For now, write it down in your notebook, in big block letters, along with the following: Eat regular meals. Get enough sleep. Take vitamins."

CHAPTER 7

A DAY IN THE LIFE

Shorey manages an irrigation store in Mill Valley, a Marin County town thick with lush, brimming gardens. For his upscale customers, he needs to be on the job five days a week, looking spiffy and cheerful. Though he designs irrigation systems and advises on pond construction and garden lighting, the job is also physical. He has a staff, but he too is expected to lug hundred-foot rolls of black poly-ethylene tubing, PVC irrigation pipe and the staggeringly heavy batches of rubberized pond liner. He lifts UPS boxes filled with metal or plastic gadgets. For work he wears a pair of sturdy twill pants, a T-shirt, a sweatshirt bearing the logo of his company or one of his suppliers, and a zip-up vest with generous pockets. On a normal day he will sweat through three layers, and once a week I haul a big heap of work duds to the Bubble Factory.

He earns more than I do, so when it came to the di-vision of labor that summer following the fire, Shorey said, "Go back to work in the fall, okay, but right now we need somebody on-site. There'll be workmen, and one of us should make sure things get done right. Then there's

Bridie. She has to be let out of the garage once in a while. If she gets too frustrated, she might just split. And one of us has to do laundry and stuff. You said you wanted to write this summer. Well, here's your chance."

The Mill Valley store had to be opened by seven, in time for the early-morning contractors and landscape gardeners. Each day on his way to work, Shorey would drop me off at the garage by 6:30, then return around five. That left nearly eleven hours to be filled. For years I had yearned for such an open schedule, the opportunity to keep writing beyond the usual time should I find myself "on a roll." That summer, though, there were no rolls. I felt washed-out, dispirited. The writing-machine seemed to have broken down, but I did my best to put in four or five desultory hours.

Writing did take me out of myself a bit, but being holed up day after day in a hot, dark, airless room with my seriously depressed cat, who lay lifelessly on the narrow divan— not even interested in picking at the looped threads of the boucle upholstery—did not do wonders for my creativity. And Mr. Vyas had categorically refused when I asked if Bridie might join us at the motel.

That summer the garage functioned as a control center. Bridie's food bowls and litter box sat primly under a tool shelf, and in the garage we had a telephone and computer. Gas and electric to our address should have been cut by Day Two, but due to some bureaucratic mix-up, or maybe the grace of God, PG&E spared the electric line that fed the garage. Continued juice to this room allowed me to use the computer and phone family and friends.

Many good reasons to be in the garage during the day, but each day I faced the prospect with dread.

On a morning of pale sun in early July, six weeks after the fire, I arrive as usual at 6:30. No one's around. The dew has not yet evaporated from the climbing roses and dahlias, and scatterings of sandy soil, still moist from the night, lie across the cement path leading to the garage. In a heightened way, I notice that the pile of charred beams and flaps of tar paper roofing has been augmented and can now be seen over the fence because the men of the soccer team who live in the upstairs flat of the building that fronts the street, have taken to pitching milk cartons and other trash out their back door and onto the pile. And their landlord has made no move to clear away the fire debris. A perfect shelter for rats, that pile—but that's not what's needling me. I feel an answer prickling just under my skin, the answer to a question I can't begin to formulate.

All praises for this early hour when no other tenants are around. Decent folks, they feel constrained to eke out a conversation with me, but as the weeks lengthen into months and workmen don't show and not much gets done on our cottage—what can our fellow tenants say? Empathy carries only so far before it deteriorates into pity, or outright resentment. Seeing me, they suddenly become awkward, embarrassed. Even worse, they are forced to reflect on the fragility of their own condition: the fact that given the right mix of wind, flame and flammable materials, the same thing could happen to them. Seeing me is like seeing Death. After all, Shorey and I came rather close. Ten more minutes, as the arson investigator pointed out, and we might have been scorched by Death's hot breath.

Did I imagine, yesterday, that my sudden appearance in the yard acted as a pall over the sprightly chat my landlady had been having with two other tenants? Did

I imagine they drew closer and seemed to coalesce against an unnamable threat that I represented?

A mere six weeks ago we were viewed as witty, personable. Others sought us out for dinners and parties. Did I imagine, yesterday, that a neighbor crossed to the other side of the street when she saw me coming?

I am the black hole that sucks all joy from life. Easier, by far, to keep myself inside the larger black hole of the garage where I can sit at the computer and disappear into fictional characters I have created.

Now I look around the garden, standing frozen for long moments as I take stock of the work not done on our home. My gaze shifts to the plywood sheets stapled over Ajax's windows by two day-laborers. Those boards have worked their way loose and now hang at crazy angles. The ground-level plywood "door," ripped off by wind that blasted through the wide-open back of the place, lies atop a pile of soggy, blackened vegetation. The ghostly opening is clearly visible from the street. Even if it were not, word of shelter travels like wildfire through the homeless encampments. After all, Ajax heard of the place from a man who'd squatted there previously, a meth manufacturer who needed to make a quick move.

On the night of the fire, even as our place was torching the sky, the arson investigator confided: "I'm worried that if that cottage isn't torn down and they let him out of jail, he might come back and try again. Finish the job. It happens."

Ajax, back on the scene. Another fire. The unrolling of an endless cycle: he and we entangled in a Shiva-like dance of destroyer and destroyed. Each morning, I try to wrench myself free of these dark imaginings and get on with the day.

Bridie senses me outside the garage and starts to yowl.

"Mommy's here," I say. "Mommy's looking for her key."

As I sift through my black bomb of a purse, coming upon cookie crumbs at the bottom but not the key itself, she starts to claw the door.

"Mommy's going as fast as she can, sweetie."

When finally I crack open the door and bend down to pet her, she slips through my hands like a black-and-white projectile and jumps the fence into Ajax's territory.

Free now after her long night, she'll be threading her way through the wet grasses and fresh green weeds that form an undulating carpet over the rubble in that yard. She'll be skulking toward the forbidden doorway. No use wondering why she and the other tenants' cats are so powerfully attracted to the squalor of Ajax's place. Do cats, like humans, sometimes experience an unaccountable *nostalgie de la boue*? Recalling the slop bucket and the flies, I will not scoop her into my arms or try to kiss her when she returns. She will come back covered in dust, strings of old spiderweb entangled in her whiskers— but eyes glittering.

Consorting with the enemy, luxuriating in his digs— and why?—when we are trying so hard, practically arranging our lives around her needs this summer.

"Disloyal little punk," I mutter.

I leave the door open to air out the garage while I top up Bridie's dry food, fill her water bowl with Crystal Geyser, and clean the litter box. The garden is still asleep, certain leaves and flowers having curled in on themselves for the night, though the creamy Peace roses exude a pure, virginal fragrance, the appropriate incense for this hour. It's not yet seven. Soon I'll go find something to eat.

Breakfast these days is a bagel, tea, coffee, anything quick, and I don't eat again until dinner, which we have in a restaurant, at Shorey's insistence.

Dinner in a restaurant used to be a once-a-week treat. Now it's a nightly affair, and the thrill is gone. It's not only that restaurant food is heavily salted and slathered with too much fat, not only that our faces and fingers are puffy from water retention and that we're gaining weight—it's the logistics, the getting there, the parking, the wait for a table, the frustration when we drive across town only to find that a particular eatery is closed because it's Monday, or Tuesday, or whatever day of the week the place shuts down. By the time Shorey gets off work and I emerge from the garage, we're sweaty and tired and just want some grub.

One evening stands out.

Late June, and muggy. Shorey thinks the Olive Garden would make a nice change, so we zoom over to Stonestown and park Tillie Tercel in a spot near the restaurant. The Olive's a big place. There seems every reason to believe we'll be seated and chowing down within fifteen minutes.

The hostess advises us there'll be a forty-minute wait, minimum. Yet we see no one waiting. Shorey has that look. I can tell he's about to project his voice, so I touch his arm, meaning, *Let's wait to hear the whole story.*

She hands us an electronic device, saying, "No need to wait inside. When this begins to pulsate, it means your table's ready. Come right away."

I trust no electronic devices. They're either too subtle for someone like myself who was more comfortable in the mechanical age, or they are apt to electrocute me. "Will it be really obvious when it's pulsating?" I ask.

"Absolutely. Just hold it in your palm."

I look around. The sky over the massive parking lot has a yellow-gray cast, as if a storm were imminent. People dart from their cars in every direction. Lots to do here in Stonestown. The bookstore is especially inviting.

"Fine," I say to the hostess. "We'll go hang out at Borders."

"No, don't do that. You have to remain within twenty-five feet of our door. Otherwise, the device won't work."

So we prowl the perimeter for forty minutes, and by the time we're seated I no longer feel like eating. All I can think of is money. I've been keeping a rough tally of costs, and though we consume only two snacks and one meal per day, by the end of summer we'll have laid out around thirty-five hundred for food.

If we disagree about one thing, it's this business of eating out every night. Why can't we simply buy bread, fruit, cheese, as Europeans do, and picnic in the park?

"Three thousand, five. That's three computers," I say to Shorey, as he twirls pasta onto his fork. "Or a trip to Hawaii."

"That's the cost of survival," he snaps. I will not chomp carrot sticks or wolf down a sandwich after a long day's work."

Not the first time we've gone to the wall over money. We each grew up without much, but while Shorey's response has been to thumb his nose at caution, mine is to save every cent.

"You think spending a few bucks is the worst that can happen?" he says, while waiters dodge around us and the dinnertime noise intensifies.

"All right, what's the worst?"

"Not sleeping in my own bed."

His own bed, with the foam mattress that conforms exactly to the contours of his body. Thick cotton flannel sheets from Portugal. Down pillows. The fact that sleeping high up in a loft bed makes him feel like the king of the night. I know he misses our cat climbing the ladder and into the bed, and that he, too—though he'd never say it— wonders if those luxuries will ever be restored to us.

I miss being able to brew my own tea in my own house. Slipping out of bed at three a.m., as I sometimes do, and choosing a tea to suit my mood: usually a Japanese variety at that black hour. Regulating the blue flame under the kettle. Pouring, without spilling a drop. The secret offices of the night: the insomniac's tea ceremony.

Our Asian neighborhood harbors many sources of tea, but I've settled on three places. At the Chinese coffee shop you can buy a small tea for sixty cents. They do not provide milk; you have to whiten your beverage with powdered creamer, a chemical cocktail I cannot bring myself to use. The Vietnamese coffee shop sells a large tea for only fifty cents, and they do provide milk, but even the smallest splash from the carton will cost you can additional fifty cents. The Vietnamese shop is friendlier than the Chinese shop, although I object on principle to the milk surcharge. For that reason, I drink my tea neat. Along with the 1970s prices comes the Styrofoam cup and the generic teabag— not even Lipton's. On days when I crave coffee, I will walk the five blocks to Boudin, the 150-year-old French bakery that opens before dawn, filling the dark street with a sweet yeasty fragrance. There, I can sit at an outdoor table and write in my journal.

These days, I'm so grateful to be sitting at a table, alone, sipping coffee like a regular person, that I'm apt to write in the journal: *So grateful to be sitting at a table, alone, sipping coffee like a regular person.*

The journal entries concern themselves with blatantly physical details.

Even more so than tea, coffee exacerbates the need to pee. Or worse. If I time things right, I can control my various sphincters until the branch library opens at ten. They have a public bathroom. Woe is me, though, if I miscalculate and show up at ten on a day when they don't open until one. The unshaven blokes who drink openly from bottles and lie about on the library lawn must sometimes run into the same problem, but they at least can pee in the bushes. By virtue of their feral appearance, they have established the right to do so.

Today I will not have tea until nearer to ten o'clock, and in the meantime will do a little reading, which is how I routinely start my writing day. Good reading unfreezes me. It's like a pep talk from a trusted coach: empowering. The trick is to read to the point of empowerment—say, twenty minutes—but not so long that the writing itself goes out the window. I read people whose work inspires me and who in one way or another I'd like to emulate. Some days I merely read people who have found their way into print, the idea being: if they can do it, so can I.

"Bridie," I call out wanly. "Bridie-girl?" My voice pulls away from me and sinks into the weedy savannah next-door where my cat is busy pretending to be Stanley fighting his way up the Congo in search of Dr. Livingstone. Sometimes she stays way until evening. Does she fall asleep in his place—on his soiled mattress?

I slide her bowls and litter box back under the shelf and shut the door on the brightening day and the roses and the ruined cottages, then settle myself on the divan and scrabble through the pile of cookbooks, choosing *The Greek Vegetarian*. As I pore over the list of ingredients for "Harvest Pumpkin-Chestnut-Olive Puree from Crete," the morning bells begin tolling at nearby Star of the Sea.

None of the books I've been reading has featured Big Plot. I kicked off the summer with the King James Bible, but Genesis hit a slough with the endless genealogy and sent me hastening back to modern lit. Shortly after we landed in the motel, I discovered Amit Chaurhuri and began going through his first novel, *A Strange and Sublime Address*. I wanted prose that featured only moments, such as the mundane clothes-hanging moments in the life of a traditional extended family in Calcutta, where an afternoon breeze becomes the main event.

After Chaudhuri I read *Falling Slowly*, a novel by Anita Brookner that begins with an extended meditation on a painting a woman happens to see in a gallery window. The subdued, smoky tones; the dirty snow; the diminutive figures frozen in their historical period—all these exactly match the woman's mood. Literary Valium. And Brookner, British to the teeth, goes on in this way for pages. No starting off with a bang. No dragging the reader over the bony spine of Plot.

One week bled into the next. Unable to focus on novels, or on anything with a sustained narrative, I gravitated to the library's well-stocked cookbook section. *Bitter Almonds*, part narrative, part recipes, tells of Maria Grammatico's life as a child growing up in a Sicilian convent, the long days of hard work and the drab clothing, the only concession to the senses being the miraculous pastries that the nuns taught her and the other girls to make: cannoli, "Sighs and Desires," marzipan paschal lambs, glazed and ready to go.

Finally, I gave up altogether on narrative and began hauling home armloads of recipe books. I longed to cook. Domestic details began creeping into the novel I was writing until the midsection bulged with ecstatic descriptions of chopping and mincing, the parsimonious sprinkling of vanilla bits and strands of saffron, the folding of wet ingredients into dry ones. Even as I wrote, I knew these sections would have to be pruned, but couldn't help myself. I wanted to try out one of Maria's recipes. Wanted to grate orange cheese into the big white bowl. Wanted my kitchen back.

At some point, Bitter Almonds must have slipped out of my hands and onto the floor. At some point, I must have fallen asleep.

A metallic clang. Dragging footsteps. I shoot up out of my reverie. Was that him? Couldn't have been. He's in the slammer. To make certain, I slip on my shoes, creak open the garage door and peek through the staggered boards of the redwood fence. Nothing. No one.

My chest has constricted around a massive esophageal spasm. Bending over, I force myself to focus on the daisies and ceanothus at my feet, this rapid shifting of the attention my only strategy in getting the pain to let go its grip. The daisies swim before my eyes in a yellow Impressionistic wash. These spasms have been getting worse. Last week I had an EKG.

Once I can breathe again, I slump down to the rotting board that forms the threshold to the garage and sit there, blinking out at the ground-level flowers that appear more brilliant, more singularly individual, now that the pain is erased. I mop my forehead with the tail of my shirt.

Shorey is at work, heaving some Herculean load in order to make a buck, while I sit here in a fog, immobilized by a free-floating dread to which I have given the name and shape of Ajax. With Ajax away in jail, though, the real enemy stares back at me with its gaptoothed doorway and boarded-up windows.

Ajax's place sustained less damage than ours did. The fire was ignited at the adjoining wall, and worked its way up that wall before spreading across our roof and consuming the top of the cottage. His place still has a roof, three walls and part of a fourth, and a perfectly intact façade. Not my idea of gracious living, but at least it's dry inside.

As long as that cottage remains standing, we're in danger, if not from Ajax, from someone else.

The soccer lads have told us the property is a bare-bones, collect-the-rents operation. A real-estate agency on Taraval Street acts as manager for an absentee landlord, and apparently no one cares. Nothing gets done. Countless times, before and since the fire, I have tried to reach the woman in charge, but she is well shielded by her staff—never in her office, never answers her cell phone.

Quite simply, I want that cottage torn down. If Madam Landlady won't see to it, then the City of San Francisco had better get on the stick.

The dread I've been experiencing now has a name, and a place, and I know what I have to do. I feel a re-animating surge of blood into my extremities. I open the green notebook to a fresh page and uncap my pen. I am going to phone every official in this town until I get what I want.

Three hours later, and I'm all phoned out. Basically, each agency referred me to another agency, or sent me deeper into the capillary system of their own agency, where I'd be stuck explaining myself to a clerk who had no choice but to redirect me to the higher-up with whom I'd spoken in the first place. Before long, I was feeling much like the hapless protagonist of Kafka's *The Trial*.

The low-level clerks, mostly women, I found to be sympathetic. They had no trouble identifying with my dilemma, and sincerely tried to help. However, as I progressed upward, into the rarefied air of the bureaucratic mountain peaks, all empathy dried up. Apparently, there was no one whose job it was to deal with a problem such as mine.

The Health Department: "Nothing we can do. Try Environmental Health."

Environmental Health: "Sorry. Try Pest Control."

Pest Control and Unsanitary Conditions: "It's not us you want. Give a ring to General Complaints."

General Complaints: "You should be talking to Building Inspections."

Building Inspections: "Call the Department of Public Works."

Department of Public Works: "Contact Construction Management."

Construction Management: "Who told you to call us? Get in touch with Housing Inspection."

Housing Inspection: "Let me connect you with the Building Inspector."

Building Inspector: "I can't act alone on this. You need to follow the chain of command."

"Chain of command, upwards or downwards?" I ask.

"Upwards, naturally. The Chief Building Inspector."

The Chief Building Inspector's office directed me one step lower to "the man who can make it happen. And he's a real nice guy."

Man-who-can-make-it-happen: "Why are they telling you to call me? This sounds like a police matter."

"I agree," I said, "but the police in our precinct haven't done a thing. And they're not empowered to tear down a cottage."

"Then get on the horn to whoever owns that property."

"I've tried. They're unreachable. It's some absentee landlord—"

"Look, my hands are tied. Get in touch with the Health Department."

"Sir, that's where I started, three hours ago."

The worst part of the process was having to repeat the dreary facts to each person who picked up a phone. Each clerk, receptionist or administrator needed some idea of the problem in order to palm me off on the next clerk, receptionist or administrator. I quickly became adept at the one-minute précis, but just hearing myself repeat the details connected with the fire brought on the sweats, and then I'd shiver and experience chest pain. I worried that if I kept repeating this litany, I'd go nuts or have a heart attack.

By one in the afternoon, drained, hungry, thirsty, I realized the game was up. *Finita la commedia.*

I needed to conserve my energy and muster some cool, even some cunning, for the next day when I'd have to face Cora Jamison at Central Relocation. She had made it clear at our last meeting that there'd be no more motel vouchers. I did not even have an appointment, but tomorrow I was going down to Gough Street, and I was not leaving there without a voucher.

CHAPTER EIGHT

MONDRIAN'S WINDMILL

At Gough and Eddy there's an empty lot where a teetering signboard proclaims the message, *You are not alone.*

Down the hill and through the buffer of big trees, mostly shaggy eucalyptus, I can see the solid white hulk of the Central Relocation Agency. As I trudge up its wheelchair ramp in the flickering filigree shadow of a leafy maple, I think of folks such as welfare recipients who are forced to beg for food and shelter on a routine basis, and I can't begin to imagine what that does to a person. Perhaps over time they toughen up, repeat and affirmation or two, throw back their shoulders and decide that, damn it, they, too, are human beings with human needs, and while they'd rather their life were neatly in place, no rough edges, no limp clothes or empty bank account, life in its inscrutable wisdom has decided otherwise, and despite any quotas or budgetary restraints at Central Relocation, they are not leaving the building without that piece of paper.

That is how it will be. Do or die.

And here I am again in this sliding coffin of an elevator, but today it takes me directly to the second floor, no stalling, no heart-stopping metallic noises. The doors open to reveal

121

Cora Jamison, her large, luxuriant person draped against the reception desk in a manner that's reminiscent of the Grande Odalisque by Ingres. She is schmoozing with a worker.

Cora Jamison is a beautiful woman who dresses well. In concert with her tasteful silk and light wool ensembles, she will flounce a boldly patterned scarf around her neck, a bit of frippery that suggests an underlying exuberance yearning to burst forth from the social correctness demanded by her job. I am counting on that exuberance as proof of a deeper, less bureaucratic Cora—a Cora who will grant me the motel voucher to which I am no longer entitled.

She turns and sees me. Frowns.

Raising my hands defensively, I'm quick to say that although I don't have an appointment, I'd be more than grateful for a few moments of her time. I then fold my hands in front of me . . . and wait. Her look tells me I'm transparent to her, that this is hardly the first time she's been faced with the fake humility of the needy.

Behind those jade-green eyes I see the two Coras contending: the one who wants me back in the elevator and out of her sight, and the one who's wearing a scarf splashed in bright swirls of Matisse colors.

"All right," she says wearily. "Come on back."

I follow along behind, a dung beetle in drab gray fleece, while Cora sails ahead, all shimmer and susurrus of silk, an expensive scent wafting off of her, gold bracelets clinking when she raises a manicured hand to motion me toward her office. Inside, we take up our positions: she, behind a desk stacked with forms and folders, and I in the wooden chair.

Grimly, Cora searches a metal file drawer for our folder that must now be among the defunct. "I know you're having a hard time," she concedes, as she sets the folder in front of her and eases it open with a tapered red fingernail. Placing both shapely hands on top of the innards—the papers that represent our life, at present—she gives me a stern look and says, "Others are also having a hard time, so I hope you're not here to ask for anything."

No, I feel like responding, *I'm here because I like the smell of your perfume.*

Behind her, fine old maples fill the twin frames of her window with their greenery and tuberous begonias line her windowsill. The window is closed against street noise.

"How's your husband, by the way?"

On our first visit, Shorey and I sat facing her in matching wooden chairs. Stressed and cranky, we started bickering during the interview, and Cora, in the gentle but nononsense voice people use when dealing with unruly children, told us that although the fire had destroyed our home, we should not let it destroy our marriage as well.

"He's okay," I say, hastening to add, "Truth is, he's under an awful strain, running back and forth from Mill Valley to the San Francisco store to pick up supplies, then over to the garage where our cat's staying. What's really made it bearable—"No—too strong a statement. Too *obvious.* "He told me that all day he looks forward to coming home at night."

"By 'home,' you mean—?"

"The, uh, motel. The Ocean Breeze."

She's not going anywhere near that. Looking off to the side, she fiddles with the scarf, rolling the silk between her thumb and forefinger. "What about food?" she says. "I gave you that list of places you could go for free food."

Oh, boy. The list. Places including Glide Memorial and St. Anthony's Dining Room. Good and worthy places. But Shorey and I, standing in line that snaked round the corner? Sitting down with actual homeless people? We were the sort who volunteered in those kitchens, not the sort who *ate* there. We were, well . . . *us*. Sitting in front of Cora that first day, and obviously wide open to her gaze, I experienced a greater shame at my own snobbery. Who was I to disdain a plate of free food? Yet I felt an absolute resistance to standing in a Depression-type line, waiting for the doors to open at Glide or St. Anthony's. If need be, we'd spend all that we had on restaurant food. It was the old business of contamination-by-contiguity. If you're near them, you might *become* them—homeless.

Cora's eyeing me shrewdly. I'm sure she can divine my thoughts.

"So. You're eating okay?"

"Yes," I tell her. "We're eating fine."

She's not making it easy. Will not come right out and deny me the motel room, thereby opening the field to a jousting-match in which I had hoped to win the day.

My shoulders slump. All right, Cora.

"I was hoping for one more week at the Ocean Breeze."

Just then a young man ducks in and drops a folder onto a stack of other folders on a low shelf. Every one of those folders, I realize, is an individual or a family needing "relocation." Cora gives him a nod, and the man is gone. The room darkens as the wind outside reshuffles the big floppy maple leaves, but then the wind retreats and morning light once again brightens Cora's walls and desktop.

"The maximum anyone gets, between our agency and the Red Cross," she says, "is four weeks. You've had five."

Hands folded on the desk, she lets those five weeks hang in the air between us. It's my turn. I'm supposed to counter in some way, but I don't. Instead, I take a risk.

"I have no right to ask for anything more. And I want you to know how very grateful we are for all that you and the Red Cross have done to help us out."

Cora studies my face for any trace of insincerity, but there is none. I meant exactly what I said. The wind kicks up again, mottling the walls with trembling shadows. Down in my lap, where she can't see, I dig into three acupressure points near my wrist, the ones you're supposed to engage in order to stay calm during, say, a job interview.

"You want another week," she says. This comes out sounding like a dead fact, and it's my job to bring this dead fact to life. Inclining forward in my seat, I say, "Ms. Jamison, I won't ever bother you again. Or the Red Cross. It's just that we—"

"Never mind all that." And she starts filling out the voucher.

I am not giddy with victory. Out on the street the feeling I experience is almost sad, valedictory. This is an ending. We've been cut loose. Now we're truly on our own. Still, we have seven more days at the Ocean Breeze, seven days in which to be jolted awake by the music from Mister Bo's, and to watch our wet towels fall from the metal nub that used to be a towel bar. But it's been a home, that room. A refuge. We're used to the big TV, the bed, the morning chorus of birds in the bottlebrush tree. And I'm used to going down to The Sea Dog to scribble in my journal. But not today. None of the usual things today.

Walking up Gough toward Geary, where I'll catch a bus, I cross the street so I can stroll beside the upward-sloping green sward behind St. Mary's Cathedral. Homeless men lie about on the grass, in attitudes of pure surrender to the warm sun. Off in the distance, facing the green, a tall white apartment building glistens in the clear light like a wedding cake decorated with white swags, curlicues and medallions.

A gravel pathway runs parallel to and about ten feet from the sidewalk. Up this path walks a man in a dumpy tweed hat, the kind Irish farmers wear, and clothes so old they've molded to his body. He looks this way and that, casting about, I guess, for a place to flop. I'm tired of tramping on concrete, so I cut over onto the gravel. This is the path that homeless men take. They're all around me on the grass. One lies fetally curled round his bottle, his knees drawn up like a child's as he takes surreptitious sips. Another's flat on his belly, peeling a banana. Most are asleep, conked out under the sun. The man in front of me suddenly veers off the path and stumbles diagonally up the hill. A spot up there must have called to him, and it's possible he will anchor that sunny patch until evening drains the grass of its greenness.

These men seem harmless. They are not barking obscenities or breaking into fights, and I don't see any anyone defecating in public. They are well behaved, the way we like our homeless to be. If there still exists such a thing as a safety net, these folks have fallen so deftly, so unresistingly through its meshes, they seem to have floated down onto this hillside, like feathers that have no alternative but to lie where they land.

A couple of guys gaze at me wonderingly. I don't imagine too many women choose to walk in their midst, and I'm not sure why I've taken this route. Feeling like an intruder, I quicken my pace.

When I reach the corner, I see a 38 Geary trundling up from Franklin Street, its windows dark from the crush of passengers inside. Standing room only. I could make a run for it, take a chance that I'll get across Geary before the light changes, but I'm not sure I could endure a packed bus right now.

This is not a cozy neighborhood of coffeehouses, shops and pocket parks. There's St. Mary's Cathedral, the school and playing fields of Sacred Heart Prep, the headquarters of the Archdiocese of San Francisco, and high-rise apartment houses studded with concrete balconies. No place to hang out except the church.

The plaza leading to the cathedral is of Vatican proportions. Red tour buses line the street in front. Japanese tourists, cameras slung, chat happily, and I note the many retirement-age Catholic couples. Catholic, for certain, because the wives look like nuns in mufti—cropped gray hair, scrubbed faces, well pressed slacks and white Reeboks. I get past this gaggle, past the main doors depicting the risen Christ with his arms wide open, and look around for a quiet corner. No such thing, so I settle for a pew by one of the giant pylons that uphold the vast dome resembling the inside of a beehive. I prefer a church that's dark, quiet, enclosed, but this one has clear windows around the base that afford a panoramic view including the newly gilded dome of City Hall. The organ does its best to drown out the chatter in the aisles.

"Why him?" I whisper. "Why did you have to send *him*?"

Most questions asked of God are rhetorical, since mostly there's no answer. Sometimes I'll get an inkling, or an unbidden thought will drift by which I'll take as a kind of reply. But today . . . nothing.

The many Reeboks squeak by on the polished brick floor, and people point at this or that architectural feature.

I lower my two bad knees onto the cushioned kneeler, and say to God, "You had to send Ajax. All those homeless on that hillside, and you had to pick him. Why not a *gentle* loony, some poor soul to whom I could have passed a casserole or a pot of soup over the fence, then walked away feeling good about myself?"

The organ stops. The place takes on a more contemplative aura. Visitors instinctively lower their voices to a stage-whisper. Easing off the kneeler and onto the seat, I tip back my head to see the hanging sculpture that dominates the interior: a huge swatch of light-catching pendants that's like a glimpse of the Holy Spirit.

"No," I say, addressing the sculpture, "You had to saddle us with one of the most notorious homeless men in the city. A criminal!"

People are starting to stare. I don't care. I've never perfected the art of silent prayer. As a girl I'd kneel by my bed with the rosary encircling my folded hands and try for a string of mental Hail Marys. Within moments, though, I'd revert to default mode: thinking about an imaginary boy whom I'd like to date, or even marry. The people in the aisles know who they're talking to: wife or husband, friend with camera. But who, they must wonder, is that woman in gray fleece arguing with?

Since this is the house of God, and there's no one else I care to speak to in here, I don't hold back. I let him know exactly where I'm at: the fact that all I want is an orderly life where one thing follows logically from whatever went before. I remind him that some highly productive people have lived this way. Proust, for example, in his cork-lined room. The poet Philip Larkin, about whom it was said that his life was "not rich in incident." Spare me, please, the richness of incidents. No more plot-jumps in my life.

A thought floats by: What about St. Francis, who actively *courted* change, homelessness, poverty? I protest that Francis was not a writer. He did not require a chunk of peaceful down-town in which to finish a book. As it happened, he got pretty much what he was after. He wanted poverty, he got it. He wanted to kiss lepers, fine. If somewhere at the back of his mind he craved sainthood, well, he got that, too. Even the legendary Wolf of Gubbio that Francis is reputed to have tamed, was probably less fearsome than Ajax.

Enough.

Closing my eyes, I sit quietly and breathe the frankincensed air until I plunge into no-thought, hanging suspended in that pleasant neutrality until the organist obliterates the quiet with a resounding Tantum Ergo. Under my breath I sing along, in Latin, repeating words written eight hundred years ago by Thomas Aquinas.

I don't pull the cord at Sixth Avenue. Bridie's been fed; no reason to stop by the garage. And I keep to my seat as others disembark at 33rd, where I'd planned to catch an 18 bus that would have taken me directly to the motel. In all the years of living in the Richmond District, I have never ridden this bus to the end of the line. The end of the line is the ocean.

The bus careens through bright, alphabetical streets —Anza, Balboa, Cabrillo—before emerging onto a sunny esplanade that faces the ocean. I decide to hike along the oceanfront to where Kirkham meets the beach, then cut up to the motel.

The ocean, an opalescent sheet, has generated no surf except for a thin white lip at the shoreline, and the beach, on this sunny weekday, appears empty, only one large orange towel spread out on its clean-swept surface. I don't see the people who belong to the towel, only a couple of ravens pecking away at the sand. I have never been to the ocean, even on stormy days, when I was the only person around. The ravens fly off in a huff, lacerating the air with their big black wings. Farther off, nearer to the motel, the windmill stands picture-still against the cloudless sky. I head in that direction: the western edge of Golden Gate Park.

The windmill is a disappointment because instead of dominating a horizon, as in the Dutch polders where land has been reclaimed from a relentless sea, it's stuck in the middle of a tulip garden, its giant sails poking out from a thicket of Monterey cypress and other conifers where it seems to be suffocating. Still, it's an impressive structure, one of the world's largest. The sails span more than a hundred feet.

Windmills and I go way back. So do tulips, presumably. A psychic once told me that I ("the entity") had been a tulip farmer in Holland, around the year 1712. "In that incarnation, the entity had a large family, many children, "she said, "but you preferred being off by yourself, putting your bulbs in the ground." Whether or not it's true, the idea pleases me, especially the part about how "In those days you would talk to God, when you were alone in your fields, kneeling among the flowers."

But windmills. As a symbol of proud isolation and self-sufficiency, they took root in my mind via the paintings of Piet Mondrian, the Dutch artist I discovered when I was nineteen. The previous year I'd moved to Philadelphia, where I lived in a thimble-sized apartment on 20th Street, just off Rittenhouse Square. (I assured the landlord that it didn't matter if I lived in a closet, so long as I might live there *alone*.)

I left home not because it was unbearable—it had been unbearable for years—but because now that I'd graduated high school and become a bona-fide wage-earner, I felt I should no longer have to compete for breathing room with eight other people in a house that would have proved a snug fit for four. Having begun to read, to educate myself, I resented my six younger siblings who ran wild through the place, and my parents who were conducting their own Hundred Years War: dishes flying across the room, black curses being uttered, no end to the tensions. In such a festering atmosphere, how was I to imbibe the subtle truths of French existentialism? The social insights of the British novel of manners?

I had a vague sense that I was preparing myself for something, but no idea what that something might be. (In fact, the same psychic who had said I'd been a tulip farmer also told me that I was destined one day to be a writer. At the time I was 32 years old, and the idea seemed preposterous. Of course, I *wanted* to be a writer—always had, at the back of my mind, and had published doggerel by the ream in our local newspaper. But real writing? Virginia Woolf-type writing? That was for others.) Nothing in my upbringing suggested that a girl could do anything more than hold onto her sales clerk or office job until somebody scooped her up into marriage and made her safe. Meanwhile, at eighteen, I was working, living at home, and competing for space.

Worst of all, by my reckoning, was the fact that we had only one bathroom. There I was, forking over a quarter of my monthly salary for room and board, and still having to adhere to the bathroom schedule. Each morning, under ideal conditions, you got ten minutes. You got the right to lock the door, and to shout, "Get away from here!" to any whiners, unless that whiner happened to be my father. If you overslept and missed your slot, tough luck. Now, though, since I had a two-hour daily commute into central Philadelphia, and needed to do hair and makeup for my office job, I got first dibs on the bathroom and more time, but practically in the middle of the night, and even then I had people banging on the door, needing to "go poo" or threatening to throw up.

And so I left, got my own place.

In the city, I could visit the bathroom fifty times a day if I liked. I could live in there, and pretty much did. I could sing, shout, recite poetry, sit on the john reading whole chapters. No one to stop me from soaking for hours in the clawfoot tub. No one screaming that I was not to exceed two inches of water. In my own bathroom, I could parboil myself in a foot and a half of steaming water, since water, hot or cold, was included in the rent. Perched at the top of a fourth-floor walkup, I felt like a lighthouse keeper, or an eagle in its eyrie. I possessed an unfettered view of the downtown skyline. At night I'd lie there in the dark, submerged to my neck in heavily chlorinated water, while I beheld, through my uncurtained window, the razzle-dazzle of lights, the oddly comical statue of Billy Penn, the black outlines of skyscrapers against an indigo sky.

I had arrived. Untethered to family, hometown, Church, I free-floated in my tub, and in my new life, allowing my thoughts to lengthen out and take their natural course: no longer measured against religious strictures or the opinions of my father, who set the bar so high you were bound to fail.

He'd say that his children had better succeed at *something*, to justify his hellish nights in the factory, the sacrifice of his life, his soul, then in the next breath evoke the

NIGHT LIGHT • 133

family jinx, stating there was no use hoping for better things when anyone could see he was saddled with a bunch of no-good bums who'd never amount to anything.

I would lie in my tub till the water turned cold and my fingerpads shriveled. Where was I going in life? What did I mean to accomplish? Downtown Philadelphia swarmed with students from Penn and Temple, and the various art and music schools for which the city was renowned: other eighteen-year-olds who were going places, and not dressed like myself, in stiletto heels and mincing little skirt, setting off each day to type legal briefs in a tiny room I shared with a woman twenty years my senior who was involved in an extramarital affair and using me as her excuse whenever she was mysteriously away from home. Her husband would ring my doorbell, nearly pleading with me to say that it was not true, that she'd really been with me on such-and-such a night and not off with . . . some other man. I lived in fear that I might end up witnessing a crime of passion, that one day he'd come storming into the office with a gun and blow both of us away, his wife for cheating and me for providing the alibi.

Meanwhile, others my age were schlepping bookbags, portfolios, sketch pads as big as windows. I came to recognize the Wharton School boys by their wingtips and attaché cases, and the Curtis Institute students by their general dowdiness and unwieldy instrument cases. I had no money for college, and no scholarship. Had done poorly in math. I told myself these people had no relevance to my life. Still, I observed them narrowly, the college kids, as I cut through Rittenhouse Square and walked along Walnut Street on my way to the office. All the women with whom I worked were much older. I had no one to talk to, and was sick of one-way conversations in which I was the captive audience while my co-worker endlessly replayed her nights of passion and then asked coy questions of me, the greenhorn, about her lover's "true intentions."

Then came the nightmares. I never connected them directly to Mr. Dietter, the man from the other apartment on my landing who stood outside my door each night and . . . breathed. From my bed I could see his two black snub-nosed shoes in the bright slit of hallway light, and felt the oppressive weight as he flattened himself against my door and made it rattle, before finally moaning his relief.

I did not want to think about what he was doing out there. I knew of course that it was something sexual, with me as its object, but this was 1961, before the so-called Sexual Revolution. I had recently graduated from a Catholic high school and escaped a small town. Though I considered myself a city sophisticate because I now lived in a city, in fact I had never encountered the word "masturbation" in conversation, and was unclear on a number of concepts.

Dietter was about sixty, a poor, lonely old fart, and I figured, What harm could he possibly do? I came to view him as a part of the building—the creaking stairs, the discolored wallpaper in the hallway. He was simply a part of the decay rampant in that place, like the elderly woman who lived below me and cried incessantly. Rivers of tears: an underground stream. Sex was everywhere—in the office, on the streets, outside my door—but my goal was Literature. I wanted to imbibe as much as possible, and had no time for side-issues. Whenever Dietter and I passed each other on the narrow staircase, I too would lower my head, as if I were somehow implicated in his nocturnal visits.

My instinct told me to keep all this quiet, certainly not to tell my parents. I didn't want my father blustering

down to Philadelphia, imposing his presence on my apartment, passing ironic judgment on my décor or my choice
of books. And I felt squeamish about reporting the incidents
to the landlord and possibly getting Dietter evicted. Where
would he *go*? The man had no doubt been moldering in
his maisonette for decades. I never considered calling the
police. Women in the office had warned me about "The
Pickup"—city cops prowling the downtown for young
girls. As a matter of fact, it had already happened. When
I was hurrying home one night after a concert, a cruiser
pulled up alongside me on Chestnut Street. Both officers
urged me to get in the car, they'd drive me home. "It's not
safe out there, not for a young thing like you."

Still, Mr. Dietter was interfering with my life. He had
an eerie instinct for times when I happened to be in my
living-room, which also served as my bedroom. I stuffed a
thick towel under the door, and when that wasn't enough,
I'd crank up the volume on my record-player: Brahms'
Fourth at concert-hall decibel.

Even Dietter had a purpose in life. What was mine?

In the bathroom, I hung a muslin curtain. How many
more Dietters were out there? I didn't want some goon
peering at me through his spyglass while I bathed each
night. The gauzy cloth acted as a filter that muted the
bright lights, softening the sharp outlines of the downtown
buildings. I was now enclosed in a steam-clouded room,
no longer an eagle in its eyrie, just another ingénue in the
city. I set up a stool on which I placed a lit candle. Instantly
the room transformed itself into a chapel, a grotto, and I'd
pray, then feel ashamed of myself, I who'd been drinking
deep from the atheistic well of Camus and Sartre. I could
not get enough of any writer who directly or indirectly
repudiated religion.

This morning in St. Mary's Cathedral was hardly the first time I had prayed for an orderly life. While Mr. D. ravaged the door, I'd lie in the tub beseeching God, if there was one, to remove all barriers to clarity and order. At least, I prayed, take away the nightmares, which now involved Dietter breaking down my door.

But to which God was I praying? I had renounced Roman Catholicism, not merely drifting away, as some Catholics do, but taking a stand, to a nun at my school, against the doctrine of Transubstantiation.

"I can no longer believe it," I told this woman, my English teacher and also the moderator of the school paper, for which I did art editorials. She was the only nun who'd more or less accepted me for what I was, and I not only didn't care that her attitude toward me would change—I *wanted* it to change.

Her face tightened, this most hip of sisters. "Please," she urged. "Let me put you in touch with my brother. He's a priest in Chicago who's been very successful with young people in danger of losing their faith."

"I don't think I need to talk to him."

"Don't be obdurate!"

"I'm not, Sister. I just—What could I say?"

Transubstantiation. I had never given the doctrine a thought, just took it on faith, as Catholics were taught to do. But now I wanted *out*, so I picked away at this tenet as if it were a tenacious old scab. How could I have let myself believe, all these years, that through the sacrament of the mass, a white wafer should become the *actual* body and blood of Christ? A ridiculous concept, was it not? No rational person would accept such a proposition—certainly not my revered Camus, or the redoubtable Sartre.

The lawyer in my mind neutralized the conflict by pointing out that if I left the Church I'd no longer have to confess, no longer have to stand in the shadowy line on Saturday afternoons waiting my turn to be browbeaten, no longer have to worry so obsessively about sins of a carnal nature.

As the water turned tepid in my tub, I wondered what I might be like to live without a God. Lots of people did. And a thought insinuated itself like an ice pick in my brain: What if in fact there *were* no God?

∾

I lived in the 20th Street apartment for eight months. I had to leave because of Mr. Dietter, who was not only a horny old bloke, he was crazy.

Early on a Saturday morning, somebody rang my doorbell. The bells were downstairs and outside, by the mailboxes. In this building of paper-thin walls, when a bell sounded in one apartment, it reverberated in every other apartment. No reason why anyone should be ringing my bell, especially at six in the morning. I turned over in bed.

The bell continued its low-pitched squawk.

"Leave me alone," I muttered.

I then heard Mr. Dietter's door burst open. I heard him bounding down the stairs, insofar as he was able to bound, considering that he walked with the aid of a cane. I heard shouting.

I had not expected city life to be the zoo that my parents' home had been. I was paying dearly for privacy, and for peace. I flopped the pillow over my head.

More loud words, and then Mr. D. clomping back upstairs, punctuating his progress by rapping his cane against the walls as he went. Someone had caused his slow

burn to boil over, but he was so uniformly strange that
I didn't bother to speculate about the shouting episode.
Not my business. Once inside his lair, he let loose a barrage of phlegm-choked coughs before subsiding once
more into the brooding choler that seeped like poisonous
mist from beneath his door. I lay back and dozed. Figured
it must be part of a dream, the army I heard tramping up
the stairs.

"Open up!"

"Wha--?"

"Open up! Police!"

I struggled out of the covers. Threw on my quilted bathrobe. Standing by the bed in bare feet, gripping the collar
of the robe, I said, "You've got the wrong place. There's
nobody here."

"*You're* here," boomed the man, "and we need to ask
some questions."

More shouting. I recognized the high-pitched voice
of my co-worker's husband. No doubt she had not come
home the night before, and he was here to check up.

Immediately, I knew the What but not the Why. Mr.
Dietter had attacked this man. Hearing my doorbell, he
had peeked out his front window and spotted red-headed
Kevin, and, for whatever reason—perhaps meaning to
protect me, or to ward off another claimant—had hurried
down to confront the person he viewed as a marauder, or
a rival.

"He hit me with his fucking cane," I heard Kevin yelling.
"Bastard whacked my shoulder!"

Four cops appeared at my door.

"Know of anyone who could've done such a thing?"

I shook my head. Affected as blank an expression as
I could muster.

"Maybe we should go have a look," suggested one of the younger cops, starting up the three steps to Dietter's door.

"There's a frail old man living in there," I said, splitting hairs as I'd long ago learned to do in the confessional. Mr. Dietter *was* frail, mentally if not physically.

I had to do some fast talking to placate the officers, get them to escort Kevin out of the building. He was babbling about needing to talk to his wife, who was upstairs, but I heard the officer tell him that unless his wife was a young girl of about sixteen, she was definitely not in that upstairs apartment.

The next time Dietter and I sidled past each other on the narrow stairs, I saw his face go slack and a smile play about his withered lips. He had won. He had saved me, and I'd reciprocated by saving *him*. In his mind, at least, we two were in collusion.

I did not know what Mr. Dietter might do next. And I didn't want Kevin coming back.

Or those cops. No choice but to move.

Though I hated having to clear out of that nest, peel my Cezanne prints off the wall and dismantle my bookshelf, the eight months had seen me launched. I now took a ballet class every weekday evening. After class, exhilarated from the rugged exercise, the sweat drying on a body capable of executing a grand jete and triple pirouettes, I'd walk the stately Philadelphia streets under a continuous canopy of elm and sycamore, flickers of amber streetlight seeping through, all the way to the colonnaded library, where I'd enter a glass booth, clap on big black earphones and listen to Brahms and ballet scores, then take my time paging through the Abrams art books.

I arrived home around nine, and ate any old thing. Didn't waste a minute on cuisine. It was in the quiet evenings that I could feel the currents from Penn, Temple, Curtis, the Museum School, and all the other campuses in metropolitan Philadelphia where students were at their books in the light of gooseneck lamps, amassing college credits. Though I knew I could never catch up, I had set myself the task of reading for three hours each night. I didn't date, didn't go to parties, and by the time Mr. Dietter whacked Kevin with his cane, I had worked my way through two centuries of British fiction, read everything French from Flaubert to Genet, and begun tunneling into the cold hollows of Scandinavian literature.

Yet I remained restless, collecting a little of this, a little of that, for my intellectual grab-bag.

Where was the defining context?

On the trail of that context, I haunted the library. One night, just before closing time, the librarian began tiptoeing among the tables, her eyes, as always, on the expensive art books. This was decades before electronic checkpoints: a kid of six could have successfully ripped off a book. I, however, revered books to such an extent that I considered book-stealing on a level with murder. Edging so close to me that my sinuses twitched from the mothball scent of her blue cardigan, the librarian looked askance at my ballet bag. I could divine her thoughts. Had I put something in there? Was I *about* to put something in there?

She bent over, peering at the page. "You like Mondrian?"

I considered this a trick question, to see if I was shamming an interest in art so I could pilfer the book and maybe peddle it to one of the used booksellers who kept their crammed stalls down on 13th Street.

"I don't know much about Mondrian," I said, pronouncing the name as she had done, "but I like this drawing."

"This drawing," she said, "was executed during a period of great transition in the painter's life."

"Oh."

"Would you like to learn more about Mondrian? He's my favorite artist."

I didn't figure the favorite artist of this stick of a woman would necessarily become my favorite, but since I was lonely, and hungry for knowledge, desperate for a connection with anyone who knew more than I did about Art and Life—I said yes.

"Come back tomorrow. We'll talk."

It turned out that Mondrian had been a Theosophist, and that the librarian herself was a Theosophist, and that not far from this library there happened to be a Theosophical Society which she hoped I'd visit with her. I did go, but on seeing Madame Blavatsky's portrait, the bulging eyes in the bulldog face, the frame high up and leaning at a precarious angle from the wall, as if Blavatsky were about to plunge into the midst of her admirers, I panicked and had to leave, to the sorrow and disappointment of my mentor, the librarian.

Before that night, however, she had taught me about Mondrian. She had a habit of prefacing her sentences with "Did you know . . .?"

Did I know that Mondrian was the most spiritual painter who had ever lived?

Did I know he eschewed appearances in his search for Platonic essences?

Did I know that he never compromised, despite poverty and loneliness and lack of understanding on the part of others?

Did I know—and here she flashed me a significant look, knowing me to have been a Catholic—that Mondrian was a man very much like St. Francis?

"How was he like St. Francis?"

"How?" She arched her neck. "He turned his back on everything sensual. He spat on the attractions of this mundane world."

I wanted to learn more about this rarity, but not through the filter of Theosophy. I wanted to live inside Mondrian's head, at least until my own head had become a fit habitation. How could this man, like the windmills he painted, stand so proudly alone? Wasn't he ever afraid, as I was every night after turning off the lights in my fourth-floor apartment?

The librarian had told me about a retrospective of Mondrian's work to be held at the Guggenheim, and I talked one of the girls in ballet class into taking the train with me to New York. She wanted to see Radio City Music Hall and the Rockettes, and kept bugging me to hurry up, crying, "Why do you need to look at every picture for fifteen whole minutes?"

I needed to do this because only through the paintings themselves could I grasp the spirit of the man. As I proceeded up the giant white spiral of the Guggenheim, the logical progression of his work became obvious: curves turning into straight lines and right angles, pastels and mixed shades reducing themselves to primary colors bordered by black lines. A nineteen-year-old, a typist in a law office, was bearing witness to a spiritual journey, and after three hours I was seeing with the eyes of Mondrian, grasping his intention in a way that no art critic or teacher would ever improve upon. The process was wordless, and I now understood that I had only to look, with concentrated attention, and to listen, in order to learn most of what I need to know in life.

That afternoon at the Guggenheim, I had witnessed change, transformation, on an alchemical level. It took guts for Mondrian to give up depicting pretty scenes, and later to break with his Cubist friends in order to go down his own, lonesome road. He probably delayed his fame by decades. Alchemy: transmutation: passing from the lesser to the greater. The obvious to the underlying.

What is fire but change, combustion, the reduction of solid matter to ash? If it hadn't been for the fire I'd hardly be walking near the seafront on a weekday, identifying periwinkles, foxtails, California poppies.

The path is deserted, the area cordoned off by yellow Caution tape. I walk under a partially dismantled underpass that's dark and spooky. Dank, too, and clogged with rubble. On this sunny day, I can hear a foghorn: a warning of the impending cloud cover that's normal for this region.

Beyond the tunnel, the path turns up through the trees. I trip a couple of times over exposed roots.

Windmills are not good up close. Big, clumsy, creaking things, they lose the dramatic, anthropomorphic appeal that distance provides: the illusion of a lone human figure on the horizon line. As I approach, a gray-haired woman in pedal pushers hurries away from the garden, where no doubt her Chihuahua has just taken a dump among the agapanthus. In a high singsong, she urges him onward, in German: "Schnell, Toby! Schnell!"

And I'm alone.

I can see each individual, overlapping shingle picked out by sunlight and shadow on the shingled exterior of the mill. As I move in closer, the windmill, too, seems to move, hovering over me, Pisa-like. The thing is massive, totemic, even more so with its unmoving sails.

This mill, with its hundred-foot lattice sails crafted of Oregon pine, once pumped water from an underground aquifer to irrigate all of Golden Gate Park. In its heyday, the interior mechanism pumped 20,000 gallons an hour.

Fronted by a diminutive lawn and low-growing primroses, the mill, massive at its base and eighty-five feet tall, seems like a bull elephant put out to pasture among the petunias. This mastodon has been tamed, its scope reduced, its main function made redundant.

Up close, my palms against the gritty flank, I view the giant sails from an unusual perspective, directly underneath. The angle distorts their symmetry, and they appear to intersect obliquely, like bold, Franz Kline brushstrokes against the hot blue sky.

Loping down the path, I go around to the back, where the mill casts a cool, damp shadow. Nothing but birdsong and the gurgle of water. By an ivy-choked hump of ground, a rusted pipe shoots out and quickly sinks into the macadam. From inside an old green utility shed comes an insistent drip-drip of water. Some sort of catchment. In a murder mystery, this is where the body would be cached.

The composition of this day—flat cloudless sky, sunny breezes—frowns on the notion of death, but in fact we could have died in that fire. At his hearing, Ajax admitted to the D.A. that he'd fallen asleep while smoking, awakened to find his pillow on fire, with fire climbing the wall, then simply walked over and stuffed the flaming pillow into the crack separating his place from ours. *But did you know there were two people asleep in that cottage?* he was asked. Yes, he did. *Did you go to a call box or call 911 to try and get help?* No, he did not. *Then what did you do?* (Reading a transcript of the hearing that we were not permitted to attend, I could feel the bated hush in the courtroom.) *Went out for a beer*, he said.

And if we *had* died six weeks ago?

Water gurgles dimly in the green shed. The windmill stands silent. I let myself fall under the spell of this monolith, this former workhorse now turned into a tourist attraction, and I wonder about the tulip farmer, with his bloated family and his fields. Who's to say whether it's true, what the psychic said—but if so, how many lifetimes, how many deaths have intervened between the "me" of 1712 and the "me" who is standing here now? That individual lived two hundred years before Mondrian painted his windmills. Did the farmer love books, as I do? Did he even know how to read? Muttering to God as he pressed his bulbs into the Dutch soil, he seems more simple and wise than I could ever be, and this is the sort of transformation I'm looking for: a return to something like simplicity.

CHAPTER NINE

KEEPING HOUSE

Early July, and Jean, our landlady, has decided to flee the city—the fog, the grit, the wind—for her other home, the one in Sacramento with the swimming pool. I can't blame her; she must be tired of the sad sight from her kitchen window. Fire damage, like a parched throat, drags a person inexorably in the direction of water. The good news is that we'll have her flat for two weeks, precisely when our term at the Ocean Breeze comes to an end. In return, we'll care for her cats, hose down the garden, and oversee the rebuilding of our cottage until she returns.

Once we've loaded the Toyota, we step inside the motel to pay our final phone charges and to thank Mr. Vyas. At the ping of the bell, he emerges from behind the paisley curtain in the same way he did that foggy night when we first showed up. Wearing the same dyspeptic smile, he waggles his fingers in a dismissive gesture and laments, "People, coming and going. Always, they are coming and going." To clinch their agreement of this timeless truth, he and Shorey shake hands.

148 • MARGARET CONWAY

Shorey has eased the car into Reverse and begun backing out of the lot when Mr. Vyas, the customary woolen cap hugging his skull, comes bustling over. "Your receipt," he huffs, shoving a copy of the phone bill through the inch of open window. As we cruise down Kirkham toward the ocean, I see that once again we've been billed five dollars—that extra zero—instead of the agreed-upon fifty cents for one of our local calls. Not wanting to go back there and nullify the genial note on which we ended our long stay, I simply fold the paper into my purse.

∼

As if to spite those who would seek to escape the chill of a San Francisco summer, just as Jean leaves the city the sun burns a hole in the cloud-cover, and we find ourselves settling into her upstairs flat on a perfectly warm, golden afternoon. For the first time in more than six weeks, I'm able to cook us a meal. Nothing fancy, just pasta primavera and a salad of mixed greens, but served on gilt-edged plates, on woven placemats, at a solid oak table lit by a dangling Tiffany-style lamp, as we listen to Puccini on KDFC.

We take our time with the meal, the way we didn't in all those restaurants. The dining-room's dimensions and décor, so opposite to the tight, transient feel of our room at the Ocean Breeze, sets the scene for some actual conversation. When Shorey gets up from the table, he's stricken with a look of embarrassed happiness. He re-folds and lays down his napkin as if it were a sacred linen.

"That was . . . really nice."

"Just pasta."

"Need any help?"

Years, since he inquired about the dishes.

"No. You go relax."

"Care from some coffee from up the street?"

"Why don't I make it here."

"But . . . have your bath first."

Neither of us feels comfortable, caught in this awkward solicitude.

He bends to stroke one of the cats, who's still skittish about our presence. Then he's down the back steps to the garage, where he will spend some time with our own cat.

The sun has set in a blaze of coral behind our place, and Ajax's. Seen from above, through Jean's plantation blinds, the ruined cottages appear backlit by a distant fire. The window is open, the summer evening thick with smells of woodsmoke and charred meat from the Korean barbecue restaurant. I'm sitting plumped against several fat pillows on the bed, the brocade comforter drawn up over my legs. Jean's cats, Monkey and Belle, prowl the room, back and forth, flashing accusatory looks at the alien presence on their mother's bed.

Flushed from my bath, I am basking in the discovery of a new author. New to *me*, although Ann Cornelisen wrote the book I'm reading nearly a quarter-century ago. In *Women of the Shadows*, and in her other book, *Torregreca*, she captures the bare, stony, sun-blinded land of Lucania in Southern Italy with such imagistic exactitude that I feel I've been there myself and am merely sitting here remembering the trip. And she didn't go there as a tourist, but rather to live among the people, sharing their hard lives, as she struggled to set up nurseries and what amounted to free day-care centers in that backward region where she, too, endured the limited diet, the freezing winters, the primitive plumbing.

The book is better than dessert.

I am masticating the words, savoring phrases, reading aloud, closing my eyes after especially delectable sentences, sinking into Cornelisen's rich yet disciplined prose the way monks and nuns engage in *lectio divina*, or contemplative reading: deep immersion in a spiritual text, without mental wrestling or preconceptions, to see where the words will lead. Words, as depth-charge into unsuspected veins of understanding. And I am wondering, sitting here so cozily, how I could have spent seven years in a master's program in writing without ever having heard the name Cornelisen. Or Chaudhuri. But perhaps we were too busy paring away adjectives and adverbs, in imitation of Ray Carver.

I have found a word, *passeggiata*, that I need to share with Shorey. The crisp dictionary meaning of "walk" or "ride," doesn't begin to suggest the hard-won sunset promenade of an entire Italian village of impoverished land-laborers , processing in straight-backed dignity behind their "betters"—the mayor, his wife and daughter, the postmaster and other petty officials. But it's the word itself, with its double consonants and poetic flow, that I want to bring to my husband. This, I think, as I'm grinding coffee beans, is the hidden language of marriage and of all long-term unions: the language of saved newspaper clippings, lines of poetry, overheard conversation, each partner playing to the other's obscure, even oddball interests. A language whose native speakers number just two, and which can't be translated because anyone outside the charmed circle would be like to say, "So what?" Which may be why widows, widowers and other bereaved lovers sometimes grow very silent, and feel unwilling to try again, to create a whole new language with someone else.

But Shorey and I are still alive, I realize with a pleasant shock, as I stand by the kitchen window pouring Kenya coffee into sturdy mugs. We've survived a fire, and so much else in our twenty-odd years together. *Passeggiata*: our evening walks to Walgreen's. Seldom do we need anything at Walgreen's, except an excuse to walk up Clement Street arm-in-arm. The years, paradoxically, have rendered us a little shy of the easy intimacies of earlier days.

Shorey's out of my range of vision. He will have left the garage door ajar—that strip of molten light against the darkening garden—so Bridie can go in and out as she likes. She can't join us up here in the flat: Jean's cats have their own territorial imperative, and Bridie is not by nature the sociable type, not when it comes to other animals.

I spot a moving black form by the door to our cottage—Bridie. She sniffs every inch of the porch and the damaged banister, but suddenly edges away and, with a jerking cartoonish movement, as if she'd been scorched, hurtles down the steps and out of sight through a broken board in the redwood fence. Born next-door, in the palmier days of that cottage when young renters put up organdy curtains and baked banana bread and tended the geraniums and the swatch of velvet lawn, she's no doubt responding to an atavistic instinct that in times of trouble propels her over the fence to her birthplace. After all, she's got no beef with Ajax.

In spite of the trauma, she's still willing to approach our place. Shorey rarely goes inside. I think the devastation breaks his heart.

We had fallen into the illusion of ownership.

For me, a fierce possessive impulse took hold not long after Ajax moved in next-door. Suddenly I perceived danger, and I had something worth protecting. Before that, never having owned a house or property, I tended to look upon any habitation as ultimately temporary. I'd put up curtains, apply coats of off-white paint, keep the place neat and clean, but I regarded these ministrations as merely cosmetic. Like painting-by-numbers rather than tackling a blank canvas. After all, somebody else owned the place, and that somebody could kick me out on a whim. To implement big structural changes—knocking out a wall, installing a walk-in closet or a greenhouse window—did not make financial sense, even if a landlord *were* to have permitted such alterations.

Shorey and I married late. He was forty, and I, thirty-seven. When we met, he posited that there were basically two types of people, Leavers and Stayers, and that our histories clearly indicated we were both in the latter category. This notion may have been a trifle simplistic, but it seemed to work for us on a metaphoric level.

"A Stayer should link up with another Stayer," said Shorey. "Let the others do their serial monogamy trips."

This made perfect sense. What did not make sense was Shorey's idea of where we would live.

When we decided to marry, Shorey still lived on the Peninsula, a spacious and affordable place in those pre-Silicon Valley days, and he felt determined to duplicate that happy experience in crowded San Francisco, where rental vacancies were running at less than one percent.

"I won't live with anyone above me or below me," he declared. "No—more—apartment—houses! What I'd really prefer is a cute little cottage."

I suggested that he was out of his mind, adding, "There *are* no such places. Even if we had all the money in the world, cute little cottages never come vacant because the people living in them never, ever leave."

Such naivete, such willful self-delusion I found maddening.

"I'm the one who's being realistic," I asserted. "I'm the one who's lived in this city for the past ten years."

This conversation took place two months before our presumptive wedding date. Presumptive, because Shorey had stated he was not getting married unless we found a place to his liking.

"In fact, we'll be lucky to find anything," I told him. "Especially at such short notice."

"But we're so deserving."

Perhaps we were, because incredibly, two weeks later, a friend told us of a vacant cottage in his neighborhood. "Get over there right away," he urged.

"See?" said Shorey. "It's called visualization."

Anyway, the old lady (Jean's mother) seemed to like us, but regretted that she'd already promised the place to another couple. Why, then, I wondered, had she agreed to see us? Hot and sweaty in our best outfits, in her airless flat, we sank back into the fathomless sofa. She sighed; gazed out the window.

"Wouldn't have worked anyway," I muttered. "We've got cats."

Every rental ad I'd seen prohibited pets, and Shorey had two of them. Right there, two strikes against us.

The landlady whipped her head round. "You say you've got cats?"

We hung our heads like the criminals that we were.

She leaned forward, gripping the arms of her wing-chair. "Male or female?"

"Two females," I admitted.

"I just *love* cats," she rhapsodized. "Got two myself. They ran and hid when they heard you coming."

We struggled up from the depths of the sofa. Shorey puffed out his chest, ready for the next round.

I piped up with, "Ours are called Tess and Tillie."

"Tillie!" Her hands flew to her cheeks. "Would that be short for Matilda?"

I had no idea; she was Shorey's cat; he'd only ever called her Tillie. These were the cats that predated Bridie. Since Shorey and I had never lived together, only he knew the particulars about his adult cats, their full names and lineage. But: "Yes," I said. "Short for Matilda."

Seemed the woman's mother had been named Matilda. Seemed her mother had lived in the now-vacant cottage until the time of her death. Seemed this was a clear sign that could not be disregarded. Beetling her brows, she stared into her lap. Shorey and I didn't dare to breathe. The problem was, she finally said, how was she going to break it to the other couple?

To prevent any change of mind on her part, Shorey upped our rent right on the spot. "Will that be enough?" he asked meekly.

As I wrote out the check, he leaned in and whispered, *"Visualization."*

In the dark I take care going down the long flight of narrow wooden steps from Jean's back door with the mug of steaming coffee. More damp and cool back here than on the surrounding streets. Hard to believe that Geary Boulevard, a straight-shot arterial that thrums with traffic twenty hours a day, is so near, and that on its parallel street, Clement, the many Asian restaurants are thronged with dinner patrons. At night, in the garden, the mulched soil gives off a stronger scent than the roses. When I inadvertently step onto a tuffet of English thyme, the herb releases its sharp Mediterranean fragrance.

The warm mug, with its raised Native-American turtle designs, feels satisfyingly solid between my hands. Alone in the dark yard, I'm virtually invisible in my black plaid pajamas. A momentary lull, a cessation of traffic and other noises, one of those rare quiet patches that sometimes, inexplicably, grips even the busiest districts in the city. The garage door stands open, but protocol prohibits me from bursting in on Shorey. He's sure to be on the Net, working his crosswords, and watching CNN, all at the same time.

As individuals, we are not neurotic about our "space," though we do value our private times. Having spent the decade of his twenties as the father of two children—their infancies, their rough-and-tumble grade-school days— Shorey is more flexible about intrusions on his solitude. Still, his twenties were a long time ago.

Not exactly a snap for two strong-willed persons to make it as a couple. The early years tested us, and he or I had been known to bark, "If you don't like it, you can leave!" Whereupon the other would spring forward like a pugilist and reply, "No way. *You* leave, if you want to. This is my home."

The cottage, a place neither of us could imagine walking away from (even when we could imagine walking away from each other), claimed us for its own, carried us through that bumptious period. And now that we're okay, our cottage is in trouble.

I cough a couple of times to alert Shorey that I'm coming in with hot coffee. And for dessert, a new word: *passeggiata*.

Sleeping was easier at the motel. Now that we're back on-site, the stench from the Korean barbecue floods my insomniac mind, blends with the lingering smell of burnt timber, and

I'm up every half-hour, kneeling by the bedroom window, straining to see through the grainy darkness. Nothing *to* see, though Meredith, the psychotherapist, did warn me about flashbacks—visual, auditory or olfactory hallucinations that can persist for a year, even eighteen months. "Or in some cases, for a lifetime."

In such a mood I'm counting the hours till daybreak, when I can go in and re-claim our place from the dangers of the night. For one thing, there's no lock on the front door; that was axed off the night of the fire. "No need for a lock," said Shorey, with maddening logic. But I'm thinking of vandals, and whatever voodoo can be practiced upon an empty, unsecured residence. An analogy that seems apt is that of *The Godfather*: the unguarded hospital room where Don Corleone lay wounded, and where Michael, his son, urged the nurse to go get a gurney so they could move him, hide him, since "Men are coming to kill my father."

But one can't hide a cottage, and so in the ashen light before dawn I'm in the place, looking for anything out of the ordinary. Then I'll slip in again around dusk. I feel diffident abut entering in the middle of the day, having accepted on some level that during business hours our cottage belongs to the contractor and his workmen.

At first, some real work got done. Men in heavy boots and surgical masks planted themselves in the sandy muck, amid the flies and feces of Ajax's place, and from that awkward vantage, all the while complaining about the filth, managed to slap a new side on our house, adding a firewall to keep us safe and bring us up to Code. Mentally, I blessed them every minute. Then came a spidery young man in a white jumpsuit of the type worn in high-tech "clean rooms." He shimmied along the blackened rafters that had been a crawl-space beneath our roof and coated them with a whitish mixture. I blessed him, too.

Two weeks of banging, hammering and the whine of the power-saw, then the project was becalmed. We entered the horse latitudes of construction work.

Now the men tend to log in no more than one or two half-days a week. I once counted eight straight days during which no one showed up. On those days the summer fog seems to coalesce, cloaking our place in a white gloom. The sight depresses me immeasurably. The Gucci-loafered contractor, on the rare occasions when he puts in an appearance, will raise his face to the sky, as if to demonstrate that God is his witness, and toss off yet another assurance: "Expect my guys on Thursday. You've got my word." Believing him, I leave the garage door open a crack while I type away on my novel, meanwhile listening for men's voices, the scrape of a ladder on concrete, the clump of workboots up our front steps. But Thursday passes, then Friday, Saturday, and on into the following week. I keep a record of their non-attendance, so that when I phone the bossman on his mobile, he can't blow me off with the usual disclaimer: "Sure they weren't there? Because, see, I've got it written right here on my pad."

Homeowning friends tell us such behavior is quite normal on the part of contractors, and that we should have believed the man when he said the rebuild would take *at least* three months. "This is a job," advised one friend, "that could be knocked off in three weeks. Jimmy Carter and his Habitat people have put up entire homes in less time. But your contractor's probably nursing along sixteen other jobs."

"What can we do, then?"

"Not much. Go to Europe. Take a cruise."

July 6. Gray day. Wet splat along the floor in front room. In this foggy light it resembles a trail of blood, the black blood of a black-and-white 1940s detective film. It's actually water that has leaked through cracks between the horizontal beams which some day, if the workers ever come back, will be our new roof.

July 7. Noon. A sunny Wednesday. Not my usual time in here. Turning the knob into the bathroom, I set off the echo. Hard to imagine we once inhabited these rooms. Feel like a ghost—redundant.

July 8. Looks like a truck stop bathroom, but I am <u>not</u> cleaning that toilet. When all this is over, I'll scour the shit out of it (literally). Cigarette butts floating in unflushed water. Still, I make sure they have toilet paper, a cake of Fels Naptha, and paper towels for drying their hands. If only they'd come back . . .

July 9 Bucking the order that "Everything must go," I fought to keep the ten-foot umbrella plant inside. Outdoors, it would not have survived. The guys don't mind its being here because the Japanese-style planter box provides a receptacle in which to flick whatever cigarette butts they don't dump in the toilet. Greasy black soot coats each leaf, but as I wash them, one by one, the large, palmate leaves reveal their original, deep green gloss.

At my last visit, Meredith counseled me to jot down my thoughts, so that I don't become a repository of unexamined fears and fire-related phobias. "After all," she said, winking, "you *are* a writer. So pay attention to any images that crop up."

"Images. You mean, like, in dreams?"

"Dreams, or the waking state. Or in nightmares."

July 10. Something about a grasshopper . . .

I'm in the front room, gazing up at broken windowpanes patched with brown Safeway bags, when I'm overtaken by the most potent sensation of déjà vu. Something to do with neighbors: the feeling that if anything of mine has been broken or trashed, then I am similarly broken, trashed. And it's *my fault*. This goes way back, and I'm not sure I want to shine a high beam onto this feeling. I only know that right now I don't want any neighbors seeing me when I exit this smashed and blackened house.

It's a question of identity.

I would ask Meredith, but I've used up my four free visits. She helped me get my act together vis-à-vis city services and strategies for staying sane through the next few months, and then we ended on a note that, if we'd had more time, would have signaled the beginning of real psychotherapy: the business of images.

No dearth of images this summer. They are competing for headspace in my cranium. Last night I entered a dream-scape full of giant flying insects, big dead bugs dropping from the sky. One of them, as it plummeted, turned into a silver-gray jumbo jet of the kind I once saw flying so low over Kowloon, on its way to Hong Kong's Kai Tak Airport, I could have reached up and touched its massive underbelly.

An insect becoming an airplane.

July 10. Something about a grasshopper.

Not just any insect, but a grasshopper.

As I play with this image, I soon realize it's about the car.

The year I turned twelve my father purchased his first car. As with nearly every major move in our life, it was my great-uncle who acted as facilitator. He taught my father to drive, steering him away from the heavy traffic onto narrow lanes that meandered past dairy farms and fields thick with tall green tessellated corn. The roads being most empty out around Douglassville and Birdsboro, I'm sure the two men had ample leisure to check out the scenery, and re-play the latest race they'd been to down at Monmouth, Uncle John referencing the racing paper spread out across his narrow lap. John would have sat on the sidelines during the driving test, while my father maneuvered the dented brown station wagon with the pails in the back and the big paperhanging brushes clogged with paste that gave off such a cloying smell, I once had to vomit out the car window. Though a fair-weather Catholic, my father must have prayed that neither the back flap of the wagon nor either of the back doors would fly open, as they often did, giving the vehicle the look of a large flightless bird desperately trying to become airborne. Following the miraculously successful test, they sped off to the used-car lot. They had no particular make or model in mind; it was more a matter of getting the most they could for the cash my father had in his wallet: four hundred dollars.

Since I'm unsure of the origin of those four hundred bucks, I can only surmise that out of my father's factory wages he put aside a five or a ten each week until he'd amassed the necessary sum. But squirreling away fives and tens, keeping track of a thickening bundle of bills in his sock drawer, would have been out of character. My father's character fault lay in the fact that, though he was dutiful and hardworking, he seemed to care not at all for money or material possessions. A bankbook balance was, to him, the ultimate abstraction. Invisible money. He never minded handing over his pay packet to my mother because once he had "rendered unto Caesar," as he put it, he could freely, and without guilt, do what he loved to do—read for hours, spend an afternoon at the racetrack, lose himself in the neon-lit womb of a neighborhood bar.

Any money he made passed through his hands with the fluidity of water; he functioned merely as a conduit. His kids always needed something. Not much left over by the end of the week. So it's most likely that John, the uncle who'd raised the orphaned boy my father once was, lent him the four hundred, to be repaid at some time in the hazy, indeterminate future.

One thing I do recall on that summer-into-autumn day: my mother, back at the house, grousing about how Uncle John didn't know crap about cars. "Driving all those years, and still doesn't know what's under the hood. Can't even change his own spark plugs. And *this* is the man who's going to advise your father?"

Even at twelve, I knew what my father would do. I envisioned him in the lemony light of the wide-open car lot up on Ridge Pike, putting a question to the salesman about "miles per gallon" or "horsepower." The question being pedantic, since my father couldn't have cared less about horsepower, or anything else to do with an automobile's innards or performance. This was simply a face-saving device, so that afterward he could say he'd acquitted himself well in the high-stakes exchange of buying a car. I'd wager that he itched to part with the four hundred. Get it over with. Then it would be off to the bar, he and his uncle, for a couple of cool ones.

The 1950s was the decade of the family sedan. To own a car became an American birthright. Without an auto you were somehow inauthentic, and I saw us that day as having moved into a whole new category: the independent and self-propelled, the driver as opposed to the driven. No more waiting for Uncle to take us food-shopping. No more being crammed, all nine of us, in the back of Uncle's flapdoodle of a stationwagon. No more stinky paste pails.

But that was me. My father didn't buy a car simply to fit in. He needed one for work.

By the time we got a car, my father had been working at the B.F. Goodrich plant in Oaks, Pennsylvania, for eight years. He was to put in fourteen additional years at the tire factory, but had he known that, he'd probably have committed suicide, as the man who gave him rides to work ending up doing. They had gravitated to each other because they both loved books, good music, foreign languages. They were what has been termed, somewhat patronizingly I think, working-class intellectuals. Because no man is an island, I know my father grieved for his dead friend, but meanwhile his transport had dried up, and he couldn't very well walk the five miles to Oaks. Not at that hour.

He worked the midnight-to-eight shift, so that his "day" was the reverse of ours. He got up a little before eleven, spooned instant coffee into a cup, and donned his workclothes while the water came to a boil. By 11:20 he was hiking the quarter-mile to Main Street where he caught an Oaks-bound bus. At that hour the buses could be unreliable. Arriving even a few minutes' late for your shift pissed off the foreman, and a hostile foreman could render your work-night considerably less pleasant.

Besides, eight other people depended on the tire-factory paycheck.

"I think," said Uncle dryly, "you'll be requiring a car."

I hope I can be forgiven for the letdown I felt on seeing what pulled up in front of our house that September afternoon. I had pictured something streamlined and loaded with chrome. A cool car. One that was two-toned, in the style of the day, or a dazzling shade of, say, royal blue or fire-engine red. Instead, our new auto, the same dull green as my father's work pants, looked stunted and misshapen, far too small for a family the size of ours.

But we had a car, I told myself. An actual car! Now we need no longer feel inferior to our neighbors up and down the street, as they ostentatiously backed out of their deep-black driveways.

My mother and we kids crowded the front walk as my father, triumphantly returned from Bob Gale's Used Autos, strode toward us, long-legged Uncle loping close behind, his few strands of white hair blown to the far side of his pink skull and his sand-colored cardigan buttoned unevenly. Both men wore the sappy, red-faced look that meant they'd made a stopover on the way home. What surprised me was that my mother, normally eaten up by resentment over the second-rate goods that furnished our lives and made us "laughingstocks" in the eyes of the neighbors, seemed not at all to mind the distinctly un-beautiful car—a turgid, crouching thing that resembled an oversized grasshopper.

Worse still, she, in short shorts and a chartreuse halter top, her five small sons clustered about her bare legs on the browning lawn, became positively kittenish with my father—a sickening display, considering the way they normally were at each other's throats.

John, the bachelor uncle, catching the intimate tone between my parents, began backing away in embarrass-ment. "Oh well," he said. "Guess I ought to be getting along." No one paid him the least attention.

Instead, my mother and the other six kids listened raptly to details of the purchase.

"I test-drove it, you bet I did," my father was saying. "Gunned the motor, and boy did she go. Children, don't ever be fooled by appearances. That car can outpace any young punk doing chicken-runs down Ridge Pike."

My mother giggled.

Pathetic, I thought. Byron Wilde or any of the guys who hung out at the steak shop could run him right off the road. Traitorous, though, to entertain a thought like that on my father's big day, so I piped up and politely asked what make of car it was.

"What, it's a Studebaker," he said. "Not exactly built for beauty, but you'll never find a more serviceable car."

"Can we go for a ride?" my mother pleaded.

"I take it you mean now," my father teased.

"George, the kids have been waiting all day."

Right then it hit me that while we were off at school or with our friends, or my father was at work, the bar, the track, my mother had been trapped all these years inside the house with a bunch of kids. She and my father never went anywhere. What did she care if the car looked like a grasshopper? Hell, it had four wheels and it could go.

"Margaret," said my father, in a dangerously controlled tone of voice. (This man, so detached about material possessions, was not so about insubordination on the part of his children. The belt was coming off with increasing frequency.) "Do I detect some reservations about our new automobile?"

My mother shot me a warning look that said, *Don't go spoiling our fun.*

"It's a nice car," I said. "Honest. I like it."

My father's face collapsed into a smile. He patted the Studebaker's flank, and said, "Now that Margaret has put her seal of approval on this baby, what d'you say we all go for a spin?"

A great cheer went up from the other kids. In their Keds, they jumped up and down around my mother.

Daintily, as if she were fussing with the flounces of an evening dress, she settled herself in the passenger seat, one of the boys between her and my father and another on her lap. The others squeezed into the back. I remained standing on the grass. No way I was about to crowd into the belly of that grasshopper with all those little kids: their sticky hands, their milk-breath, their sweaty bare legs. I looked at them, crammed in the semi-gloom of the back-seat behind a sort of porthole window, and tried to hide the contempt I was beginning to feel for people who so easily, so cringingly, surrendered their dignity in return for a quick thrill. At twelve, I expected a little more from life.

There'd be time enough to ride in the new car. Though he himself no longer attended mass, my father might roll out of bed on a Sunday morning to give my sister and me a lift to church. No more walking the long road between corn fields and horse farm, scuffing up our patent-leather shoes. Eileen and I, in our topper coats and veiled hats, would be chauffeured to St. Francis' in stately fashion.

My father ducked his head to see past my mother through the diminutive window. "You'll not be joining us, Margaret Anne?"

"Not today," I mumbled. "Told Ginger I'd meet her in Norristown."

"Well, la-di-da," he said, fiddling with the shift. "Your loss." The heavily freighted car bucked and shuddered—he was not yet used to the gears—and then surged down the road toward the open countryside.

⌒

Wearing sleeveless blouses and cotton shorts, Ginger and I walked miles that day to showcase our legs. We strode past Montgomery Lunch, the Pennsylvania & Western depot, the Conte Luna spaghetti factory, all the way to the east end of Norristown where the Italians lived. But the only audience we attracted was a car full of greasers who veered near enough to shout, "Hey, girls! Grow something up top and we'll come back and marry you!"

"Told you," said Ginger. "We shoulda wore falsies."

"I don't have any." And couldn't imagine the embarrassment of buying them.

"Then stuff some socks in there."

Tired and dispirited, I accepted a ride home from Ginger's dad. No use walking all that way when nobody'd notice me anyway. And besides, it was well after nine. By now, Whitehall Road with its rare streetlights would be densely, scarily dark.

Driving along with the windows up, my shoulders began to slump at the prospect of the shrieking reprimand I was sure to receive from my mother. From within the smoky enclosure of Mr. Nowicki's car, I struggled to devise a strategy for blocking out the sound of her voice.

My dread increased as we crunched onto the gravel where the met the road outside our house. Bad news: it was Saturday night. My father would be there, waiting to add muscle to my mother's gripes against me. And even more so, considering how lovey-dovey they'd been today.

"Looks like you got company," said Mr. Nowicki.

Blinking into the darkness beyond his windshield, I spied the hulking, unfamiliar shape. Intent on my own ambitions that day, I'd almost forgotten about the grasshopper. So . . . they'd had their ride. They had christened the new car, the other eight of them. More and more, I was distancing myself from these people, and I wasn't sure whether that represented a good or a bad thing.

"Nah," I said dully. "It's ours. My father bought a car today."

"He did? Well, isn't that nice," said Nowicki.

As I crept up the front walk, I hugged my bare arms. Early September, though tonight might turn cold. The damp air shivered, threatening autumn, then winter. Nevertheless, I felt tempted to make a run for the woods across the road. Hide out there until morning.

I hated the fear I felt. Hated them for making me feel this way!

Odd thing—the door had not been pulled shut, and a strip of light punctuated the darkness. Almost like an invitation. Perhaps they'd been worried about me.

When I stepped inside I saw my mother sitting in a corner of the couch with the youngest, a toddler, in her lap. She barely glanced up. She looked beaten. "Did you see it?" she asked.

She held onto the child as if he were a teddy bear, absentmindedly stroking his fine brown hair. The other boys would be asleep by now, but Eileen sat at the dinette table examining what looked like a laceration on her elbow.

"See *what?*" I said. "What's going on?"

My mother lifted her face, fixing me with a dead-eyed look. "Weren't you the lucky one. You knew to stay away."

"Where's Dad?"

"Your father crashed the car."

"He—crashed it?" The first time out? What about the four hundred bucks, and we Conways as proud owners of a family sedan?

"I don't feel like talking any more tonight. Stephen chipped a tooth. I wrenched my shoulder."

My father's armchair, his reading chair, sat ominously empty.

"But where's Dad?"

"In bed. Where else?"

Studying the broken windowpanes, I realize it will be quite a job, and expensive, to restore our Victorian windows, but since they constitute the most charming feature of this otherwise plain-fronted cottage, I hope they *can* be restored. The alternative—sliding glass windows encased in aluminum, with those fingernail-tearing locks—is too depressing to contemplate. Another innovation I'm seeing more and more here in the city: crisscrossing black tape, or paint, applied to windowglass, to give the illusion of individual panes. Hideous. All about bottom-line. But was life so very different in 1955 when we got our first car? My father purchased the cheapest vehicle, because that's what he could afford.

How my mother suffered over the loss of that Studebaker.

The morning after the crash, she was sitting at the table in her duster, seemingly revived by a cup of Nescafe. When I came downstairs dressed for mass, she said, "Sit down. You can go to church later."

"But, Mom. This is the last mass."

"God'll forgive you. Sit."

She passed me a glass of milk. The clink of glass on Formica was the only sound in that house. The others must have been sleeping in.

Seemed they'd been having a grand old time, Eileen and the boys, singing "Davy Crockett," all the verses, while my father kept urging everyone to notice the "turning leaves," the first reds and yellows of the season.

"I was just quiet," said my mother. "Glad to be going for a ride."

After they'd driven north for about twenty miles, they came into Souderton. That's where it happened. She remembered an underpass, then a pole. My father, struggling with the wheel, crying, "Mary! I can't turn this goddamn wheel!" The steering mechanism had locked. She let the facts tumble out, without employing any of her usual rhetorical flourishes: embellishing even the tiniest details and drawing out the narrative into a thin, vibrating wire of suspense. Had she lived in another time, another place, my mother would have been the village storyteller. Now, however, she hurried to bypass the part where they smashed into the pole, the part where the Souderton people ("so nice") drove our family home and even arranged, at my father's request, to have the car towed home as well.

"So the car can be fixed?"

"No, it cannot be fixed," she said indignantly. "It's totaled."

"Then—"

"Don't ask me why he had that thing brought back here." Now I could feel us closing in on the real story, the narrative that rumbled beneath mere accident facts. "And don't ask me why he won't go up to Bob Gale, that crook, and get our money back."

"Maybe Uncle—"

"Don't mention that man! I blame all of this on him. But guess what reason your father's giving?"

"Reason for what?"

"For not getting our money back! Are you paying attention?"

"I am!"

"Says it's like placing a bet at the track: you may win, you may lose. 'Luck of the draw,' he says. "Meanwhile, that shithead on Ridge Pike is laughing up his sleeve at the two live ones who bought that lemon."

Now we were getting into old grudges between her and my father, between her and my great-uncle, stuff I was not remotely interested in. I peeked through the Venetian blind, to see what daylight would reveal. Someone—probably my father—had draped an old Army blanket over the wreckage.

The ravaged car remained in place for three months. Within a week the blanket had blown off. Late autumn rains drummed against the body of the Studebaker, and large red maple leaves drifted down, pasting themselves onto the wet roof, the crushed hood. One night a prankster, or maybe a neighbor sick of that eyesore, caved in the windshield. December snow sifted through the gouged glass, piling whitely on the passenger seat. During a blizzard a foot of snow buried our auto, so that it now looked like every other car in sight: a fat white shape in a white landscape.

The snow melted, and once again kids at school were needling me about the junk-heap in front of our house. People walking by expressed their distaste. One woman used a term I'd never heard: "Tobacco Road."

My father, who re-read James Joyce's *Ulysses* every year of his adult life, who spoke Berlitz Italian and could sing operative arias and quote with ease from Dickens and Shakespeare, could not manage to get that car removed. My mother nagged, raged, implored, but his famous inertia had set in. Was this something to do with the Irish temperament—an inherited lowering of the give-a-shit factor after eight hundred years of English rule—or simply that after standing on a factory floor in front of a high-decibel machine, surrounded by other high-decibel machines, my father had developed a sort of Yogic detachment, the power that made it possible for him to read difficult books while seemingly oblivious to my brothers' tumbling and brawling all around his chair? (Later we would learn that all those years in the factory had impaired his hearing.)

One morning the car was gone, vanished in the night, and my father waved away any questions about its removal.

Oddly, I missed the wretched thing. After all, I was the one who had never ridden in it, who hadn't smelled its leather seats or experienced its speed. The one who could know it only posthumously. Toward the end I'd been sneaking out there to witness its disintegration, having already learned that breakdown can be far more fascinating than unobstructed growth. I was thinking of the log I sat on in the woods—how its crumbling underside supported an entire ecosystem including wild grasses and earthworms, ants, beetles, armadillo bugs. And how I loved the rich, ripe smell of decay.

The impact of the crash had torqued the body of the car to the left, so that its windshield reflected the trees across the road. On windy gray December days the tree-skeletons swam black and watery in the unsmashed portion of the glass, and I stood for long periods, puzzling over why this sight pleased me more than our Christmas tree, or the window display at Novell's, or even a winter sunset.

Ever the smart-aleck of the schoolyard, I spouted big words I'd heard my father use. I won spelling bees, and kept a vocabulary list. For the first time, though, I needed words in the aggregate: sentences, entire paragraphs to capture the mutable beauty I had seen. And I failed to find those words. At twelve, I didn't realize that it took years to bring words under domestication, and that even then one sometimes failed.

CHAPTER TEN

THE CATHOLIC MOUNTAIN

The Toyota tunnels through solid fog along Fulton, as we drive past avenue after numbered avenue traveling east from the Beach. The heater's on the blink, so we sit rigid in our seats, two isolated cocoons in the deep-freeze of the car's interior. Who would believe this is summer? Tatters of mist hang in the trees that blur by on our right, the eucalyptus and conifers of Golden Gate Park. At this hour, in this weather, the park looks impenetrable, forbidding, yet within its more than one thousand acres, homeless people are sleeping, or trying to sleep. It's a little before six on a dark, wet morning when it seems the sun will never rise, never again shed its life-giving heat on this peninsula called San Francisco.

Shorey, his neck muffled in a knitted scarf, flexes his fingers on the wheel. They are crimson from the cold. He's got the radio tuned to some Born Again station. At this fragile hour, it's natural to latch onto whatever feels comfortingly familiar. He is humming along to songs that hearken back to his fundamentalist upbringing, songs written in a down-home vernacular. Songs about Jesus being our friend, and the weathered old cross.

173

We are now staying with Sam, at the western limit of the Sunset District. Our clean, bright room overlooks a terraced garden and the occasionally blue Pacific. We fall asleep at night to the white noise of pounding surf.

The room had always been available to us, from the day when Sam stood in the sun on our patio, putting together cardboard storage boxes, pleading with us to take advantage of his hospitality. But in those days right after the fire we were too prickly, and would have made bad company. We needed the anonymity of the motel as a neutral space in which to reconstruct ourselves, rebuild our flagging attitudes.

Shorey's on his way to dropping me off at the garage before he heads over the bridge to Mill Valley, where he'll open the store by seven.

The fog encapsulates us as we creep along, reminding me of Pennsylvania blizzards where you lose all perspective in the pervasive whiteness. We're a little white car moving through a white cloud. "Can't see a thing," says Shorey, setting the windshield-wipers to a manic speed that makes no difference at all in terms of visibility. "Have we gone past Fifth?"

"Must have. We're going uphill." I see the gold-tipped spires, lit from below, shining insistently through the mist as we climb the long gradient to St. Ignatius, a Jesuit bastion, big enough to accommodate two thousand mass-goers in its cavernous nave.

Shorey squints into the fog, checks his rear-view mirror. "Coast looks clear," he says. "I'm gonna backtrack." Craning to see over his left shoulder, he tenses for the hard work of a U-turn, the hand-over-hand exertion in a car that lacks power steering.

"No, wait!" I say.

Expelling a white breath, he veers back to the center of the lane.

"Keep going. Drop me off up at the church."

"What *for*?"

I tell him it's too early to hole up in the garage. Otherwise, it makes no sense for me to seek out a church at this black hour.

"But you're not even wearing a coat. You'll freeze, walking home. Here, take my scarf."

"Thanks," I say, and loop it round my neck, the burgundy scarf I knitted for his last birthday.

He pulls up by the side entrance. In the empty street our Toyota looks bug-tiny beside this fortress. The double doors at the apex of a wheelchair ramp appear resolutely closed. I can almost hear the medieval clank from the night before when a sexton turned the key or shot the bolt to secure this edifice. Gone are the days of the six a.m. mass. For decades, churches have been limiting their hours due to acts of vandalism, robbers prying open poor boxes or walking away with sacred hardware. Or homeless, seeking a warm dry place, a haven for the night. I understand the need to lock up, yet can't help feeling queasy about being one of the "elect" who is always welcome inside a church while others are not. No use pondering what Christ would have to say on the subject, or St. Francis, with his patch-work robe and ragamuffin followers.

Outside the car, wind picks up the tail of the scarf and slaps it against my face. The mist, almost a light rain, immediately coats my black pullover in a fuzz of silver droplets. Under the St. Ignatius spotlights, I am aglow.

Shorey leans over and cranks open the passenger window, peering up at me in a way that emphasizes his eyebrows. He is not suited to this six-o'clock routine. The patience that characterizes his dealings with people takes time to filter through his awakening system. "It's dark, it's cold, and I'm not leaving you here. Get back in the car," he barks.

"Just a minute, okay?"

Not that I'm dreading the solitude of the garage. It's just that I need to clear my head. What's happening is that Shorey and I have each received our subpoena to appear in Superior Court on the ninth of August. Which means that nine days from now I will have to sit in a witness box and testify against Ajax. He'll be there, in orange jumpsuit and shackles, focusing his hate-lamps on me with all the creeping malice of which he's capable.

"I don't know what you've got in mind," says Shorey, "but I have to get to work."

Across the street, there is a lone sign of human life. A man in an overcoat, head tucked into his upturned collar like a turtle's, stands crammed against a stone entryway. A car eases into a parking spot, and a woman steps out. Six on the dot. The paneled doors creak open to reveal a warm amber recess: a church or chapel I never noticed before.

The man and woman slip inside, and I decide to follow.

Shorey says, "Need some money for the collection plate? Can't go in there without cash."

He adheres to the received wisdom of his childhood regarding the Church of Rome, and recent scandals have only vindicated his point of view. I don't pretend to be an apologist for the Church, but I do like to sit in a pew, in the muted light of stained-glass windows. I find it peaceful.

Once the doors thud shut and I'm in out of the drizzle, I sniff for the signature Catholic smell: frankincense mingled with molten beeswax. What I pick up instead is the clear, rigorous scent of cleanliness, an absolute lack of dust, surfaces washed within an inch of their lives. A posted sign asks us to keep silent. The place is designed so that you have to step down into the basin of the chapel, as if to demonstrate your lowliness before the Lord.

As I will later tell Shorey, there is no collection plate. Happily, there are no parish announcements. This is not a parish church but rather the chapel of a Carmelite monastery where the walls rise straight up without the interruption of windows, enclosing us as the Carmelites themselves are enclosed by the Rule of their religious order. These nuns do not go out. They work, pray and maintain this chapel. That is their gift to a faltering world.

Right on my tail as I enter are eight Mother Teresa nuns, the Missionaries of Charity, wearing dark sweaters over their saris and squeaking along in plastic sandals. Next comes a young nun in dove gray, a priest in his black suit, then a priest in a cassock who genuflects deeply, his knee all the way to the tiled floor. I watch as the side across the aisle fills up with all these religious. They, and the laypeople, file in quietly and get down to business.

Here, there's a conspiracy of preparedness, making oneself ready for the one mass of the day that begins at 6:25. Some use the minutes before mass starts to carry out private devotions—touching the plaster feet of a statue, observing the Stations of the Cross, dropping off a written petition for the Infant of Prague in his elaborate doll clothes —but most sit at attention, eyes closed, motionless as dolmens. I can tell they are not simply praying, but meditating. The Church now sanctions a form of meditation called Centering Prayer, previously the province of cloistered monks and nuns, and lay Catholics by the tens of thousands have taken to this inner practice.

Seeing these meditators flashes me back to my teens, when I was locked in combat with my father and, I imagine, sitting here in this holy place, that if only the simple expedient of Centering Prayer had been available to me, all that turmoil might have been avoided.

There's a burst of plainchant from an unseen choir, while a tiny Carmelite in brown wool distributes mass booklets. The mass begins, in Latin, and the place brims with the spiritual yearning of all these people who have ventured out on this dismal morning. In no time, the atmosphere has settled like sand in an hourglass, the only rogue element being my own mind.

While we were toiling up Fulton Street in the fog and I saw the illuminated spires of St. Ignatius', my first and only thought was, *A place to think.* Someplace away from the garage. Because writing is struggle enough, I try to leave unrelated mental struggles outside the writing room. The notebooks and research materials, the Post-it notes curling on the computer screen, the photos, drawings, diagrams and scribbled affirmations—all relate to the novel I'm working on.

No room in the writing sanctum for a singing arsonist.

I have not forgotten what the fire marshal told me the morning of May 25th: that arson is notoriously hard to prove, usually for lack of an incendiary device, and that the worst possible scenario would be for Ajax to have his chance before a jury. "He plays them like a musical instrument," said the marshal. "I've seen him do it, when I used to be on the police force. He's funny, charming, and they don't see the other side of him: the meanness and violence. In jail he lets his beard grow out, all white and fluffy. 'Look at me!' he'll crow to the judge and jury. 'I'm Santa Claus! Would Santa hurt anybody?' He'll convince them he was just a poor old homeless guy trying to keep warm. Which is partly true. He'll say the fire was purely accidental. In fact, he can't remember much about the night in question except that he felt awfully sorry about those folks next-door. 'I was in the Army,' he'll tell them. 'Served my country.' And he's so cute. He could be their grandfather. The jury members will be practically in tears. To cheer them he'll sing a song—something maudlin. No, we definitely don't want him in front of a jury."

As I sit, kneel, stand, and mechanically follow the mass, all I can do is to wonder what weird unraveling of karma has thrown Ajax across my path, and who will protect me from this miscreant.

Shortly before he died, my father and I happened to be talking and he came out with this non sequitur: "I always thought I could protect my children, but in the end I was unable to protect them."

What could he have meant? I had rarely experienced him as a protector, more as someone to be protected *against*.

Of course he would not explain himself, since having the last word was his modus operandi. And, of course, I couldn't press for an explanation, in the face of his obvious deterioration. I had stayed with him that day for his five-hour dialysis treatment. Swooning from exhaustion in the Naugahyde® chair, he sat surrounded by a tangle of clear plastic tubes that passed his red blood to and from the crude mechanism of the dialyzing pump. At any given moment, a large percentage of his blood had a public life, outside his body, where a machine took over the work of his ruined kidneys. A river of purple bruises ran down the inside of his right arm, and a shunt bulged beneath the papery skin. My father, the most private of men, who craved only to be left alone so he could read, and think, with his life's blood so blatantly on display.

He endured seven years of this. Whenever I went home, I'd hang out with him for a couple of sessions in the dialysis unit. Once, just down from Boston where I'd been visiting with my brother, I broke one of the trackless silences by enthusing about a city I knew my father approved. In Boston, he had discovered the Sligo Bar, a haunt of Irishmen from Ireland, some of whom spoke Gaelic, the language of his Donegal grandfather who was alive when I was a small child. In the Sligo he had drunk "black stout, as black as the devil's own blood," before going back to my brother's and passing out on the floor. No offering of mine could match the excitement of the Sligo, but I did my best to describe some of the tamer aspects of Boston: the swan boats in the Public Garden, the fine old homes along Commonwealth Avenue.

He looked blandly thoughtful, then said, "If there's one thing I can't stand, it's somebody beating my ear."

For a moment I couldn't speak.

"Were you referring to me, Dad?"

"No. Just speaking in general terms."

Leaning back in the tilted chair, he crossed his tooth-pick legs and closed his eyes. He'd had the last word. I told myself he was tired. He was sick. Then chided myself for being caught off-guard. After all, when had it ever been different?

I could only assume he didn't like me.

Maybe I wasn't likable.

Maybe I should stop caring.

On a cold, overcast morning in November of 1986, after having flown across the country from San Francisco, I stood at a nurses' station in the Norristown, Pennsylvania hospital where I'd been born and where my father had just died. At that moment it felt crucially important to speak with someone who had witnessed his final hours. I addressed one of the women, who looked about fourteen, asking if she'd been one of my father's nurses. With a stern show of dignity, she declared, "I was his *doctor*."

Then she softened. My face must have looked haggard with grief. I'd had no food or sleep in more than twenty-four hours. The plane-ride had been a grueling trajectory, made worse by the laughter and boozy ebullience of my seatmates. My father was lying dead, but up there in the Friendly Skies they were having one helluva blast.

"You must be the daughter from California," said this doctor.

"So—he told you about me."

"No, actually. Your mother did."

"I see."

I'd come to ask if I might see my father's body, one last time. I already knew from my sister that in two hours they'd be transporting him from the hospital morgue to the place of cremation. He had not been "prepared for viewing," said the doctor. I'd have to wait at least twenty minutes while they made him presentable. Meanwhile, the women at the desk regaled me with stories about "George."

"Such a wonderful man."

"Such a beautiful, blue-eyed smile."

"Always charming, no matter how sick he felt."

"He'd been coming here for years; he was like family."

"We'd go to him with all our problems, and he never minded."

And then: "He was like a father."

Leave it, I told myself. He's gone. Be happy that a certain hospital anonymity had made it possible for him to open up to these women. They had been the mirror of his better self. Through them, he had excelled in his chosen role: protector of the young.

We've reached the penitential part of the mass that prepares us for the changing of bread and wine into the body and blood of Christ. Along with everyone else, I thump my chest three times for the *mea culpa*: "Through my fault, through my fault, through my most grievous fault."

In the shadowy chapel the red sanctuary light glares back at me in rebuke. All right, I feel like saying, I know I'm guilty of many sins.

I am willing to admit, as the congregation pleads for God's mercy through the words of the Kyrie, that it might have been my fault that my father disliked me. The sin is called Pride. It dwells in me still. I like to be right.

Had I been one of those ultra-feminine 1950s girls who giggled like a willing accomplice in response to daddy's macho posturing, he'd have forgiven anything. Even had I lacked that endearing quality but deferred to his every opinion and pronouncement, he'd have accepted the fact that at twelve, I was still climbing trees and trying to beat up boys. I had no clothing sense and could barely comb my hair. I looked like a haystack on two legs.

"You're just like him," my mother would scold.

In my naiveté, I figured being "just like him" should qualify me to be my father's buddy, his whispering confidante.

He saw otherwise. Rued the day he had spawned such a know-it-all freak of a tomboy. Stung by the rejection, I decided what the hell and said anything that popped into my head. Having placed first in the school's intramural running meet, I flew through the front door like winged Mercury whenever he came roaring after me in response to one of my sassy remarks. He couldn't have caught up with me on a bet.

We continued these low-level hostilities till I crossed the wrong finish-line and made him an enemy for the remainder of my time in that house.

On a sunny morning at the end of June, I had ridden to where Egypt Road splits off from Main Street on its way to Valley Forge. Back home again, my neck grimy and the bangs glued to my forehead, I had just stashed my bike by the side of the house when I heard singing. Nothing unusual about that. Singing was the lingua franca of our family, a means of releasing unspeakable emotions. My mother once hoped for a career as a popular singer, and at sixteen had placed second in a big-city singing competition. Early mornings, she warbled along with the awakening birds, singing all day through her mounting unhappiness. My father had a fine tenor voice. I sang; my sister sang; my five brothers shared a room where, as a group, they sang themselves to sleep each night.

Taking care not to crush my mother's rust-colored chrysanthemums, I drew closer and peered through the window screen. Inside, my father paced the living-room, conducting an imaginary orchestra while he sang along with Caruso in a wildly declamatory fashion. It was a Saturday, his favorite day. Having put in his five nights in the factory, he wouldn't have to go back there till Monday. Lodged in the temporary bliss of the sixth day, he could look forward to the buffer-zone of Sunday. The minutes would click by, the hours accumulate, and come Sunday evening he'd sink into the bleakest depression, thinking of the week ahead, but right now, in this parallel universe of Saturday, he was free.

That historical recording of *I Pagliacci* crackled with age, but the violins conveyed all the pathos of the sad clown as my father's voice overrode the voice on the record in belting out *Vesti la giubba*. As a part of the role, he had to laugh maniacally until his laughter shattered into naked pain. Believing himself to be alone, unobserved, he brought sounds out of his chest and throat that bespoke his own anguish. In those moments he was no longer my father but the wounded street-creature of the opera. I started feeling weird inside, as if I might cry, or even scream.

Why was he doing this? Why couldn't he go down to the track with Uncle, like he did on other Saturdays? No one else's father spent his Saturday emoting in unison with a dead tenor.

Watching him, I felt my lip curl. My father had never been to a proper opera-singing school, I told myself, or even to an opera. He'd never been to a college where they taught real Italian, I reasoned, but only to Berlitz where anyone could go for free if they'd been a G.I. during World War II. And what about his James Joyce? People went to college for that, too. Why should I listen while he blathered on about Molly Bloom or Stephen Daedalus with his stupid ashplant? Nobody cared about such things. I had my own life. Ginger and I were busy learning the Bristol Stomp, in preparation for the Labor Lyceum dance.

Look at him, pretending to be Enrico Caruso. He was an embarrassment. At the next histrionic laugh, I also laughed. More like a snort of derision.

He turned, arms still outstretched. Frowned, as he peered through the dusty screen, adjusting his eyes to the bright yellow daylight outside. At first he seemed confused, as if in a trance. I thought he'd go turn off the Victrola, but he let Caruso continue pouring foreign syllables into our living-room.

His eyes clouded over, his face went slack. I had brought a ticking clock into his timeless Saturday.

Just then the phone rang. Probably for me—and I knew what he'd do. I had recently changed my name to Margo, a French-sounding moniker more consonant with the person I felt myself on the road to becoming. (I didn't learn until I was an adult that he had named me Margaret after his mother, who along with her husband had died at twenty-five from TB, leaving my father an orphan. He had adored his mother, who'd made much of him, propping him on the counter of the local grocery as if he were a miniature king.) Whenever a phone call came in for "Margo" and he happened to pick up, my father'd clip the other party with, "Nobody here by that name."

I decided to race him for the phone.

I burst through the chain-link gate that hung by one hinge, past my mother and the others frolicking like fools in a plastic pool five feet in diameter, up the step, in the back door, but a second too late because he had the receiver in his gnarly grip and was already barking, "Nobody here by that name."

"Can I have the phone, please?"

"No, you may not."

I made my grab, and in so doing collided with his new routine, the business of catching my arm in a bone-breaking squeeze that normally caused me to cave in due to his superior strength.

"You little son of a bitch!" he cried, his face blanched and sweaty as we struggled for possession of the receiver in the overheated room. Later that day, I'd surely see his fingermarks empurpled on my upper arm. No matter. This was war. In a war, people got wounded.

From the backyard came the cheers and exclamations of my brothers, the sound of their splashing in that dinky little pool decorated around its inflated margin with blue and green sea-creatures. My sister, already launched into popularity, was off with her friends. I, on the other hand, had only one friend.

"Ginger, don't hang up!" I called out, desperate to keep the connection as the phone rose and fell in my father's and my joint grasp.

Just as books and opera were all he had—this isolated intellectual who on his income-tax return listed himself as a "tire beader," the person who uses big industrial scissors to cut strips called "beads" that reinforce the inside of the tire—my father may have realized that Ginger was all I had, really.

"Take the damn thing," he muttered, letting the receiver drop silently onto the rug as he stumped form the room.

Rain now beats against the outside of the chapel, as the priest performs the *Fractio panis*, the breaking of the bread, the sacramental snapping of the pure white Host, a sound that reminds me of how on that June day I broke my father's heart, and how breaking a heart can be accomplished as easily as snapping a twig.

Ginger, on hearing Caruso in the background, wanted to know who was singing: "Your good-looking dad?" My father had just re-entered the room, as if he sensed Ginger's words. I glossed over her inquiry about my father and said: "Want to go to Norristown?" While riding my bike I'd seen guys all over the Saturday roads in modified coupes with racing stripes and raucous glass-pack mufflers. We could stuff our bras with socks, I told her. Go for hoagies. See what was playing at the Grand. A beat or two of silence. She insisted that first I put my father back on the line so he could sing, especially for her. This, I wanted no part of, but she wouldn't let it go. Wow, what a voice, she gushed. He should be on Ed Sullivan. On in the movies! In less than a minute she rebuilt his ego, brick by brick, so that he walked around the living-room preening himself.

What he'd craved was a little praise: cheaper than a hoagie.

∾

The rustling sound brings me back to present time, where people are slipping from their pews and filing to the front to take communion, the body and blood of Christ. I am the only one who remains behind. Am I still the teenager who refuses to believe in Transubstantiation? Do such things matter in the modern Church? But these are questions for theologians.

What happens is that I become a regular at the monastery. Every morning after Mass, I walk out into a monochromatic world where sky has descended to earth and sits whitely on the quiet residential streets, while wind whips the cloud-cover as if it were cream in a blender. Fog on the flatlands of the Richmond District becomes highly condensed up here on the heights: what I now think of as the Catholic mountain.

It's an area known variously as Lone Mountain or Ignatian Heights, after Ignatius Loyola, founder of the

Jesuits (there's even a Loyola Street), and over the decades
the Jesuit-run University of San Francisco has bought up
much of what used to be oak- and lupine-covered hills that
leveled out into ranches maintaining a tenuous foothold
along vast sandy stretches leading to the beach. Later, the
mountain would be a Masonic and then a Catholic cemetery,
with much shifting of bodies on a hotly contested hill that
finally became a fiefdom of the Catholic Church.

Fog this thick has a peppery effect on the nostrils. I stop
to fish for a tissue. It's barely seven. Not a soul on Parker
Avenue as I turn in between two houses onto the narrow
passageway of Lone Mountain Lane, a stair-street that
cuts knifelike through three downward-sloping blocks.

Halfway down the incline, between tall fences and
stuccoed walls, at the point of a Dangerous Dog warning,
I turn to look at the bell tower atop Lone Mountain College,
once a private women's school that's now submerged
under the greater mandate of USF. In the early morning
emptiness, it's a nameless tower in the fog, cloaked in a
Japanese stillness. The Monterey cypresses, nearly black
in this light and beaten back by ocean wind, hug the hill
up there for dear life. A hundred years ago, that hill functioned as the sole landmark for people hiking back from
the beach amid the treacherous sameness of the dunes.
This lane frames the shot, directs the eye to the tower the
way streets and alleys in European cities converge like
spokes of a wheel on a central plaza with its cathedral.

Never mind Europe—no way I'll make it there any time
soon, considering how we're running through money this
summer. We've got kitchen privileges, but have been
eating out again. After dinner Shorey will drop me off at
Sam's, then drive the five miles back to the garage where
he remains until late. Most nights, soothed into sleep by

the lullaby of breaking waves at the foot of Sam's street, I don't even register Shorey's arrival when he slips into the darkened room after midnight.

I know he's depressed. So am I. But I am more immediately troubled by something Sam said.

Last evening at around 7:30, Sam was sitting on his cushioned bench doing paperwork at the kitchen table while attending to a BBC newscast. The oversized radio with its old-fashioned knobs sat high on a shelf to his right. I sat hunkered on a low stool, the kind a kindergartner might use, just outside the arched entryway to the kitchen as we carried on a desultory conversation about our casual reactions to the news. All around us, the evening breathed a peaceful silence. I do not belong to the same radio generation as does Sam, but was beginning to enjoy these sessions, the aural entertainment that left my eyes and hands free to do a little knitting.

Part of the reason Shorey has been staying away in the evenings is that, accustomed as he is to simultaneous strands of sensory input—TV, computer, newspaper, music—he finds the monastic silence at Sam's a little unnerving. Paradoxically, the greater the barrage of words, bytes and tunes, the more soothed he feels. Mere radio patter would never suffice.

Sam, at eighty-six, leads a monkish life. He does not indulge in TV or go to movies. Though he cares about world affairs and keeps informed, and though he's helped any number of people along the way, most of his energy gets funneled into the spiritual side of life, meaning meditation. Sam worked as a newspaper typographer until the age of eighty-four. I figure he's entitled to spend his remaining years in any way he likes.

The statement he made last night, coming from anyone else, would not have unsettled me half as much.

I have known Sam Freedman for thirty years. He's been a friend, a mentor, and yes—the father I had wanted for myself. Never in those years have I seen him act badly. Never has he given ill-founded advice. The man lives a blameless life. His words carry weight.

Sam didn't acquire his brand of wisdom via the armchair route. He has led a full and sometimes far too exciting life. As a teenager during the Depression, he "rode the rails" back and forth across the continent in search of work. When the freight train would pull into certain towns, local vigilantes came running with guns to keep out interlopers who they feared would bleed the town of what little work was left, or become a nuisance, begging at back doors for food. Sam, forced to dodge bullets, sometimes resorted to dangerous inter-car maneuvers to avoid being shot.

During World War II, well past the draft age but strongly committed to fighting fascism, Sam joined the Army and saw several years of active duty in New Guinea and the Philippines, often under daily bombardment from the Japanese.

His nine decades on this earth have taught him, apparently, that vengeance rarely works. Not in the long run. He relies on the mercy that droppeth as a gentle rain from heaven, rather than the Mosaic eye-for-an-eye.

After the broadcast ended and Sam reached up to switch off the set, I expressed what had been on my mind ever since Shorey and I received the subpoenas: my fear that at the upcoming trial Ajax might be let off. I expected Sam to commiserate.

As I perched on the stool, a rod shot up my spine. I was all attention. Well, was he going to say something?

He was not.

I took his silence to mean he was withholding a painful truth from me, one I might not be capable of taking in right now, and I had an idea it had something to do with forgiveness. Without waiting to hear his position, I began arguing my own, fiercely, from every imaginable angle, while Sam sat serenely affixing stamps to his outgoing mail. I felt myself edging toward hysteria as I cited statistics about the homeless: the need to draw a distinction between "harmless ones" and the more violent among their number. I wanted to protest that this time he was carrying his bleeding-heart liberalism to a ridiculous extreme. I wanted to say, Damn it, Sam, can't you see that I'm right?

But he turned in his chair to face me, looking suddenly exhausted from his eight-six years on this earth, and said, "I hear you, Margaret, but where's the compassion?"

As I blow my nose by the Dangerous Dog sign, I keep an eye on the broken fence. Why bother to post a warning when you've got a hole in your fence through which a dangerous animal can escape? Two dangerous dogs could squeeze through that opening, with no trouble at all.

One last look at the tower.

I want to cast myself in its image, to be that bell tower: a solid casing with a soul-stirring mechanism within. A structure that's motivated from the inner core. After all, the tower's only reason for being is its bell.

Meditating in the chapel, buoyed up by the other meditators, it was easy to connect with the still point that T.S. Eliot, for example, speaks of in his *Four Quartets*, or that Mary Oliver extols in her poem, "The Loon."

The soul, mother of so many metaphors:

A pearl.

The omphalos.

The drop of holy water in the ancient cave.

Fine and good, but this morning during meditation my mind kept replaying last night's conversation with Sam, coming up with ever more ingenious arguments in my own defense. During the imaginary debate, T.S. Eliot went spinning off into space, and Mary Oliver's loon began flapping its white wings. I hadn't been meditating at all, but *thinking*. Then, by an uncomfortable coincidence, the priest launched into a sermon on homelessness.

The monastery does not have a resident chaplain. Each morning a different priest officiates. They are all Jesuits, massively educated and highly articulate. You never know what you'll get. We've had Latin masses, English masses, Gregorian chant, and songs from being the enclosure's grille that sound like Tex-Mex *corridos*. One priest in his sermon will hew to the liturgy, while another takes a free-form approach. My first day at the chapel coincided with the feast of St. Ignatius Loyola, July 31st. The priest, a gray-haired man, expatiated on the saint's life, with emphasis on his time as a soldier. Another priest, on another day, slipped into confessional mode, bemoaning his own Pharisaical hypocrisy but quick to laud the healing power of the Holy Spirit.

Each priest seemed to have an issue.

Today we got one who urged us to pray for the homeless. Who are these homeless? he asked rhetorically. They are Vietnam Vets, paranoid schizophrenics, the working poor, those with an unshakable drug habit, senior citizens, children, people who as the result of a disaster have lost their homes. They are the gentle fellows who sell the *Street Sheet*, and who, whether you give them a dollar or not, still smile and wish you "a nice day and a nice life."

He told us some things I already knew. Homelessness in San Francisco had exploded during the seventies with the closing of state mental hospitals. Nor did the policies of a certain administration (he took care not to mention the name of former Governor Ronald Reagan) help matters. Did we realize that the Richmond District, "Region Four," was the most poorly served in the city in terms of shelters and other facilities for the homeless?

"They are our brothers and sisters," he said. "We are beholden to them because through them we remember . . . Our Lord . . . as well as that most illustrious of homeless persons, St. Francis of Assisi."

At this point his argument seemed to fall apart, as no Jesuit's should ever do, and he left the pulpit in confusion, almost in tears.

Actually, I do know a few facts about homelessness, having done a research paper on the subject. According to whose figures you consult, San Francisco has between seven and twelve thousand homeless persons. It's not easy to come up with an accurate count because some live in cars, behind steamed-up windows, and who's about to go around at night banging on car-windows in order to ascertain how many "units of homelessness" might be curled up inside?

We also have a Rio de Janeiro-style favela: a homeless community of about sixty who live in thatched-roof shanties on the hillside overlooking Laguna Honda Reservoir. There, they garden and grow fruit trees. They have constructed a pond.

During his eight years as President, Ronald Reagan reduced HUD (Housing and Urban Development) funding from an initial $32 billion to $8 billion. And *voila*, fewer affordable housing units.

Nearly concurrent with Reagan's accession to the presidency, Californians cast their votes for Proposition 13, which slashed property taxes for those who already owned homes and in turn limited funds for affordable housing. In the aftermath, many low-wage workers slipped over the edge into homelessness.

And these numbers, current at the time of our fire, from a San Francisco Office of the Controller's booklet:

Estimated number of homeless persons in the City's jails nightly: 959

Estimated number of beds used by homeless in the City's jails annually: 350,035

Estimated cost per bed: $88

Estimated total annual cost of jailing homeless persons in San Francisco: $30,803,080

The priest had offered a cross-section of homeless persons in San Francisco, nice people who'd fallen on hard times, none of whom resembled Ajax, the man I will have to face in court, in three days' time.

Monday, August 9th. Shorey's at work. I'm in the garage. This morning the court convened at the Hall of Justice, on a grimy stretch of Bryant Street surrounded by bail bond offices and windblown litter. There, the "People of the State of California" will go up against Ajax.

We are on telephone standby, a circumstance that might extend to days, or weeks. However long it takes. We were not given the option of bowing out, letting blind Justice take its course. Our notices stated that "Failure to obey this subpoena may result in a warrant for your arrest and punishment by civil and criminal contempt [sic]."

The court has us on a short rope. We're all in the soup—
Shorey and me, Ajax, and the jury. Just by knowing Ajax
we have become potential criminals, subject to arrest.

We are not permitted to watch the trial, except on the
day when we are called to testify.

Ajax has been incarcerated in the County jail since the
night of the fire, eleven weeks ago. By this time he'll be
stone cold sober. I have never seen him sober. I doubt he'll
be doing much singing, but he will be rigid with rage.

Shorey plans to hightail it across the bridge the minute
he receives my call. Meanwhile, I'm dressed and ready to
go. Having done some thrift-store cruising, I'm looking
very downtown in a dark green suit.

The door stands ajar. From the gloom of the garage I can
see a strip of deep blue sky above the trumpet vine that's
so heavy with summer growth it's exerting a downward
pull on the fence. The fleshy red trumpet flowers hang
despondently, waiting for any passing hummingbird to
take an interest, make stabbing motions with its needle-like
beak. Jean was pruning her rosebushes, but went upstairs
for some lunch. The afternoon is so quiet I could hear each
snip of a rose-cane with her Felco pruners.

As a way of staying calm, I'm sifting through my box
of research materials. Since the protagonist of my novel
is a former nun, I've had to reconnect with the Catholic
Church. I've got papers, books, file folders, and at the bottom of the box a jumble of antique rosaries, holy cards, miraculous medals, scapulars, holy water bottles, a tattered
St. Andrew's missal, even a vial of Lourdes water—all
stuff I picked up at flea markets.

I should be writing.

I remember Molly Giles saying, in one of the last writing
workshops I took at San Francisco State: "Don't kid your-

selves. Research is not writing." Once, I had to write a few sentences about lace. All fired up, as if on a mission, I took two buses to the main library and spent hours in the remote stacks, then hauled my books to the café in the library's basement, where I spent more time nursing refill after refill while I scribbled notes from volumes on the Belgian lace industry, the making of Valenciennes lace, and catalogs of various lace exhibits that had taken place before I was born. By the time I'd finished, I was half blind from peering at Victorian lace patterns. When I got home I found myself too exhausted to write even those few sentences.

The problem is, I'm too jazzed-up to write. Too spooked to do anything that requires more than the most glancing concentration.

In the center of my palm lies a miraculous medal, a large, brilliantly silver oval.

"Well. Do your miracle," I say.

That very moment the phone rings.

"Hello?"

"Just me," says Shorey. "Anything happening?"

"Not a thing."

"Give the D.A. a call. See what's what."

I had assumed that on the first day there'd be nothing but legal saber-rattling, taking up of positions, much stating of the obvious, and generally a lot of paper-shuffling. I never expected any real progress on the first day of trial. Au contraire, the trial ended almost as soon as it began. Our testimony was not required. The D.A. is delighted with the outcome. Ditto, the fire marshal. My neighbors congratulate us when they hear the result. My landlady feels appeased, and so does Shorey. I feel like the one-eyed man in the land of the blind because I consider the outcome to be disastrous.

Ajax has been let off on three years' felony probation. He will be remanded to a residential facility run by the V.A.

To get my head around what I've just heard, I transcribe the D.A.'s phone message and read it again and again:

"He's serving an 18-month to 2-year residence program through the Veterans Administration. He's nowhere near you. He can't come anywhere near that location, according to the Stay Away Order. If he comes anywhere within 150 yards of the place where the fire was, you can call the police and he will be picked up immediately. He'll then be in violation of his probation and basically he'll be incarcerated and subject to State prison. So it's a pretty good stronghold on him. And the police will have that on their records, in their files, that he can't be anywhere near where the fire happened."

They have placed him in a swinging-door facility. There is no booze in such a facility. This is like the dangerous-dog warning next to the hole in the fence. Do they have any idea who they're dealing with? Can they possibly imagine that Ajax will meekly remain in rehab, away from the streets and his beloved 540 Club? He'll be back in the neighborhood inside of a month.

Wednesday, August 11th. Feast of St. Clare, founder of the Poor Clares, the sister-order to the Franciscans.

Today's priest calls her by her Italian name, Santa Chiara, and says that everything becomes more beautiful in that language. I can see in his expression the same adoration of all things Italian that my father possessed. He tells us that when, for example, Italian drivers yell something like, "Move that pile of junk, you cretin!" the words sound like lyric poetry.

He's trying for a light note, but doesn't elicit even a titter from the serious crowd in this chapel.

Santa Chiara, he goes on to explain, was higher in the Umbrian social order than St. Francis, the son of a wealthy cloth merchant. Though she hailed from the noble Offreducia family, she, like Francis, insisted that her order maintain its vow of absolute poverty when reformers tried to push for a relaxation of the Rule, and the ownership of property.

I'm listening quietly, hands folded in my lap. The story of Francis and Clare has a pleasing symmetry: two rich kids from Assisi who saw the light and drew a rood-screen between themselves and their opulent lifestyles.

My mind feels settled, clear, and perhaps this is a gift from the saint whose feast-day it is, and whose name translates as "clarity" or "light." I can honestly state, in the presence of the sanctuary light, that I bear no real hatred towards Ajax. It would be like hating a force of nature: a tornado or an earthquake.

I simply want him put away.

Perhaps felony parole is best. I did not have to face him in court or testify. As long as he's far from here, what do I care whether it's prison or rehab? Though after all the wild nights, the decades of drinking, I'm not sure he retains enough brain cells to rehabilitate.

∽

Early afternoon. I'm driving with Karin and Virginia to the Legion of Honor for an exhibit that's called, incongruously, "The Treasury of Saint Francis of Assisi." The day is strangely muted, muggy and windless, with a cloud cover so low there is no Golden Gate Bridge except for the rust-red tips of its high towers.

In the exhibit room, I recognize faces from the society page, people who are decked out and expensively coiffed. I mingle with men and women whose very shoes qualify as *objects*. Everyone is fitted with a headset, trying not to jostle others as they take the Walking Tour. We see jewel-encrusted reliquaries, paintings, illuminated manuscripts thick with gold-leaf, and huge color photographs of frescoes form the Basilica in Assisi that Francis expressly forbade his followers to build. "Il Poverello" would be rocketing over and over in his grave at the sight of these priceless art objects displayed in his name.

Or perhaps these eight hundred years have mellowed him out, and he realizes that the big fancy church and the frescoes by Giotto and Cimabue and Lorenzetti were actuated by love, and that sometimes love overrules the Rule, and that not everyone can live up to the austere ideal put forward by him and Clare.

After blitzing through the exhibit—too crowded—we make our choices at the museum café and take our coffee and poppyseed cake out onto the patio where blackbirds rustle in the dull green foliage of the olive trees and peck for crumbs on the concrete at our feet. Suntans, all around. Conversations are pitched to a low, worshipful tone. The exhibit has had its effect.

Three months have passed since I sat with these women at Karin's triangular table and first told them about Ajax. Now I'm telling them, as we sip from clear glass cups, about the trial Shorey and I didn't get to attend, and the three years' felony parole. Karin frowns, sets her cup down with a careful clink. There's an answering rustle in the olive trees: blackbirds, not wind. Virginia, sitting across from me in the clear gray light that traces every line on her beautiful ageless face, says, "I'm not sure I like this outcome, Margaret. This is a dangerous man we're talking about." And Karin nods her agreement.

CHAPTER 11

ZEN FLOOR

We are dangerously close to going home. I say dangerously because things still can go wrong, and they do. This job has dragged on for three months. The contractor is feeling a sudden urgency to wrap it up, and all at once our project pulls out of the doldrums. By late August we've got workmen tripping over each other to get things finished.

I'm not comfortable playing the "heavy" with workmen, preferring instead to demonstrate respect for their mastery of the building arts by staying out of their way so they can get on with it. This may be too laissez-faire an approach. By the time I check in with the painter, he has obliterated our bathroom's Southwestern earth-tones with a coating of high-gloss white, the very horror that Shorey and I had sought to remedy by applying shades of sage and sandstone in the first place. Now I must tell Mr. Kim, a tall, aristocratic-looking Korean man, that he will have to redo the bathroom. Clearly, he is not used to taking instructions from a woman. Face averted, he informs me that he was ordered by the contractor to "paint bathroom with white," and I believe him. The contractor lives on Olympus and issues orders by cell-phone.

Some days are wonderful, as for instance when the floorman dances his drum-sander around our living-room while at the same time two glaziers, sweet guys, sit cross-legged on the patio toiling like medieval artisans to duplicate our hundred-year-old windows. They love talking about their work and do not find me a bother when I ask my million questions about the craft of glazing:

Will it be difficult to replicate our Victorian windows?

Do they think that many-paned windows are on the way out?

Do they think we will ever see a resurgence of stained-glass door panels?

No, no, and no, they answer. I'm about to ask if they think of glazing as a job or a vocation, but that would be intrusive, even patronizing. Just watching them is answer enough.

"Thank you," I say. They are moving us forward.

But there's a stone in the road, a ten-ton boulder, and its name is Lyle. He has been deputed by the contractor to oversee the project. It's not that I mean to knock him off his perch—I'd rather be writing—but each time I see the guy he's stretched out in the hammock he's got strung in his van, eating or sipping a latte. With Lyle, it's eternally break-time. And even that would be okay except there's a list of tasks that only he can do, and he doesn't seem to be doing them. From the comfort of his hammock, van-doors open to let in the breeze, he explains why this or that job cannot be done. Doorway's a tad too wide, or too narrow, window's off-kilter, floor is warped, must have been that last earthquake. Nothing is easy, he wants me to know, nothing as simple as it might appear to the unini-tiated. I tell him we're reasonable people and that we're not expecting perfection, but he has already tuned me out. Apparently, we must settle for the grossly *im*perfect, such as the brown plastic accordion door he hung over my doorless closet, instead of the white louvered door our landlady had ordered.

Lyle doesn't like me, and at this point I really don't care. I just want him to get off his dead ass and do some work so we can move back home.

Whenever he does manage to complete a task, the effort drains him to such an extent that he's forced to skulk back to the van where he will lie supine in his hammock until he can legitimately call it a day.

I remind him that along the length of the closet floor there's a quarter-inch crack opening directly onto the outside world, and that damp air is sure to seep in and create mildew.

"A rug oughta take care of that," he claims.

The single coat of beige paint on the floor of my room is so translucent, I can see the old brown undercoat.

"No second coat on my punch-list," he says.

I type up a punch-list of my own, details that need seeing to before the contractor signs off on the project, but Lyle folds the sheet in four and tosses it into the van where it lands among the KFC bags and empty latte cups that litter the floor beneath his hammock.

In the evening, after the workmen have gone, I'm down on my knees in the closet caulking that hole. After that, I drag out the appropriate can and give the floor of my room a second coat.

Around Lyle, I can feel my blood pressure rising. Daily mass at the monastery has become not just an esthetic pleasure but a necessity. The meditation cools down my brain, sets me up for the day, and I savor any random bit of wisdom from the sermon.

The morning is white and still, a little on the warm side. I see people shrug off their costs as soon as they enter the chapel. Tall white tapers burn serenely on the altar, and so tranquil is the atmosphere in here that I fully expect the candle-flames to flutter when a man in front starts coughing.

Today, August 28th, we celebrate the feast of Augustine, patron saint of theologians. Several religious orders go by his name and follow his Rule, and his *Confessions* ranks as the Western world's first autobiography. Brilliant though he might have been, he came up with some clunkers. Augustine is the one who postulated that babies who died without having been baptized went to Limbo. And there, in the words of my third-grade nun, "Never to see the face of God, but happy . . . in their own way."

Augustine's life is so big, so contradictory, so influential— he wrote some one hundred books—I figure the priest will tackle either the intellectual element or the personal life. He goes for the personal. Good choice. It was Augustine who famously prayed, "Lord, make me chaste, but please not yet."

I'm hoping the priest will take a more liberal approach to the story—after all, this is San Francisco—but he starts right in on "the irregular lifestyle, living with a woman to whom he was not married." This morning's Jesuit goes on to tell us that Augustine did find the courage to put her aside, "but not for a long time." Then he launches into a eulogy of Augustine's mother, St. Monica.

No doubt that Monica was a minor mystic, but I am remembering what she did to Augustine's "woman."

Monica was a Berber Christian, descended from one of the North African tribes. She both idolized and badgered her son, for whom and with whom she had big plans:

together they would find God and rise to great heights of religiosity. Whither Augustine went, there went Monica. When he attained the age of thirty-five, she began arranging for him an advantageous marriage. There was just one snag: for fourteen years he had been living in complete felicity with a woman who had borne him a son.

To dispatch that woman for the greater good, the making of a future Doctor of the Church—no big deal. Of no more importance than the "collateral damage" we speak of in wartime: the unintended casualties, the people not even footnoted by history.

The way Monica connived to separate Augustine from his partner deserves a volume all its own. In the end, he never married—embraced the Church, eventually becoming a bishop—but long years later Augustine still spoke of that parting as a terrible wrenching, as if a limb had been torn from his body. She was a woman of no rank, to whom a legal marriage would have been inconceivable. So Monica sent the woman on her way, but without the child. Monica herself took control of his upbringing. We know his name—Adeodatus ("Gift of God")—but not the name of his mother. Nowhere in Augustine's writings, in none of his hundred books is it written, not even in the intricately explicit *Confessions*.

That evening, I'm still mulling over the story of Monica and the no-name, no-rank woman.

"I wonder what life was like for her after losing both of them. After she went back to wherever it was she'd come from," I say to Annette. We've been staying at her home for the past three weeks. "I'd love to read something from her point of view. Say, a fictional biography."

"Why don't you write one," says Annette, settling back into the welter of ethnic cushions that makes her living room seem an extension of Augustine's hometown, now called Souk Ahras, in northeastern Algeria.

"Jim Crace is the one who could pull off something like that," I say. He's a British author who wrote a stunning novel about the Judean world of Jesus.

We're side by side on the sofa, drinking French roast and facing a pointedly blank screen. It's my last night here, and we don't care to waste it watching TV. Annette takes a thoughtful sip. "Back then," she says, "women lost babies all the time. So she wouldn't have been unusual in that respect."

"Adeodatus wasn't a baby. He was a teenager."

I muse out loud about what the world might have been like if Monica had let the two lovers stay together and if Augustine had remained a householder. Unlike the acidulous St. Jerome or certain other Fathers and Doctors of the early Church, Augustine is a piquant spice that helped flavor the Western mind-set, so it's interesting to contemplate what would have been lost if he'd never entered the Church, never become a priest and written a hundred books.

There'd be no Augustinian religious orders.

No babies would have gone to Limbo.

My grade-school, St. Augustine's, would have had a different name and a different saint's statue affixed by rebar to the front of the adjacent church building.

And Adeodatus would have been raised by his natural mother, and might not have died at seventeen.

But you can't argue with Fate.

Annette, who was raised in a community of four hundred Socialist families in the Bronx, in the 1930s, listens carefully. Her pinched expression tells me I am talking crap, violating some gut-level notion of commonsense. As passionate at seventy-one as she must have been at twenty, she throws up her arms. "What *mishugas*!" she cries. "You just don't stand by while somebody walks off with your kid."

"Maybe she wasn't the fighting type. I picture a gentle Pisces."

"Pisces schmisces! I'm a New York Jewish intellectual, and we don't—talk—about—astrology."

As well as being an intellectual, Annette raised four kids, mostly on her own. During the 1950s, when "natural childbirth" wasn't much in vogue, she gave birth to all of her children, without anesthesia, in a $17-a-month cold-water flat in New York's Lower East Side. Annette's style was to be everywhere at once. She knew everyone, including the writer Grace Paley. She eventually moved her act to San Francisco, obtaining a library degree in her late forties. She has always been a fighter. Hates being confined to a hospital bed in her living-room.

I've been urging Annette to write her memoirs, something she has threatened to do for years. She has purchased a notebook and gotten in touch with one person from the Socialist community. Tomorrow she will "start scribbling."

"Even if it never gets published," she says, "it's for my children. I want them to know what that world was like, the Sholem Aleichem Cooperative. It's the one thing I hope to accomplish before my time comes."

Talk about Limbo. Annette has spent the summer recovering from an injury. She and I are here together in the book-heaving living-room—she's an information librarian as well as a Yiddish translator—due to our two misfortunes. During these past weeks Annette has lent me books, while I've taught her to eat Tofutti straight from the carton and encouraged her to once again take up embroidery. Annette is someone who does not have time for embroidery, but

I now watch her at her open door on this rare sunny day in this neighborhood that borders the extreme fog-belt of Daly City. Embroidery hoop in hand, sun on her face, she chats with the postman from her tipped-back chair in her street-level doorway.

"I'm like one of those Sicilian village women," she says, without turning her gaze from the sunny street while stabbing a long silver needle into the taut linen circle, drawing the red thread under and up. "Those widows who wear black for the rest of their lives and live in their doorways."

Tomorrow we are going home. I swore I would never go back there until Ajax's place had been demolished, but clearly, this is not about to happen anytime soon. A few nights ago a neighbor spotted yet another homeless man slinking along the path toward the back. I can't even allow myself to think of the possible danger to ourselves, but I am also horrified at the desperation that would drive a human being to try and enter that boarded-up shithole.

Shorey piles into bed around midnight. By six we are schlepping suitcases and a summer's worth of bulging plastic bags to the car. Annette, a large woman, sits plumped against pillows in her adjustable bed, the big blue leg-cast outside the covers. In the shadowy corner she looks diminished, almost little-girlish. The summer has torn away a portion of her natural chutzpah. She can walk again, but not with any great ease. Her home health aide is on the way, and I'm also available.

She makes a show of perusing her *New York Times*, smacking open a page and folding it smartly down the middle. When I start to lavish thanks for having been given the top floor of her house, she raises a stern hand. Why make a fuss over what's only natural? In childhood,

Annette learned the Socialist ropes: the sharing, the accept-
ing, the making sure that no one fell through the net. She
came of age in a constant swirl of give-and-take. During
the Depression, when one of the four hundred familities
in the cooperative could not make their rent payment
one month and was threatened with eviction, had their
furniture tossed onto the sidewalk in front, all the other
families withheld payment until the landlord saw reason
and backed off. An agnostic, Annette lives according to
her code the way others purport to live according to their
religions.

"Anything you need before we leave?"

"Just toss me that *Chronicle*."

I pick up the yellow plastic bag from the mat and place
it on her tray next to the unread portions of the *Times*. As
I'm closing the door, she murmurs, almost to herself, "The
Joads are moving on."

∾

The first night is fraught with flashbacks. Shorey's in the
loft-bed, while I'm on the floor in a sleeping bag, the better
to leap up at the least sound coming from the other side
of the wall. I imagine I hear Ajax coughing, stumbling.
I smell smoke. In the disembodied border region between
dreaming and wakefulness, I hear the licking of flames, a
sound that's now as close and constant as the pulsebeat
in my ears. Thrusting up out of the mummy-style bag,
I rush to the window and yank back the polyester sheet
Annette gave us to tack up in lieu of a curtain this first
night. Nothing to see. No movement in the yard. The
plants and flowers seem under a spell. The wind chimes

hang silent. There's only the muted noise of midnight revelers at the Abbey Tavern.

I tell myself he's far away, asleep in his residential facility.

Night is his element, but the night is for drinking. Seeded throughout this neighborhood are his favorite watering-holes: the 540, Fizzee's, O'Keefe's. He's in a Veterans Administration facility, probably the one at 42nd and Clement, a short bus-ride from here. Except that Ajax doesn't ride on buses; he travels by cab.

Once more, Shorey moans in his sleep. From over by the window I can make out the low mountain range of his body under the comforter. Groaning, he turns in one smooth movement without dislodging Bridie, who lies curled at his feet near the edge of the high bed. It took some persuading to lure her back in here. At first, she was afraid of the place—its echoing emptiness, the exaggerated tap-tap of our footsteps on the bare living-room floor. When we closed the door behind her, she started to wail and tried to scratch her way back out. No words would do. I refilled her food-bowl, sprinkled her kibble with the nutritional yeast she likes, and after some wary circling, some twitching of her black tail, she bent her head and began to eat.

Last evening, for the first time in months, I took a bath in my own tub, but not by the usual candlelight. It will take time for me to trust even the smallest flicker of fire. Instead, my source of light was the last copper flush from the west through the bathroom window. After bathing I made myself tea, and it felt miraculous to be performing this simple ritual in my old surroundings. Waiting for the water to boil, I never for one second took my eyes off the bluish flame beneath the kettle.

Fool me once, shame on you, I said to the fire. Fool me twice, it's my fault.

Standing by the stove in fuzzy slippers, I got back into synch with the rest of the world. The day before was the first of September, 1999. All summer, while we merely concentrated on each day, everyone we knew had been storing half-gallon bottles of water and boxes of canned goods, in preparation for the coming disaster called Y2K. One friend had spent five thousand dollars filling a garage with non-perishable goods. Another had purchased a portable toilet. Y2K was the background buzz I tried to ignore, since there wasn't much we could do about it anyway. Now, in the moments before the kettle began its low whistle, I realized we were utterly unprepared for an emergency that might overtake us in four short months. I started making a mental list, calculating the cost, wondering where we'd store all those provisions. Also, were we to believe the optimists who were saying we'd need enough for three days, or the doomsayer on the radio talk-show who claimed we must be ready for a year's interruption in goods and services?

And then I started to laugh.

Rounding the corner at 7:30 the next morning, I see a ruddy-faced man down on his knees, a silver keg beside him as he scrubs with an old-fashioned brush and sloshes soapy water over the entryway to the Abbey Tavern. I'm just back from mass, but he's preparing for a different sort of sacrament, one that's far more ancient: a Bacchic, pre-Christian celebration of the grape.

On this resplendent morning, clear, sunny, fueled by soft breezes, the world is hardly able to stay in place, obey the iron laws of gravity. The old guy scrubbing the doorway hums an off-key tune that carries the length of Geary Boulevard and beyond, to the ocean, the sky, the empty stratosphere, bouncing off the amniotic membrane that encloses the universe and keeps us separate from the Godhead and from each other. From our own selves. The Irish tune, the hum of traffic, the news helicopter clattering overhead—pure music. The world is powered by waves of sound, some of it pitched at too high a frequency to hear. If we did catch its vibration, would we be obliterated by ecstasy?

I like clarity. Can't respond to phrases such as "blissed-out." Couldn't have made it through ten years of school on five hours' sleep a night if I'd been blissed-out. Bliss was for others, hippies with trust funds, I told myself. Now I question a frozen component in myself. How long must I coexist with this iceberg that rises up like a white mountain and blocks me from any joy I might be feeling?

As I pass the Abbey and push through our gate on this limpid morning, the facts line up like good soldiers:

I did not have ovarian cancer last fall.

Came away with a master's degree.

Survived a fire.

And now—just look—we have a new house.

Whenever folks approached our home for the first time, I'd feel exquisitely embarrassed over the peeling paint and faded trim, the undeniable shabbiness of the place. Before they got within ten yards of our front steps, Shorey or I would go on the defensive, telling them not to judge a book by its cover. Now the old façade has fallen away, literally. New boards, creamy white and set off by brick-red trim, cover the exterior. We have clear, undistorted window glass. New steps and porch. New roof, too.

Dan, the clean-up man, swept the patio yesterday, carting away wheelbarrows loaded with debris. The garden was largely unharmed, but after the fire Jean had to brutally prune the blackened princess bush that grows under our front windows. It looked every bit a no-hoper, but already the leggy stalks have sprouted fresh green leaves, and a few new purple flowers are quivering in this morning's timid breeze.

No one viewing our white cottage against the blue sky would dream there'd been any kind of ruination. The hollow-eyed hovel next-door tells a different story, but Nature will take care of that, too. I notice an acacia volunteer has shot up over there. By Christmas that pollen-breeding, glorified weed will have spread exponentially, concealing a good part of Ajax's place.

The imprint will remain, pentimento-style. Just scratch the bright new surface of our cottage, and see what's revealed. Yet I can't let such memories cloud our homecoming.

Anyway, I'm not worried. Not on this sunny day that's like an overexposed photo, bleached of every dark corner and lurking shadow. A day without nuance. A day when people run their five miles before breakfast and carry picnic lunches to the park. Besides, there's a lot to do. As soon as the stores open, I'm off on a buying orgy: sheets and pillowcases, cleaning supplies, yards of fabric and matching thread. When Shorey returns from work, he'll borrow the company truck and we will haul our possessions home. I've seen the stuff: dressers, tables, plastered with bird-shit and coated with grit after fourteen weeks under an open sky. We'll be on this patio scouring away until the moon comes up. Meanwhile, I will give our place a deep cleaning—crevices and corners, dust that collects along moldings, and that place of profound denial: the linoleum behind the toilet.

Then I'll spend the long empty stretch of afternoon, making curtains.

Unobstructed by curtains or furniture, the honeyed light fills our living-room and illumines the floor. A floor is the natural place for light to settle. Light enhances an expanse of open floor, glossing the sheen and featuring the grain of the wood. In traditional Japanese architecture, the floor is the furniture: every other object partakes of the transitory, and can be folded or stored out of sight. Less is more. In a Buddhist zendo, whether walking or sitting, a person focuses his or her eyes on the floor, so that over time the floor becomes a part of one's spiritual practice, or so I imagine, sitting here on a zafu, hand-sewing a curtain in the center of our resurrected floor, its true lustrous nature revealed now that its black surface has been sanded away.

When we first moved in, it was I who'd insisted we keep the floor's original Varathane, because it suggested the black elegance of Japanese raku ware. "Nice for a tea bowl, but not for an entire floor," Shorey pointed out, and several years later he overrode my idea that the floor be re-sanded to remove all traces of the oppressive, non-reflective blackness.

It took a fire to free that floor.

The front door stands ajar. There's a pleasing breeze. I can hear the sweet cacophony of glass, metal and wooden wind chimes. For the first time in nineteen years, our place is empty. I like it this way. The white teacup on the russet floor. The stitch-by-stitch creation of a hem. One thing at a time, in a multitasking world.

For three and a half months, we lived out of two suitcases and a few plastic bags. We managed to look clean and presentable. We got things done. Where is it written that we have to unpack the approximately one hundred boxes we put into storage and once again clutter this place with clunky objects and a million fussy little keepsakes, knickknacks, photos all over the walls—as if those friends and relatives would disappear from our lives if their likenesses were not prominently displayed?

And regarding all those washer loads of fabric that got stuffed into storage boxes: must I now cram every square inch of closet, every shelf and drawer with linen and thrift-store clothing?

Those hundred boxes remind me of St. Augustine's hundred books. Why did he need to pen so many? Does it take that much space to elucidate the fine points of Catholic dogma? All those books by Augustine, while a Zen master merely slaps the disciple's face to bring him to realization. Who's to say? I have chided myself for starting to write later in life. Others will get to write dozens of books, while I'll be lucky to finish three or four. That's greed speaking, the same greed that made me stuff our place with dust-catchers, then complain about the dust.

I am falling in love with emptiness.

I recall what the poet Shelley said in his "Adonais," that *Life, like a dome of many-coloured glass / Stains the white radiance of eternity.* My whole being longs for the white radiance, but my very nature works against me, making me reach for pretty bits of glass.

Clutter. Dust. Greed. Gandhi had twelve possessions when he died. My own father had not many more. On the night of the fire, I had to choose from thousands of items the two or three worth saving. Now I'm supposed to welcome back those thousands of items.

September 9th, and Shorey has laid down the law. Either I start putting away the contents of the mountain of boxes in our living-room, or he will throw everything out in front, onto the sidewalk.

"A week's enough," he declared. "I'm tired of slamming into boxes every time I head for the bathroom at night."

"I'll get it done."

"When? A year from now? I know how you are. Denial will set in, and pretty soon you'll stop seeing what's there. Those boxes will become a permanent part of the décor."

Actually, that's exactly what had started to happen. The fine weather held, and I shoved open the windows, propped open the front door with a pile of books, and simply transferred my curtain-making operation to the adjoining room where I wouldn't have to look at Box Mountain.

"Take me seriously," said Shorey, looming in the door-way between the two rooms while I hand-rolled a section of hem. "Do something with that stuff or I'll haul it all to the Purple Heart."

I decided that fifty to seventy-five percent of the dreck must go. All afternoon I filled shopping bags. Once some-thing went into a bag, it was gone. Never existed.

While sorting, I held in my mind an image of those few possessions laid out on a square of homespun khaddar cloth after Gandhi's death: the twin circles of his eyeglasses, the spinning wheel, the sandals, the other humble bits and pieces. Giving now became easy. Things simply dropped into shopping bags on their way to becoming someone else's storage problem. Chipped coffee mugs landed in the same bag with my wedding gown.

When Shorey comes home, he sees the progress I've made.

"This," he says, "deserves a dinner at Minh's."

Over coconut curry we congratulate each other, with much clinking of cups, for the fact that we've been "at the scene of the crime" for nine days, and look at us, we're doing just great. Some freaky feelings in the night, sure, but that's to be expected. The worst is behind us. In the dim restaurant, to the background sound of a castrato voice wailing pop tunes in Vietnamese, the congratulations flow like Oolong tea. Sucking on orange segments, we go so far as to say the fire could be viewed as a good thing.

New house.

New curtains.

New us.

We step out into sudden evening along this restaurant corridor, neon reflected on the wet sidewalk, windows ablaze, showcasing deep-fried pastries, roasted ducks suspended by their necks, baskets mounded with Chinese medicinal herbs.

We are months away from the rainy season, yet rain has darkened the sky. A few reddish streaks of sunset bleed through, but faintly. Shorey opens the big black umbrella over our heads. With a touching show of chivalry, he tilts it more to my side to make sure I'm fully sheltered. Only two blocks to walk.

Thunder rumbles, more like a movie sound effect since the current weather is totally out of character for a night right in the middle of our bone-dry Indian Summer season. People flit by like phantoms, lugging plastic bags a-bulge with groceries, no doubt trying to hoof it home before the sky rains down more than these few desultory drops.

"Want to go by the Toy Boat?" says Shorey.

This is a ritual. He buys a decaf every night after dinner, asks me if I want one, and I always answer no, I'll just "borrow" a sip or two. In the Boat, we run into Jesse, the owner, who's rarely behind the counter after six at night. He frowns, as if remembering something, then says:

"Hey, guys. You back home?"

"Yes, indeed," declaims Shorey, for everyone to hear. "Ain't life grand?"

Most of the time." Again, that frown. It's probably been a long day. The place opens at 7:30 in the morning, and Jesse's here, greeting downtown workers before they board their buses. "Listen, coffee's on the house. You folks take care, okay?"

Since it's on the house, we each pour a cup, snap on a plastic lid, and down the street we go, talking softly about hardware items we will need: a drain-cover for the bathtub, some wood cement, steel wool. The Toy Boat Café anchors a corner of our block, which seems densely dark after the artificial brilliance of the Boat.

Shorey stops for some reason, the oversized umbrella teetering in his grip.

"I don't believe it," he says through his teeth. "Is that him?"

When I'm not wearing glasses my eyes feed me blurred images even in bright daylight, so that now, in the dark, I'm able to make out only a vague form waddling towards us. Could be anyone. But my body revs through its full range of panic symptoms: jitterbug heartbeat, legs turned to tree trunks, feet footed to the pavement. At this moment,

I couldn't manage to run if Ajax were threatening me with a meat cleaver.

Under the black cave of the umbrella, we instinctively step back, as if to let a squadron pass.

"Don't say a word," cautions Shorey.

And I manage to whisper, "Act like we don't know him."

I desperately want this to be a mistake. That's not Ajax coming closer, just a nameless drunk lurching along, picking his uneven way among demons only he can discern.

The distance closes. Exhaling liquor fumes, Ajax is in our faces. He's wild-eyed. Unkempt. Not the least bit intimidated by Shorey, who looms over him from a greater height. They are practically toe to toe as Ajax croaks, "I'm just . . . pullin' up my pants." Like a Western movie bucka-roo, he feigns a bowlegged gait, stomping his feet as he exaggerates the motion of hitching up his trousers. I see that his flies are undone.

We don't speak. Don't breathe. Somewhere in that addled brain, he knows we're afraid of him, and he's loving it. After all, his reputation precedes him, and it's quite a rep. Yet here he stands: free, juiced, with his drawers hanging off his butt.

He lets his eyes glaze over, as if to say, *Guess I've scared you enough for one night*, then mutters, "Have a nice evening, folks," and rolls on up the street.

We stand frozen, our psyches hanging wide open, then stumble the rest of the way home. By our gate, Shorey says, "I saw him stop here, on his way up the street just now, but I didn't realize it was *him*."

"Think he was scoping it out?"

"Yeah. Little trip down Memory Lane."

It's September 9th, a month to the day since Ajax was granted felony parole and placed in a V.A. facility. One month since I opened my big mouth and predicted that he'd be back here in a month.

Our house no longer looks like the happening sort of place we left a short while ago before we left to go for dinner. All I see is a dispiriting hodgepodge of possessions on the living-room floor, and still there's that echo. Worst of all, I feel the lingering presence of Ajax, his bad magic flooding back. Just minutes ago, and well within the forbidden circle drawn by the law, the 150 yards stipulated by the Stay-Away Order—he stood looking back here, bold as you please, thinking his thoughts, making his plans. So what's the use of putting everything together again if, any time he chooses, he can send all the pieces flying? And who's to stop him? The cops? They don't give a flying buttress. To saunter down the familiar path to his hovel—easily done. There are no locks or bars to prevent his entering.

Shorey reaches for the light-switch.

"Don't," I say.

"You're just going to hang out in the dark."

"For now, yes."

"You're going to let him win."

"I don't need a hundred watts blazing down on me right now."

"Do something constructive. Don't just cringe."

"Leave it alone, okay?"

"Okay. I'll leave it alone."

He blasts out of the house. Before he bangs through the front gate leading to the street, I'm calling his name. He doesn't hear, or doesn't want to hear. Now I'm scared. What will he do? All summer Shorey has been the embodiment of Mr. Cool. If he now steps over the line, it'll be my fault. Mea culpa.

In the dark of the other room, I crawl into the sleeping bag I am still using because it's on the floor, near the door, well placed in case of an emergency. No need to lose precious time blundering down six rungs of a ladder from the loft-bed. Eyes closed, I am wide awake. I'm thinking that I've seen Shorey lose his cool. I've seen him angry. Though he'd never resort to physical violence, the righteous anger in that unfettered voice can be frightening. The history of his family in America dates back nearly four centuries. Four hundred years of men shouting their opinions in New England town-hall meetings reverberate in Shorey's baritone instrument. When he sings, he can easily reach below a low C. When he shouts, you don't want to be in the same room. It could be dangerous to use such a voice on Ajax. Or on a cop.

Shorey shows up at ten, hair moistened against his forehead, face gone slack the way it does after an ordeal.

"I nearly got arrested," he says.

While I make tea, he tells the story.

After bolting from the house, he went by the 540 to see if Ajax was in there. He was, of course, and hard at it, deepening his inebriation. To confront the man would have been useless, foolhardy, so Shorey continued along Clement until he turned onto Sixth, sprinting toward the police station. Halfway down the block, he spotted the multicolored flashers of a patrol car. Flagging down the cruiser, he told his story, in an agitated way, facts piggybacking onto facts like a twenty-car pile-up on the freeway. In the telling, he might have expressed "a little bit of anger."

"I'm trying to give the guy a sense of what we've been through, how it feels to see that little pisser on our street. I said, 'I'm a citizen! I pay my taxes!'"

Anyway, the policeman at the wheel, neck wider than his head, according to Shorey, jumped out of the car at the suggestion—or possibly the demand—that he get himself up to the 540 Club, pronto, and clamp some cuffs on Ajax.

"I don't like your attitude!" said Neck-Man.

To which Shorey retorted, "Listen, you're well paid and well trained to deal with situations like this. It's your *job*."

"You calling me lazy?"

"Those are your own words, sir."

"Buddy, you're looking at some real trouble here."

The man's fellow officer, catching the drift of things, stepped out of the car and calmed down his partner, then said to Shorey, "I'm the one who arrested Ajax the night of the fire. I understand what you're going through. I'll go right now to the 540 and make the arrest."

Shorey, his face bathed in the disorienting sequence of lights from the police cruiser, replied, "Thank you, officer. I'd appreciate it. So will my wife. She was pretty shook-up, seeing him again."

Sometime after midnight, I hear the squawk of the ancient doorbell that no one but delivery people or Jehovah's Witnesses ever use. Shorey must still be in the garage, calming his nerves via computer Solitaire. Struggling out of the down bag, I pad barefooted to the door in my wrinkled pajamas. A young cop peers at me through the doorglass.

My first thought is that he's here to arrest Shorey.

He huddles under the meager porch-roof. Removing his cap, thwacking it against his thigh to shake off the rainwater, he says, "Boy, this is some kinda night."

To complete the melodramatic scenario that started earlier in the evening, the weather has turned wild, with lashings of rain, white jags of lightning and thunderclaps splitting the sky. Bridie's been howling with fear. All week I tried to convince her the house was safe, the world was safe, but she knew better. Now she dashes out the door, tangling with the policeman's legs as she plunges down the front steps and into the storm.

"Won't see *her* again tonight," I say.

"Sorry, ma'am." I like the way he takes the blame. He must be the nice cop Shorey was telling me about.

"What is it, officer?"

"Just wanted to let you know that Ajax is in custody."

"Thanks so much. How long will they keep him?"

"I'm not sure. Actually, I arrested him on some out-standing traffic warrants. Old stuff. That's all we had to go on."

"Excuse me? What about the Stay-Away Order?"

He turns his blond head to hide the pained expression. I can see that he's searching for the right words, reassuring words, but that in the absence of such words he's going to give it to me straight.

"There *is* no Stay-Away Order," he admits. "What I mean is, we couldn't find one. We've got this new computer system, and it's terrible. Even if there were such an Order, we'd never be able to find it."

"So, what now—traffic warrants? He could be out in no time."

Again he says, "Sorry, ma'am. Really, I am." Lowering his voice, as if afraid our porch might be bugged, he tells me that the problem is downtown. With the D.A.

"You mean, the woman in charge of our case?"

"No, no, no." He's shaking his head. "I'm talking about the top guy."

Terence Hallinan. Our city's controversial District Attorney. God help you if you're a crime *victim* in San Francisco.

"See, if this were San Mateo County, Ajax'd be doing one to three in State prison right now."

"Do you realize how dangerous he is?"

"I certainly do. He's totally crazy. He should be in a hospital for the criminally insane. But he's a master-manipulator. No one can hold him. And I don't mean to make excuses for my fellow officer, but it's frustrating for all of us. Our hands are tied."

I can see he's the new kid on the block. The young idealist. A blond Serpico—or just a cop who cares. One who's still green enough that he'd venture out into a storm like this, not for points with the chief but simply for us. How long, I wonder, will he be able to keep up that stance in the ener-vating atmosphere of a district station-house known around town as "Club Richmond," the do-nothing precinct?

"Look," he says, "I want to help. You can leave mes-sages at the station." And he gives me his name. "Be sure to say the message is for me."

Once the more theatrical elements of the storm have let up, a thick, monotonous rain falls all night long. We search, but Bridie does not return. And because she's out there, we can't sleep.

Shorey calls down to me from the loft-bed: "Did you notice Jesse acting a little strange when we were in the Boat this evening?"

"He seemed to have something on his mind."

"When I passed on my way to the 540, he called me in. Said he hadn't wanted to tell us before—we looked so upbeat—but earlier in the evening Ajax was in there, drunk, yelling, scaring the customers, the little kids with their ice-cream cones, and Jesse had to escort him out. He thought about warning us that Piss-ant was on the prowl, but seeing us happy and relaxed for the first time in months, he held back."

In the sodden center of this rain-drenched night, I get up, go to the kitchen, start the tea-water, ease open the back window and call for Bridie, quietly enough so I don't disturb the sleeping neighbors but audibly enough for a cat to hear.

No response.

After I strain and pour the tea, I call her name again.

No response.

I close the window and stare at the phone for a moment, then call our D.A., quoting her words of a month ago about the Stay-Away Order and the fact that if Ajax were to come anywhere near the site of the fire we could call the police and "he'll be picked up immediately. He'll then be in violation of his probation, and basically he will be incarcerated and subject to State prison."

"Call me," I say, "as soon as possible."

The next day passes.

I leave another message.

Another day passes.

Ajax—man or myth? Now that we're back, the neighbors start telling us stories. Seems he has terrorized this block for twenty years. We were just too busy to notice, or lucky enough not to have fallen within his crazy purview. He broke into the studio across the street where Wayne repairs musical instruments, some of them rare and expensive. Smashed in a woman's door to draw her attention, then pulled down his pants and pooped on the sidewalk in front of her house. Some of the stories are fantastical. One thing I do sense: Ajax's ego is so colossal that I'm certain he relishes his mythological status on this street. He's a contrarian who seems to thrive on being despised.

But even *he* must have a limit. The man isn't all that young.

Will he ever tire of acting out?

Will we ever be rid of this man?

The rain's over. Puddles sparkle in the shallow declivities of our Oriental carpet, spread out on the patio for washing. I've applied liquid soap and have gone over the green-patterned surface with a scrub-brush. Shorey aims the hose, drilling a jet of water so hard that it ricochets off the rug's low pile and soaks his pant-legs. Craters of suds form round each watery jab of the hose. I'm in bare feet, slogging over the sloppy wet rug in the back-warming sunshine. No matter how much we rinse, the suds just multiply. I take the hose and broadcast water here and there, use my feet to edge the suds off the rug, onto the concrete. It's a battle. We can't stop laughing. This is like the *I Love Lucy* grape-stomping episode where Lucy and Ricky travel to Italy and Lucy hikes up her skirts and hops into a vat full of wine-grapes and experienced grape-crushers.

Slung over two sawhorses on the patio, the rug will take days to dry. Days, ideally, of sun and wind, though fog and mist may intervene, and then we're back to a wet rug. Could take weeks. I won't mind. Soon enough, the house will fill up and the atmosphere will contract around our possessions. Dust will collect. Our Zen floor will disappear under a thickness of carpet.

CHAPTER 12

SHAPE-CHANGER

History suggests that once again Ajax will kick over the traces and make a fool of everyone. Even while in jail the previous summer, he managed to keep people off-balance—changing his lawyer *and* his appearance. The mountain man/Santa Claus we first encountered in no way resembled the shorn, winter-pale Ajax who began haunting the neighborhood after his escape from the V.A.

A police inspector named Dave Parenti is keen to see him contained. We've been in phone contact since I called him right after our unexpected reunion with Ajax in September. Perusing the computer, Parenti, like the cops, could find no Stay-Away Order. He let slip that "Somebody must have dropped the ball."

"It *must* be in there," he declared. "Just a question of where. I'll find out. By the way, call me Dave."

Time passed. No Stay-Away Order was located.

One morning in mid-October, Shorey tracked me down at the branch library. "You were gone," he said, "when Parenti called. Wait'll you hear."

"Good or bad?"

"Little of both."

Dave Parenti reported to Shorey the news that Ajax was in custody and his parole had been revoked. Shorey tore out of the house and headed for the library, stopping on the way for a decaf at the Toy Boat.

In the café he questioned his own sanity. How, he asked himself, could a human being be in custody downtown while at the same time in the Toy Boat, barking a greeting to Jesse, the owner, and demanding strong black coffee?

"He was standing one foot away from me," said Shorey.

Because one can never tell with Ajax, it was impossible to say whether he knew he was being tailed by Shorey as he left the Boat, or so drunk he didn't care. "Could've been putting the whole thing on, thumbing his nose at me," said Shorey. "Or maybe challenging me to *do* something. Boy, would I like to rearrange his face for him."

"But you'd never."

"No, and I think he knows I wouldn't."

Shorey trailed behind as Ajax passed several cronies who raised their hands in greeting, chanting his name, while Ajax himself, like a personage who'd moved far beyond them in knowledge and experience, merely waved them off. He turned onto Sixth, heading for the bus-stop, where he stood for a while, waiting for who-knows-what, since it's a well-known fact that Ajax does not stoop to riding buses. Finally, he sheltered under the nearby awning of the Five Happiness Restaurant.

"That's when I went and got the car," said Shorey, as we careened round a corner onto Geary. "Because if he's still there, I'm dropping you off at the police station. Right now I don't trust myself to go in there."

I saw under the awning yet another face of Ajax: the respectable pensioner, clean and spruce in a green windbreaker and floppy white rain hat.

Before the car stopped moving, I had already scrambled out the door.

No beehive atmosphere in this precinct. Behind bullet-proof glass were two officers: a male at his desk in the back, and a female in front who raised an index finger for me to wait while she completed a phone call. The call continued. I raised my hand, waving it about like a kid in a classroom, but the officer, crunching her forehead into a unibrow, silently warned me to cool it. Finally, the male officer ambled out to where I stood, closing the heavy door behind him.

I told him Ajax was down by the corner. The name needed no explication. Every officer in this part of town knows Ajax by name and face.

"We don't dispatch from here," he informed me.

"But there's a warrant out. Who *does* dispatch?"

"Downtown."

"Are you saying I have to call 911?"

"That would be better."

"You won't pick him up?"

"That's correct, ma'am."

"But by the time they arrive, Ajax'll be in the next county."

He then volunteered the following, damning information:

"That's how it's done. Last time, though, they sent someone who didn't know what Ajax looked like. Officer picks up this homeless guy who just happens to be there, but leaves Ajax behind because he looks so clean."

Fully aware that sarcasm would get me nowhere, I blurted, "That makes, like, brilliant sense, to send someone all the way from downtown who doesn't know Ajax from Terence Hallinan."

He shrugged.

"Give *me* a badge and some cuffs, and I'll go make the arrest."

"Ma'am . . . " he warned.

Meanwhile, out in the world, where you can't hide behind bullet-proof glass, Shorey was frantically pointing toward the corner. He, from inside the car, and I, from the steps of the police station, watched helplessly as Ajax flagged down a passing cab.

Throughout the fall, we'd hear about Ajax—bounced from the 540, belligerent in Fizzee's, D & D in front of the convenience store. He was like our local UFO. At around two on more than one morning, the neighbor in front saw a black shadow dash across our patio toward Ajax's burnt-out cottage. The shadow, unhindered by the rebuilt six-foot fence, "passed right on through." Late on another night, Ajax appeared simultaneously on Fifth as well as Sixth Avenue, decked out in a black tam o'shanter.

More than one woman on our street refused to step outside her apartment while he remained at large.

Two days ago, on my way to buy an afternoon paper, I ran into one of these long-time residents, a woman called Noni. She'd been lying low, she told me, but Ajax or no Ajax, she needed her Metamucil, and so she trekked the four blocks to Walgreen's. The sky had spilled a little rain, and by the time I came upon her she looked like a frightened mole in her tight glove of a coat with its spiked wet fur. I could see that she wanted nothing more than to burrow back into the safety of her flat, but first she had to tell me something.

Noni resembles the French writer, Colette—the Colette of later years—with her wedge-shaped face, frizz of hair and black-rimmed eyes. Whether from rain or tears, the mascara on her lower lids had run, pooling in the hollows above her prominent cheekbones. Black ran wetly in the tributaries of her eye-pouches. While she warmed to her story, setting the scene, I had the strongest urge to whip out a Kleenex and wipe away those smudges.

Ajax, she said, was "even as we speak" lying dead-drunk on the sidewalk at Sixth and Clement, one block away.

"At the risk of my life, I'm telling you, I snuck to the pay-phone to call the cops. How do I know he's not playing possum? Maybe he's got one eye open and is watching me. Looks like he's dead, but this guy is Lazarus! He could come in the night, slice my throat!"

I held her freezing hand while she rambled on.

"They come, these cops. They say to me, 'We gotta look in the computer,' so they go away again. Meanwhile, I'm hiding in Schubert's across the street, choking on my napoleon, I'm so nervous. They come back, the cops, so I leave my coffee, a full cup, with half a napoleon still on the plate, and run back over, fast as I can. They tell me he's not in the computer."

"I ask them, 'What kind of a computer you got? What kind of a computer is my taxes paying for?'"

"'He's not wanted,' they say. 'Leave him alone. Let him walk.' I look down and there's Ajax, on all fours, struggling to get up. I don't think he saw me, but how do I know for sure?"

"It'll be okay, Noni."

"I'm afraid to look out my blinds."

"It'll be okay. I'm in touch with a police inspector."

"Honey, tell the inspector to take him away. I think maybe he's got X-ray vision. I think he can see through blinds."

December 6th, and I'm later than usual mailing my Christmas gifts. Many in this international city start sending packages to Asia and other offshore destinations as early as mid-November. Our gifts are only going to the East Coast, but at this point the sneezing, coughing, kids-in-strollers line will be out the door and down the block at the Parker Avenue post office.

Still, I feel joyous seeing the crisply brown-wrapped packages in their pyramidal stack. I've got an armful, but will hike the half-mile rather than jam my way into the crush of shoppers on a 38-bus. It's cold out, the air a silvery tingle against my nose. The kind of winter morning that drains the warmth from your face and makes you un-willing to inhale too deeply after the first chilled breath into the lungs. Waiting for the light to change at Geary, I wave to Wayne, who's huddled in the recessed entryway of his building.

"Hey, Santa Claus," he calls out.

"Wayne! Connecticut weather, huh?"

"Been so long, can't remember."

Green for Go. In the brief absence of oncoming cars I'm able to shave a few steps from the trip by cutting a diago-nal that brings me to the doorway of Cala supermarket.

The usual scene—five or six red-faced men sit knees-to-chest at the base of the building, empty coffee cups in place in case any spare change wanders by. The mood seems upbeat in the extreme. Normally at this time of morn-ing the guys are asleep on the job, basically just bodies proximate to their begging bowls, but today they're in full shout, raising their fists in response to an orator in a tomato-red jacket and white cap.

I can't make out what they're saying because their voices erupt out of growl register, husky and raucous as they laugh themselves into coughing fits at the instigation of the spiffy fellow who stalks back and forth in front of them like a stand-up comedian.

Then he turns, as if he has sensed me. Instinctively, I raise the pyramid of parcels to hide my face. We are mere feet from each other. I tell myself it can't be him. When did he ever have short hair? But one thing I know by now: every time you encounter Ajax, he's new. He's the Houdini of shape-changers, magically and endlessly able to reinvent himself.

I lower the packages so I can see. The face appears coldly white, carved from stone. He regards me as if I were a worm, or worse: a spatial absence.

Since I'm not wearing my glasses, I can't be certain. However, who can inspire admiration amounting to reverence in other homeless men? Whenever he reappears— from out of town, out of hiding, or out of jail—they gather round him as if to a king or deity, chanting his name, as they are doing now: "Ajax! Ajax!"

Holy shit, it's him.

Feet, move me down the street.

I know what I've got to do.

By the side entrance to Cala, at the edge of the parking lot where automatic doors continually open and close, there's a payphone. At the other end of the city is perhaps the only person who can help. I start to set the packages down on the ground, but lose my grip. Big and little boxes tumble in a heap at my feet. He could whip round the corner of the building at any second and assault me, as he did to the female police officer, as he's done to his fellow drunks. To anyone, actually, who gets in his way. Imperative, therefore, that I make this call—and quickly. As I fumble for correct change, coins leap spasmodically from my hand

and land among the fallen packages. Folks clatter back and forth with their metal shopping carts. One man, with almost gleeful vehemence, rams his cart into the tail-end of a nested row of carts. Though my hands are shaking out of control, I manage to insert two coins in the slot. Blessed be the dial tone.

Over the noise of traffic and the racket of the carts, I can hear Ajax, just out of sight, yelling imprecations. His mood is turning dark. I hear the answering roar from his well primed audience.

Shorey and I are no longer so hopelessly alone. D.A. Inspector Dave Parenti has told us, "I've got your number locked into my pager. Call any time, night or day. If you see him on the street at two in the morning, call me. I'll be there."

As I punch in the payphone number so Parenti can call me back, I see the notice that says this payphone will accept no incoming calls. Ajax, canny as he is, will have intuited that I'd call the cops. He will linger for the last cocky moment of glory in front of his group, then flee the scene. Leave them cheering.

Our house is just across the street, but I can't go back there to make the call and wait around for the response because in doing so I'd have to walk past Ajax. I am shaking with frustration.

A computerized female voice squawks inside the receiver that dangles from its inflexible metal cord. I hang up the phone. I hesitate a moment while trying to pull an answer from the unresponsive day: the wan winter sunlight and chaos of cars, carts and groaning diesel buses. All I want to know is: Where can I make a simple phone call without having to walk a mile out of my way?

But it's like the Zen saying: *Whatever you need is right at hand*. The answer is right in front of me.

For a decade, until three years ago, Shorey managed the hundred-year-old lumberyard on the opposite corner, its warehouse of a back room wide open to the side-street that runs past this parking lot.

You can't live in this neighborhood and not know Shorey. Like Ajax, he's a larger-than-life character, except he's the flip side, the one who tries to make life easier for people. He's not a do-gooder, but he does a lot of good. For his patience with customers and his ingenious solutions to their problems, he earned a sort of celebrity status in these streets. Whole buildings in this area have gone up under his guidance. I'll walk over there, tell them who I am, and ask to use their phone.

I go in through the back, into the cool, dark, forest-fragrant cathedral of lumber with its high catwalk that runs round the perimeter where sheaves of seasoned boards are stacked beneath the ceiling.

But where are the workers?

"Hello?"

Never this kind of quiet in the days when Shorey worked here. He left—or, was invited to leave—when a new owner decided he could make it only by hiring low-wage humps willing to work without benefits. "No hard feelings, I hope," said the man, "but I can't afford someone like you. I'll manage the place myself."

Clearly, the place has run itself down. It feels dead.

I push through an opaque plastic curtain dividing the back from the front: the old womb with its worn countertop and hanging back-order slips and endless hardware items that Shorey knew by heart.

No one in here, either.

"Hello-o?"

A rodent-like rustling behind the gadgets island, back by the assortment of wooden dowels. Out comes a guy of about thirty-five with a beefsteak complexion and lank, sandy hair who's obviously a veteran of hard living.

"Yeah?"

"Excuse me," I say, "but you might know of my husband —Shorey? Used to manage this store?"

He frowns, deepening the furrows between his brows. Whatever happened to the warm welcome for which this lumberyard was renowned? "I don't know no Shorty," he grumbles.

"No, his name is Shorey."

"Don't know him either."

"He worked here ten years, he's kind of well-known, but . . . never mind." I'm dancing from foot to foot, desperate to make the connection with Parenti. "I'm wondering, would you let me use your phone?"

"Phone's only for employees."

"Like I said, my husband—"

"And like *I* said, I don't know your old man."

He has taken refuge behind a mask that hasn't creased in a smile in a very long while. He stands guard over the endangered company phone. Beads of sweat twinkle on his forehead.

"Pleez! I'd be happy to pay." I whip out my wallet, drop a couple of Ones on the counter. "Is that enough? This is urgent!"

"What's so 'urgent' about it?"

There's a psychopath over by the supermarket, and we're in here arguing semantics.

"Look, lady, go use the payphone at Cala."

I explain why this is not an option. I tell him, in as telegraphic a way as possible, about the fire and how I've got to reach the police inspector so he can come pick up Ajax.

Instead of scooping up my dollar bills and providing me an outside line, he says, "Dude burned your house down?"

"He did," I confirm. "With us in it."

"Where is this asshole?" He stalks to the front window, hunching over the dusty display as he peers up and down Geary. Ajax is not visible from that angle, so he says, "You stay. Watch the store." The bell above the door jangles wildly as he bursts outside, onto the boulevard. I'm right behind him.

"Where are you going?"

"Get back there! Place can't be left unattended."

"But—where are you going?"

"Smash the fucker's face in. Somebody's gotta do it."

This is all we need—more violence. This volcanic individual, pummeling Ajax. A felony assault, and presumably at my behest. At any rate, that's how it'll look to a cop.

We're at the corner. A block away, Ajax is entertaining the troops.

As Monday morning traffic flashes by, I beg this man to go back inside the store. The longer we remain in plain sight, the more likely that Ajax will spot me and realize I'm plotting his arrest. When he's finally nabbed, it should seem to him a matter of rotten luck, not something I have instigated.

"You'll only make things worse," I tell the lumberyard worker.

He jerks away from me. He's a turbojet just waiting for runway clearance. At the first lull in traffic, he springs, practically airborne, off the curb. I catch hold of his arm, the bleach-spotted olive sweatshirt.

"Don't go down there!" I plead. "Don't get involved."

"Big fish eating little fish," he mutters, "and nobody's got the balls to stand up and say, *Stop messing with the people!*"

I can feel him shaking inside his shirt. Am I holding onto an unhappy childhood, a meth habit, a minimum-wage worker itching to trounce his boss—or all three? Motionless in the middle of the street, he flexes and unflexes his fists. An SUV racing out of Cala's lot could run us down. To break through his trance, I speak in the tone of a platoon leader:

"We are going back to the store. I am calling the inspector. He will pick up Ajax and put him in jail."

In clockwork unison, we turn and walk back. He seems beaten. He has not been permitted his catharsis (though it might have been pleasant to watch this six-footer put the fear of God into Ajax).

I make the call. While I wait for a response, the man moves down the store aisle, repositioning spray-cans of WD-40 so they all face front. Still no customers. Half the shelves are empty. Sad to see the pallid, century-old walls that in Shorey's day remained hidden behind thickets of product.

Within five minutes, Inspector Parenti gets back to me.

I give him the coordinates, warning that the show down by Cala seems just about over. Ajax is likely to bolt.

"I'll be there like the wind," he says.

∾

Walking back empty-handed from the post office, I keep to the opposite side of Geary in case Ajax is still doing his schtick in front of Cala. He's not. His buddies now sit mincingly against the pale stuccoed exterior, gripping their knees, heads swerved in the direction of the arrest. Parenti has pulled it off. A gleaming police cruiser straddles the far right lane, parked parallel to the unmarked car of a plainclothes officer. The two vehicles obviously made a sudden, freewheeling stop. Did Ajax break and try to run? I slow my steps but do not stand and stare: grudging respect for a tough adversary keeps me from openly gloating. He's facing away from me, hands cuffed behind his back. With the backup support of a uniformed officer, Parenti—I know him by his white hair—appears to be reading Ajax his Miranda rights.

The roaring of the captive Ajax carries in all directions. Two elderly Asian women with bulging grocery bags keep right on going. Getting comestibles to the kitchen table ranks as far more important than watching some rabble-rouser get pinched. I can't see detail from this distance, just a bright swatch of primary color, the red jacket, writhing like a snagged kite in the wind.

His admirers look stunned, utterly subdued. Their hero is shackled like an animal, bound for downtown. I experience the briefest stab of sadness, realizing that Ajax possesses what high-school teachers love to call "leadership qualities." What might he not have achieved, if only . . .

But life rushes on, autumn leaves fall, and we are what we are.

I don't need to stick around to see him eased, or forced, into the squad car. I don't have the stomach for the *coup de grace*. As I jaywalk to my gate, face averted, I can't help but feel exultant. If Sam were here I'd explain that at the

root of my feeling for Ajax there is compassion—maybe—
but right now, damn it all, *I just want this punk off my street.*

Several hours after the arrest, Parenti calls. I've been waiting
to hear from him. He guarantees that Ajax will remain behind
bars through the first of January ("So you can have a peaceful
Christmas"), but can't promise much more, though he'll do
his best to get him locked up for a few additional months.

"You can do that?" I ask.

"Oh, I think so. When we put the cuffs on, he threatened
to kill me. I'll note that in my arrest report."

Sounds good.

"He got pretty wild," Parenti adds. "Started yelling,
'You can't touch me!' 'Oh, no?' sez I. 'Well, I'm taking you
in.'"

"I appreciate all you've done."

"One more thing, just to show the arrogance of the guy.
We're putting him in the car, he's resisting, and he bellows,
'You can't do this! The Richmond is my place, and this is
my street!'"

Bridie is stretched full-length along the ivory quilt in my
room at the back of the house. She feigns sleep, her right eye
a glittering slit through which she observes my movements.
Behind her, an ebbing breeze sucks the diaphanous curtain
back out through the open window. There's a sour, salt
smell to the air. On this quiet afternoon, the ocean feels
close, although it's more than forty blocks away. It's a
gray day. Mild, for December.

The room, with its new paint and moldings and louvered closet door, looks as pristine as it did seven months
ago after I'd gussied it up for Bernadette's visit. At that
time, she'd driven up here from Arizona for my graduation,

only to find a burnt-out shell. So we're trying again. Bernadette is coming for Christmas. She'll be here in a week.

The day has an empty, entr'acte feel to it. I want to match its emptiness, my mind a fallow winter field with maybe a gull or two cruising the soft gray sky, but I keep flashing on Ajax—trying not to picture him down at the County jail. Can his situation be all that bad? After all, he's got food and shelter, and by now should be over the worst of his alcohol withdrawal. What I see is fresh color in his face, and a return of his usual belligerence. He'll be safe and warm and off the streets this Christmas.

"I did it for you," I whisper to Bridie.

She gives me one of her noncommittal blinks.

"To keep you safe."

She yawns, exposing the rich pink interior of her mouth, that last terrifying sight glimpsed by the mice and birds she has killed in her lifetime.

Cats are not dogs, who grovel in gratitude for every scrap of grub or show of affection. Cats don't care to know the why or wherefore of what we do for them, so long as we keep on doing it. And Bridie's not buying into the idea that I had Ajax thrown in the can on her account. Extending one white paw, she languidly flexes her claws just above the vintage quilt but without digging into the fabric.

I reach to pet her. She flicks a warning swipe with the paw.

"I know," I tell her. "You're a cat. It's not your problem."

Across the street, in Mary Dawson's high-ceilinged parlor, we can hear the clock ticking. Bernadette, in a wing-chair, is as dressed-up as she gets: gauzy off-white Mexican blouse with botanical embroidery, chocolate velour pants, and the customary Birkenstocks, their suede surface powdered with desert dust. In honor of the climate, she's wearing socks. She arrived after a long delay on her morning flight from Phoenix.

The dull gray day conceals a potential for rain, and a fine winter mizzle has fluffed Bernadette's hair, wetting the gauzy fabric where the heavy mop rests on her shoulders. She's still brown from Arizona sun stored in her skin; it'll take a week for her to register the bone-softening cold of this town.

Offstage, in another room, Mary's two roommates chatter away. Delicious to my ears, the soft burr of the Dublin accent, as opposed to the rough brogue of the more northern Irish counties. They sound girlish, full of easy cheer, and I feel a fleeting stab of envy over not having been born in Ireland. I'm certain no such thought would ever occur to Bernadette, who's so sufficient unto herself. No doubt she identifies more with the clay soil of Arizona—the stuff out of which she fashions her pottery—than the sentimental Irish sod.

She's being quiet, taking her bearings. Later, she'll talk, probably a lot.

Between Bernadette and me, on a round table draped with a forest green cloth, sits a miniature Scotch pine. It's late afternoon on Christmas Eve. Perhaps Mary does not mean to decorate this tree, just leave it as-is, green and proud, a reminder of her tree-loving, Druidic island.

She's in the kitchen brewing Barry's Tea ("Blended in Cork Since 1901"). I can see her through the archway, dumping big spoonfuls into the white pot. Now she pours the boiling water that infuses the tea and releases an earthy aroma that makes Bernadette smile her first real smile after what was admittedly a stressful trip.

Seven months ago I didn't even know Mary Dawson, and now here we are, the three of us, china saucers balanced on our knees, sipping this rich cinnabar brew.

"Would you not care for a raisin scone?" says Mary.

Bernadette and I demur. The clock ticks portentously.

Momentarily I'm a character in a story from *Dubliners*. I start asking my many questions about the Dublin I haven't seen since my 1966 visit to that city. Mary answers politely, but, clearly, she'd rather discuss her graphic design program at City College.

Pouring us each a second cup, Mary asks if we wouldn't care for "a coupla biscuits" with our tea. Each cookie is a caldera that oozes the sugary lava of raspberry jam.

It strikes me that I scarcely tasted the tea Mary gave me on the night of the fire, merely gulped the wetness, the sweetness of the sugar, the heat that I needed as I sat shivering and in shock on my landlady's front steps, desperate to believe Mary Dawson when she assured me that things would be all right, really they would.

It's Christmas. I'm drinking Barry's Tea with Bernadette O'Neill and Mary Dawson, the angels of the fire, as I've come to think of them. This evening Shorey, Bernadette and I will attend a carol-singing service at a neighborhood church. Shorey, the minister's son, is not one for church-going, but he looks forward to this particular service at this particular church because it's carols by candlelight. Carols by fire-light.

CHAPTER THIRTEEN

STEVIE

We are not the only ones who've been blindsided by fire. Daily—nightly—red engines scream past our street on their way down Geary. We are a city of elegant wood frame dwellings: in other words, a pile of kindling. Fires happen, neighbors gather, and if a blaze is sufficiently dramatic, the TV cameras appear. But in the aftermath, once the ladder trucks and engines have left the scene and the TV van has sped back to Channel Two, survivors are left staring at what used to be their home. Frozen in shock they may be, but before the smoke clears they will need to come up with at least a provisional plan for getting through the coming days and weeks.

While firefighters doused our house, I huddled on the steps of the building in front with the fire marshal, telling him I felt our situation was doubly bad on account of the added criminal element: Ajax, and the possibility of arson. He did not exactly disagree, but said that during his career he had investigated more than four hundred potential arsons, and, in his opinion, "Every fire, whether it's an arson or not, has a story attached."

245

This is Stevie's story.

We had seen her on TV in June of the previous year when we were staying at the Ocean Breeze Motel. She looked the way I must have looked on my own night of fire. Her face in its stark whiteness resembled a Kabuki dancer's, and she wore the expression of someone who'd been punched awake. To her left, smoke issued from every window and fissure of the house she had just escaped. She clutched a cat carrier as it if represented life's last hope, and I could see the cat's nose straining at the peephole.

With a mike stuck in her face, she spoke about how she'd lived in her top-floor flat for twenty years—she gave a sideward glance at the smoking Edwardian ruin—and how she could only assume she had lost everything. "Except for Sparky," she said. And right on cue, the cat meowed.

The reporter gave the location: three blocks from our own place and, like ours, in the middle of the block, the western side of the avenue.

Fire had made us kin. The day after her residence burned, I stepped off a bus at Third and Geary and started walking westward, to our own ruin, when I felt the pull to turn back toward Second Avenue.

At the scene, smoke was still wisping from the second-story windows. I saw the sad heap of fire-trash: the charred, blistered timbers and wet, sooty clothing. Fires blaze redly while robbing everything in their path of color, turning the world black. Some things do survive, in this case a toaster, perched on the pile and gleaming in the brassy sunlight. The silver symmetry of its rounded outlines would have made it a 1950s model. Someone had loved this appliance.

You could tell by the shine, not a fingerprint visible. If I were to snatch it from the pile, I might be accused of looting. I asked myself: Does fire-trash belong to anyone? Having been dumped on the street, does it not fall within the public domain? If I could have been certain the toaster belonged to the cat-lady, I'd have made my grab and done my best to find her.

But I walked on.

Months later, I learned that the toaster had indeed belonged to Stephanie Willett-Shaw, or Stevie, as she's known to friends. She wished I *had* retrieved it from the pile, saying, "One less thing I'd need to replace."

In December, while I arranged pine boughs along the mantelpiece, the phone rang. Mark Grim. For years, he and Shorey had worked the front counter at the lumberyard. Anyway, he had a slew of new paintings he wanted us to see before his upcoming show. We should come over. And hey, what had I and "the Shoremeister" been up to in the meantime?

How to encapsulate an entire year in a couple of sentences? And it struck me, talking to Mark, that he knew nothing about the fire.

"Why didn't you call?" he whined. "Carol and I would've helped."

I explained that we'd spaced out a number of people, not intentionally, but that during those difficult months our lives had moved along a narrow channel called Barely Keeping Afloat.

"Wish I *had* called," I murmured. An evening in their art-filled apartment, eating from hand-painted plates, might have taken the edge off.

A good-natured Scandinavian giant, Mark's not one for holding grudges. He harrumphed a bit, then said, "When did you say that fire was?"

"Late May."

"We've got this friend who had a fire last summer. You guys should meet. I'll give her a ring. Stevie, her name is."

"She wouldn't have a cat called Sparky?"

"Ah, the Sparkster. She's nuts about that cat."

"I'll be wearing a flared black raincoat—like those swagger coats from the 'fifties. And frog earrings."

I scanned the lobby for a woman fitting this description. The room reeked of wet fabric and dripping umbrellas: the sour fragrance of city rain. We'd agreed to see a movie, *Haiku Tunnel*, a comedy about a man who takes an assignment as a temporary legal secretary.

While I waited the line lengthened, and I hate being late for movies.

She must have arrived before I did and gone straight to the Ladies' Room, because who else could that be, standing in a yellow-lit pool on the figured carpet, searching her satchel of a purse? I like to see people before they notice me, remain for a moment in the vestibule of relationship and gather impressions from purely visual clues before nervous, first-time conversation colors the picture. I like to catch a prospective friend in their most unstudied mode, since things will never be quite so artless after the introductions and the piling on of biographical details. After we *know* each other.

Taller than I, she had crinkly auburn hair piled into an upsweep. Hanging from her earlobes were silver frogs the size of the actual amphibian. Rings on every finger, and a black raincoat with scads of fabric, suitable for waltzing.

Then the moment of recognition, the big hug, umbrellas dangling by straps from our wrists. Some disconnected conversation, and we were inside the theater, safe in our seats.

Stevie told me she preferred polenta to popcorn and avoided white sugar. I, however, cannot cold-turkey my way through a movie. The snack-holders affixed to our seats looked tragically empty. Dashing back to the lobby, I bought a triple pack of York's Peppermint Patties.

After the film, we inched our way along Stockton Street, rummaging through bins of bok choi, bitter melon, mustard greens, and fingering the cheap, glittering items made by slave-labor in mainland China. Guiltily, I bought a beaded bracelet for a dollar. Stevie held back.

The heavy sky, which looked like the underside of an old mattress, now split open, spilling an ethereal light over the shoppers and tawdry goods, painting the wet pavement a Mediterranean shade of rosy apricot. Hot light on a cold, damp day.

In the noodle house, we sat by the front window. Ruddy, late winter sun flared in the storefront windows across the way, while we, on the western side of the street, sank into gloom. The place had four tables, three of them empty. The tables were more of a courtesy, the main business being a noodle-making operation in back. Still, they served a few dishes. A couple of times, an aproned waiter came out from the back to refill our teapot. He didn't seem to mind that we lingered far too long over our food. White flour coated his hairless forearms: he no doubt doubled as a noodle-maker. Stevie and I talked until dark, till bright lights came on in all the surrounding stores. In the back, they kept recycling the same Cantonese music tape, a soprano competing with a high-pitched violin.

The place felt homey—the sort of home where no one pays you any mind. I wanted to hear about Stevie's fire, but she was talking tea, and pouring us more. Did I know, she said, that tea is related to the camellia? *Camellia sinensis.* Green tea comes from the tips, or shoots, of the tea-shrub, while black tea comes from the leaves and must be fermented. And did I know that used teabags are soothing to sore eyes?

She did a lot of loud laughing. The sound, tinged with hysteria, went right through me. I'd been able to talk things out with Shorey. Was it possible that Stevie had had no one with whom she could share the trauma?

At Stevie's instigation we discussed the strangeness of February, the current month, with its extra day every fourth year. By some stretch, she connected that intercalary day to an astrological period when the moon is out of phase. "My whole life has been out of phase," she admitted, "since that fire."

The restaurant was nearly dark now, as if shut down for the night. Had they forgotten us completely, that we hadn't yet paid?

"Stevie?"

She snatched the paper napkin from her lap, crushing it in her fist, letting it fall like a white dumpling into the empty bowl.

"I should go feed Sparky," she said, as she got up and thrust her arms into the raglan sleeves of her raincoat.

No sign of our waiter. We dropped a couple of bills onto the table, enough to cover the meal plus a tip of nearly the same amount—rent payment for having stayed so long.

Outside, Stevie suggested we go by way of Grant rather than continue along Stockton and trudge through the bathroom-tiled, heavily traveled tunnel where a constant roar made all talk impossible. We were headed for the same bus: the #1 that cuts up Sacramento before beginning its vertiginous climb out of Chinatown towards Nob Hill.

We crossed the street, turning down by the high-rise tower of the Ping Yuen housing project. A colder night surrounded us as we passed the empty, ground-level spaces of the project, and it was here that Stevie opened up.

"I had this premonition," she said. "For weeks, I was expecting a fire. You know, we had a convicted arsonist living in the basement of our building."

"That's unreal. You think he did it?"

"For some reason, I don't. Though he *was* weird. They're claiming it was a faulty heating pad, but I blame it on poor maintenance. Decades of neglect."

"Bad wiring."

"We'll never know."

Somebody yelled. Probably kids fooling around, but we stepped up our pace toward the lights of Grant Avenue, half a block away.

Her fire fits the usual profile. On June 29th, at 4:22 in the morning, she heard muffled cries coming from below and people running through the hallway. Looking out her bay window, she saw black smoke. The rest is history, but that history forms the more compelling part of her story. Four years later, she would still claim that fire was tracking her, and there seem plausible reasons for such a claim.

We passed two stores in a row that sold embroidered white bed linens from China. Both stores were empty except for the sales clerks, who tried to entice us inside with smiles and beckoning hand-gestures. One even bustled outside with a brochure: everything half-off. Were these women working on commission? If so, I didn't like their chances of making rent this month. February lies deep in the off-season, and Grant Avenue, on this rain-threatening night, did not exactly hum with tourist trade. A rare quiet pervaded the street. Most establishments hadn't bothered to activate the canned music—waste of electricity, perhaps —and we could hear our footsteps clicking along the pavement.

Back home now for five months, Shorey and I were still fixing up, replacing items we'd lost to the fire. I'd have liked to go in and price some pillowcases, but didn't want to make Stevie feel bad. Since her own fire, she had been housed, but not in anything approximating a home.

"I live in a room without water," she said.

Stevie worked as a legal secretary. The law firm, located in a rambling, decrepit building, had a fully equipped kitchen and bathroom, including shower, as well as a storage room two floors above the office. Stevie put in fifty-to six-ty-hour weeks, so it almost made sense for her to reside in the building where she worked. After the fire, her employer allowed her to live, rent-free, in the 10 by 16 storage room, and there she would remain for a total of three years.

She developed a routine. The routine became iron-clad.

Her days started at 4:22 a.m. She woke spontaneously at that time, always. Some days she'd wake at 4:21, before the clock ticked over into that devastatingly memorable moment on June 29th when she'd heard the first screams in her hallway.

She claimed she never really slept, just dozed and startled awake again and again through the night.

As we spoke, I tried to picture the building: the vast hundred-year-old structure with its rinky-dink elevator and the creaking stairs she prefers to use, going down the steps each morning in the wee hours, with Sparky in her arms and a clutch of keys.

"I hang onto those keys as if they were my life," she confessed. I'm terrified of losing them and being stranded in the hallway, having to wait till someone shows up several hours later. It's more than that, though. It's a fear of being cut off, if you know what I mean."

Again, I imagined the building, subdivided into the many rent-generating offices, and Stevie alone there at night, listening for sounds—the creaking of a beam or the groaning of a floorboard as the old edifice settled into itself on cold, damp nights such as this one. Stevie, sniffing for smoke, as I still do. In fact, on one recent night she did smell smoke. She went tearing from floor to floor looking for the source, which turned out to be the elevator. A minor fire, but had she not been in the building, the whole place might have gone up.

In a way, Stevie owns the place during those uninhabited hours, and I told her, as we continued along Grant Avenue, that it's nice to think of her padding around in slippers and a robe, metaphorically thumbing her nose at a building that normally sees only suited lawyers and well primped secretaries.

"But I've never worn a bathrobe or even pajamas in the place," she said. "I sleep in my clothes. If I could sleep with my shoes on, I would. I'm ready to dash at a moment's notice. My backpack's by the door. So are my shoes and purse and Sparky's cat-carrier."

Once Stevie has survived the night, morning becomes a relatively pleasant affair. She tiptoes downstairs at around 4:30, letting Sparky loose in the kitchen. Switching on the Russell Hobbs electric kettle, she starts the coffee percolating. For the next several hours she can do as she pleases, either slip into the office proper and rack up some hours, or work on her own "thing" (she is a painter as well as a fiber artist, and has a small design business).

For three months after the fire, she felt "generally afraid," able to venture outside the building only on her lunch hour to buy food and other necessities. She never went out at night, and had no social life.

Though she still remains inside most of the time, she forces herself to take a walk around the block at eight each morning. She's getting better. She bought a microwave and a bread-making machine, and now bakes her own bread. She has invited friends over for Italian meals.

"I forgave the person who presented me with candles for Christmas," she said. "Also the one who handed me a house-*warming* gift for my room."

As I listened, I thought what a burden it must be for our friends, Stevie's and mine, having to sensitive themselves to fire-issues that have never touched their lives, and possibly never will.

"So, okay, I'm a trifle better," she said. "But I'll never be the same. I will never get over this."

And future events would not allow Stevie the chance to get over it.

I asked what Sparky did all day while Stevie put in her eight or nine hours in the office.

"Oh, she goes to work with me, every day."

"And people don't mind?"

"Screw them if they do. She's a very good cat."

Our bus toiled up dark, narrow Sacramento Street toward the brief effulgence of Nob Hill—Top of the Mark, the Fairmont, Grace Cathedral, neoclassical condos fronting a fairy-lit square where Nob Hill children played during daylight hours. The conveyance was packed solid, windows closed, oxygen at a premium, each seated passenger, as far as I could see, hunched over, wrapped around bulging packages and parcels, carrying home as much as possible from the Chinatown cornucopia. Standing passengers were pressed front to back against each other. Every stop became a crisis—would those needing to leave be able to worm their way through the crush in time to make it out the flapping back door before the bus once again jerked into motion? Would I be able to make it out?

As the vehicle gasped its descent to flatter ground, it came to me that those riding crowded city buses should have in mind a disaster plan. For instance, what if the bus slipped out of gear? What if the brakes gave way on a steep hill such as this one? There'd be no room to move. People, smashing out windows. Screaming. Like rock concerts or soccer matches gone bad: people trampled underfoot. Being crushed to death, unable to *breathe*!

"You okay?" said Stevie, her hand on my arm as we sat side by side.

"I think so, but I need to get off this bus."

"You'll be home soon."

"No, I mean I need to get off RIGHT NOW."

"Okay, okay. My stop's coming up. You'll get off with me."

Outside, I gulped the mid-city air like a diver whose oxygen tank had failed halfway up from the ocean depths.

"Air!" I exclaimed, throwing my head back.

"You were having a panic attack," said Stevie. "Hyperventilating."

"Sweet suffering Jesus, I'm falling apart."

"Then you're in good company. Come back to the place with me. I'll make some tea."

"Got any opium?"

"Would you settle for chamomile?"

Titters of laughter, but I felt genuinely embarrassed, even in front of post-traumatic Stevie. Was I becoming my mother, with the claustrophobia?

Van Ness is one of my least favorite streets: wide as a football field, and the green light allows a pedestrian barely enough time to make it across. At night, the car dealerships feel creepy, with their darkly reflective plate-glass windows and the looming shapes of Mercedes, Jaquars, Lincoln Town Cars. A relentless wind made walking unpleasant. At every few steps, the phantom figure of a panhandler came at us from a doorway.

I felt for Stevie, stuck here along this alienating stretch after twenty years in our cozy neighborhood.

With one small key, she unlocked the door to the barn-like building where she'd been holed up for eight months. Carpeting and wall-sconces could not hide the fact that the place was a ramshackle, maze-like edifice that reminded me of the spooky Victorian hotel where I'd once stayed in Bloomsbury. There, too, I'd found myself turning this way and that, up three steps and, inexplicably, down four, searching for my room along the endless, echoing hallway where the floor, as here, was spongy from dry-rot.

"We'll have tea," said Stevie, "but first I want to dump my bag in the room. Mind walking up two flights, or do you want the elevator?"

"Thanks, but I'll walk."

She laughed. "I don't trust that elevator either."

Stevie's room resembled the interior of a Mongolian yurt, the richly colored bits and pieces once spread throughout a large flat now crowded into this chamber where red and purple predominated. Her mattress took up much of the floor, and two oil paintings stood against the wall. Sparky played hard-to-get for about five seconds, then pranced over to meet me and be fawned over.

"Even your cat—" I started to say.

"What about her?"

"That name: Sparky."

"I won't change her name, just like I won't get rid of everything that's red."

I remembered Stevie's having told the TV reporter that she'd lost pretty much everything except Sparky, yet what I saw here was a lot of stuff. Of course, on that morning of the fire, with smoke still billowing out of the blackened shell, it would have been natural for her to assume that the fire had consumed all of her belongings.

Sidestepping Sparky, who in her craving for attention had gotten tangled up in the long folds of Stevie's coat, I said, "You thought you'd lost everything."

Stevie took a moment to respond. The fringed length of crimson challis barely covered the room's single window, and the night outside looked implacably dark. I didn't relish the prospect of hiking back up Van Ness to wait on the windy corner for a bus.

"I did lose material things," she explained. "But when I said 'everything,' I guess I meant the intangibles—the sense of security, knowing I was safe in my own home. Think about it: You can have a lock on every door and window, so no one can break in, but if some dunderhead on the first floor leaves a pot burning on the stove . . ."

"There's no real control," I said, finishing her thought.

"Maybe not, but one thing's for certain: I can never live in peace as long as someone's living above or below me."

I wanted to concur, but there we were, Shorey and I, back home and living smack up against the abandoned cottage that two years later would shelter yet another person—this time, a known meth addict and former manufacturer of methamphetamine, who would run a TV by tapping into our electricity. We learned of his existence when he woke us early one morning with his shouted responses to a televised sports event. I realized that if he could run a TV off our juice, what would happen when winter came and he also hooked up a heater, possibly an old thing with faulty wiring, to the same line. By that time, though, I'd wised up. Instead of wasting my breath on the cops, I got right on the phone to Fire Prevention, and before we could say Smoky the Bear they had dispatched a majestic officer who flushed out the intruder.

"Fire can marginalize a person," said Stevie. "Some friends avoided me as if I had cancer." Crouching down, she upended a bag of kibble and shook some pellets into Sparky's bowl. "But there were miracles, too."

Christ, yes. We were alive. Unburned. Our cats were alive. And, speaking of Shorey and me: How often, after a major fire, are renters able to return to their old place, only now a beautifully renovated unit? We should get down on our knees before Brother Fire, who was not always so merciful. In the words of St. Francis, he is "robust and strong," and sometimes goes so far as to claim the child in the burning house. How to understand or explain why in one instance he'd take the child, and in another, spare a mere portfolio?

We needed to have our tea, and I needed to get going, but one day when we had more time I would tell Stevie the story of an acquaintance of mine, an architect who'd watched his San Francisco flat burn down. Inside had been the one thing he absolutely needed: his big zippered portfolio case. (That was back in the early 'seventies, before computers, before career-building imagines could be stored on a diskette or CD. It was strictly a time of hard-copy documentation.)

He claimed that he did not pray for an intervention, just stood on the sidewalk with everyone else, watching the flames, trying to flood his mind with Buddhistic emptiness.

But for damn sure, he wanted that portfolio. That, he admitted.

They let him go back in the next day. He could barely see due to residual smoke. The scene was one of black, blistered ruin. Picking his way from room to room, he stepped on the remnants of his life, everything drenched in filthy water. At one point, he got up the nerve to go into his workroom. There in the gloom stood a tidy circle of perfectly unharmed apartment—the hardwood floor gleaming as if it had just been waxed—and in that circle were two objects: the portfolio, and on a tall, narrow display table, his porcelain statuette of the Kwan Yin.

Every fire does have a story attached, but in Stevie's case that story turned episodic, to the point where, as she insisted, fire was stalking her. It tracked her from flat to office building (the elevator blaze) and from office building clear across the intermontane West to Colorado.

Due to her heavy work schedule and some time she'd spent out of town, Stevie did not get back in touch until two months later, in April, to say she had purchased a home in Colorado.

Just like that—a home.

A long-time renter (like myself) had gone out on the real-estate limb, sunk her life savings into a down-payment, and signed on the line.

"Colorado?" I said. "But that's so far away. When are you leaving?"

"Not yet. I'll need the money I'm making here for mortgage payments. For a while, I'll have to commute."

Suddenly I was feeling stupid. I know about business travelers and their weekend junkets from coast to coast, or from coast to same coast, but how would Stevie, a secretary, "commute" more than a thousand miles? By car? Plane?

"I did buy a four-wheel drive—they're absolutely essential out there—but no," said Stevie. "I'll have to fly back and forth."

She figured on spending three weeks of the month in San Francisco, in her waterless room, and a fourth week in the wide-open spaces of the Real West.

Stevie has a predilection for heights. For twenty years she lived on the top floor of the house that burned down, then moved to the fourth floor of her office building, and now hangs out at an altitude of seven thousand feet.

Ms. Stephanie Willett-Shaw owns a five-acre swath of mountain, too high up for snakes or mosquitoes, although mountain lions do prowl the territory, and deer feed from her garden. The air smells "ineffably sweet," aromatic of pine resin in the hot months.

It's a twenty-minute walk to the mailbox, a forty-five-minute drive to the nearest food-mart. Pasta takes longer to become al dente at that altitude. A single storm can—and did—drop five feet of snow. Afterward, the power went out for nine hours, and Stevie was a woman alone in a three-bedroom house, staring out at a monstrous pillow of snow on her cedar deck. Visibility, in that mountain community south of Denver, was reduced to a clotted whiteness.

When I pressed her on the issue of mountain lions, she insisted the only predators were snow, fire and loneliness.

After two long years of commuting, Stevie cleared out of San Francisco, for good, arriving in her new town of Sedalia on April 20, 2002. Three days later, the area fell under threat of the Evergreen fire, ignited by children about ten miles to the northwest. The following month, lightning struck a remote spot four miles south of Stevie's mountain, setting off the Schoonover fire. Had it now snowed on May 27th, who knows how far that fire might have extended?

But these were baby-fires.

Twelve days later, on the afternoon of Saturday, June 8th, Stevie went out onto the deck to water her plants. Transfixed, she dropped her watering-can. The sun had turned a malevolent copper, reminding her of a science-fiction flick: this weird orange hubcap affixed to the sky. Dense smoke thickened the atmosphere, and big gobs of cinders fell like black snow, signaling the start of the Hayman fire, the largest in Colorado's history. An arson, later determined to have been started by a female forest-ranger, the Hayman would take its place among the more than 175,000 arson fires set each year in the United States, according to the U.S. Fire Administration.

That night, Stevie and Sparky had to be evacuated. No looking back. Eleven days later, the Hayman, urged on by hot, dry winds, still burned out of control.

Along with nearly nine thousand others, Stevie and Sparky remained out of their home for two weeks. There seemed little reason to believe they'd ever be going back.

The *L.A. Times* surged into Colorado to report on the fire and to interview evacuees. A reporter talked at length to Stevie in her $47-a-night Super 8 motel room. According to that June 20th article: "Like many evacuees, Willett-Shaw is bored. At dawn, she's often at the nearby Wal-Mart trolling the aisles, just for something to do. The rest of the day she watches TV, naps, worries about the future."

After the *Times* article appeared, people from L.A. started phoning Stevie at her motel, to extend sympathy or share their own brushes with fire. She found herself at the hub of well-wishers and "fire groupies."

Many lost out as a result of the Hayman, but Brother Fire spared Stevie's house. Once she had settled back in, on a day still acrid with lingering smoke, a Denver TV crew drove up the mountain to interview Stevie. And once again, as on the morning of Stevie's San Francisco fire, Sparky stole the show, pressing her nose against the camera lens.

Stevie is still hypervigilant.

Still searches for emergency exits.

Has a permanent disaster plan in place.

However, she feels proud of this achievement: she no longer sleeps in her clothes.

We got together when Stevie last visited San Francisco, after she'd been in Colorado for a year. Sitting across from her in a coffeehouse, I noticed a new clarity in the lake-blue eyes. She said she loves living on a mountain. Loves the seasons, and the long view across the valley. Without fire, she'd never have had the nerve to make that move.

Within minutes, we were done with fire-talk.

"Your garden," I said. "What are you growing?"

She spoke of the short growing season at that high altitude. You've got a narrow window, she explained, and have to get things in the ground at jut the right time. But she grows most of the vegetables she eats, canning some and freezing others. To work in a garden, her own garden, after years of city living—this is heaven.

"And I'm growing pumpkins! My own pumpkins for jack-o'-lanterns, and for pies. Keep your fingers crossed that they make it out of the ground before the first big frost."

I promised that I would.

CHAPTER 14

FIRE-BREAK

I love studying architectural features. Especially, I love the words: lintel, pilaster, embrasure, fan-vault. In my bag there's always a notebook of architectural terms with crude explanatory doodles. Right from my early years in Philadelphia, I was drawn to dormers, garrets, any tiny top-floor hermitage. I imagined the cozy, slant-walled room, with me inside, safe and peaceful in a reading chair.

But such nooks no longer seem safe.

On a day in late November, the sky a dirty curtain over the city, I'm sailing along Divisadero on a 24-bus when we brake for a light. I've got the window seat with a window that actually opens. A pre-rain fragrance permeates the street.

Across the intersection I see a fat medieval turret with a slit-window tucked beneath its conical roof. Perfect space for a scribe, hanging three stories above the street, except that the structure is unconnected to any visible means of escape in case of fire. And that's what I look for these days—fire-escapes, ladders, widow's walks. I'm not obsessed, just cautious.

Sometimes it seems the fire happened to another couple, not us. A veil has overlaid the raw memory of that awful night, and the intervening years have acted as a kind of fire-break: the strip of cleared land that halts the wildfire in its sweep across prairie, forest, field.

Fire has drawn a line across our lives. Shorey and I now speak in terms of "before the fire" and "since the fire." We now have renter's insurance, though given the magic formula of the insurance industry and the way luck runs, if you have it, you won't ever need it. Nevertheless, we are among the 25% of American renters who possess such a policy. It's like the umbrella I brought with me today, thereby guaranteeing that it won't rain. Even though it might seem that you are throwing away money, you're not—you buy the insurance to insure that you'll never have a fire.

The years have brought other changes.

Two months short of his 92nd birthday, Sam Freedman died peacefully while taking treatment at a health clinic in Puerto Rico.

Annette MacNair died suddenly, alone in her home. She did not finish her memoir. Her life was her memoir. Much of literate San Francisco gathered to commemorate this remarkable woman, and in her honor the San Francisco Library Commission shut down on that day.

It took two years for Stevie Willett-Shaw to find permanent work in Colorado. She is now grieving the death of Sparky, who might have been killed by a mountain lion.

Mary Dawson moved back to Ireland. The Emerald Movers van sat in front of her place all that day. Before leaving, she appeared at my door with a bagful of various teas, including a full box of Barry's Gold.

Bernadette, steady as the earth, still lives and works in central Arizona.

On January 30, 2004, Shorey suffered a stroke, nearly dying in Marin General Hospital. Miraculously, he recovered all function on the left side of his body. On the day we brought him home from the hospital, he exclaimed, "I've never seen the garden looking like this. The colors—they're so brilliant!" He has become a collage artist, having had two exhibits of his work here in San Francisco.

Then there's Ajax.

Living at the calamitous center of his unexamined life, Ajax may not even remember the arson—the incident of the burning pillow. So much drama has played across his stage in the meantime. No doubt in response to all the criticism, our neighborhood police precinct has been doing more outreach. They now host community meetings where neighbors can voice their concerns. During the February 2001 session, we learned that Ajax was wanted for attempted homicide. "Don't worry, though," said the officer from his podium. "He can't evade us forever."

At the mention of his name, a group shudder passed through the room. Most accepted the rumor that Ajax had been "invited" to leave the area and was hiding out in Reno, although one man said that Ajax had fled to Texas. Two days later, Noni whispered to me that she'd been looking our of her window when she saw him saunter by. "All dressed up, and his hair looked real nice. Maybe he's using a conditioner."

One night in April, 2003, around pub-closing time, someone used terrific force to kick in our front gate, leaving jagged shards of wood all over the pavement. Madelaine heard the man choking with laughter as he continued up the street. We all figured, "Ajax."

During that same week, when Shorey and I passed the convenience store on our evening *paseggiata*, Ajax reared up from the sidewalk where he'd been sitting with his cohorts. He greeted us with sneering affection.

As Shorey said, "He's like Freddy. He keeps coming back."

Early on the morning of May 5, 2003, nearly four years to the day after the fire, I was on my way to catch a bus. Turning down Sixth Avenue, I practically collided with Ajax, who was behind the MUNI shelter swigging from a bottle. He noticed me, in a sleepy sort of way, and in the same sleepy way started following me down the sloping block towards California Street. I didn't turn to look, but sensed him behind me, maintaining the same distance between us and tipping his bottle to take casual belts of hard liquor. He didn't say a word. Just step after step, in slow pursuit. My heart clanged inside my chest cavity, but otherwise the experience had a dreamlike feel, as if we moved, he and I, like waves of energy down that empty street. I spied the straggle of people at the bus-stop, and knew I was safe. Ajax wouldn't pull anything in front of witnesses.

I also knew that he was preternaturally aware of the fear he had engendered by trailing me in that way. He had no need to shout in order to make the menace more real.

Reaching the corner, I merged with the other MUNI passengers and took a furtive look. Ajax had turned onto Cornwall, where he paused for a long moment to peer in the window of the Bubble Factory, scoping out the place where I routinely did my laundry. There's a place back by the dryers where you can't be seen from the street. Sometimes, alone in there on a dark winter morning, I had wondered what might happen if someone unsavory were to wander in while I was in the back folding clothes. I had wondered what might happen if that someone were Ajax.

Generally, I like the way we are serendipitously thrown together in the city, the way we must coexist. Buses, in particular, force you to expand your notion of who constitutes acceptable company. Laundromats do likewise. I had met some interesting folks at the Bubble Factory, but the Ajax episode caused me to switch to a laundromat closer to home. At the new place I haven't managed to connect with anyone, interesting or otherwise. It's a safe, antiseptic environment where people are careful not to interact beyond a perfunctory "Good morning," and where they come and go like washday automatons.

Seeing my house, filled now with civilized paraphernalia and sealed off from the outside world by Code-approved walls, it's hard to believe we stood on the patio that night in May of 1999 and watched tall flames devour our roof.

But next-door stands the proof.

Ajax's cottage, neither demolished nor improved, has settled like a wooden tombstone into the surrounding greenery, the plywood boards over his windows gray and striated from years of rain and fog, the acacia sapling of seven years ago having grown so copious that it now cloaks most of the façade. It's the sort of cottage that children discover in the woods, and then, to add that delicious component of fear, they fabricate a story about a wicked witch.

After the second man (the one who tapped into our electricity) was evicted from the place by Fire Protection, officers dragged Ajax's blue mattress outside the cottage and stood it upright against the doorway, where it has remained all these years. Vines have pierced the fabric and sprouted round its sides. The mattress, drained of its original color, has become a living organism, at nature's mercy. Soon it will be engulfed by greenery.

Bridie, at eighteen, has not allowed the diagnosis of kidney failure to keep her down. She receives fluids by injection, then goes out to play. She's still able to leap fences. Sometimes I see her standing in the weeds, in a cat-trance of total immobility. She has taken over the yard behind KFC which is visible from our kitchen window. That vacant, untended expanse plays host to foxtails and white plastic bags that are thin with age and that self-inflate and float like ghosts over the yard. There, Bridie Matilda waits with characteristic patience for mice that never seem to come around anymore. She seems content simply to wait.

MARGARET CONWAY

Margaret has an MFA degree from San Francisco State University, and also taught classes in Creative Writing there.

Night Light: Memoir of an Arson is her first major book. She has also been published in literary magazines in the 1980s and has published a collection of nonfiction historical memoirs in 2024.

Made in the USA
Monee, IL
09 February 2024

52746662R00154